D1463090

GENETOPIA

Keith Brooke
GENETOPIA

an imprint of **Prometheus Books**
Amherst, NY

Published 2006 by Pyr®, an imprint of Prometheus Books

Genetopia. Copyright © 2006 by Keith Brooke. All rights reserved. No part of this publication may be reproduced, stored in a retrieval system, or transmitted in any form or by any means, digital, electronic, mechanical, photocopying, recording, or otherwise, or conveyed via the Internet or a Web site without prior written permission of the publisher, except in the case of brief quotations embodied in critical articles and reviews.

Inquiries should be addressed to
Pyr
59 John Glenn Drive
Amherst, New York 14228–2197
VOICE: 716–691–0133, ext. 207
FAX: 716–564–2711
WWW.PYRSF.COM

10 09 08 07 06   5 4 3 2 1

Library of Congress Cataloging-in-Publication Data

Brooke, Keith.
    Genetopia / Keith Brooke.
        p. cm.
    ISBN 1–59102–333–5 (alk. paper)
    I. Title.

PR6052.R58133G46 2006
823'.92—dc22

                                                              2005032904

Printed in the United States of America on acid-free paper

ACKNOWLEDGMENTS

My thanks to . . .

. . . Pete Tillman, for an illuminating discussion about the archaeology of lost civilisations

. . . Peter Patrick, scholar of pidgins and creoles, for helping my mutts mutter believably

. . . Eric Brown and Alison Brooke, for their typically incisive critiques of various drafts of this novel

. . . Chris Evans and Rob Holdstock, for publishing the story that first set me on the way to Genetopia, back in 1989

. . . Sarah Molloy, as ever, for her first-class agenting and author-minding skills

. . . and Lou Anders, for, ahem, his excellent taste and judgment.

CHAPTER 1

In the day's harsh sunlight the Leaving Hill appeared white with bones. Flintreco Eltarn adjusted his sunhood and scrambled up the last of the rough incline, following the path his sister had taken moments before. It was good to get away after a morning spent working the fruit trees of the family holding.

Amberline sat on a rocky outcrop at the crown of the hill, bare toes playing with chalky fragments. She stared down at Flint from under thick chestnut hair, her eyes at once fixing him and focusing dreamily in the distance, it seemed.

When Flint sat by his sister, her head barely reached the level of his chin. He gestured to the sky, the sun. "You should cover up," he said. "You'll have Granny Han popping cysts from your skin again if you're not careful."

Flint knew how much his sister hated the healings, when Granny Han excised the little brown sun-blisters from her skin. He knew she would ignore him, too.

The dry breeze carried a soft whimpering sound to their ears. A pup in the last throes of exposure, perhaps. Probably just a herd of hogs, scavenging somewhere on the hill. Down below, the jungle hummed with the soft trumpetings of courting dawn oaks, wooing the birds with their calls, their promises of dark nectar.

"What if they were human?" asked Amber, softly, turning a bone in her hand. It was cupped, curved, barely the width of her palm. A collarbone, Flint thought, from a pup barely days into its short life.

"They are not," said Flint. "That's why they're here."

He and Amber came here occasionally, usually on whim, as they had done today. Flint felt that the Leaving Hill had more of a pull on

Amber than it did on him, but it was indeed a special place, a place with a powerful grip over all True people.

"All of them?" she persisted. "Every last one of them Lost, corrupted, changed . . . ? No one ever makes mistakes?"

"People are careful," said Flint. "A pup would never be exposed unless a parent is certain that it is Lost. Human life is too valuable."

"Then . . ." Amber dropped the collarbone and shook her long hair in the sunlight. "Then people must err in the other direction. Some of the Lost must pass as True. What if that happens, Flint? What if I were not human? What if you were not human? Do you think that ever happens?"

Her eyes were fixed on him now. Eyes stained piss-yellow by childhood illness. Eyes that both entranced and scared, hinting at corruption, at change. This was Amber's big fear: in a world where illness can steal humanity, where change is prevalent and feared, at what point does a damaged human cease to be True?

Flint, in his ever-steady way, gave her questions serious consideration. He met her look and nodded. "It's only natural to wonder," he told her. "Only natural to fear the change and to question your own status." He paused and spread his hands wide, palms upwards.

"But don't worry," he concluded. "If you were not True we'd just sell you to the mutt trade."

A flash of anger quickly transformed into a wild, mischievous grin, and then Amber hurled herself at her brother.

She struck him in the chest, and together they tumbled from their rocky perch.

Flint cried out as bones and rocks broke his fall.

Wrestling, they rolled down the slope a short way before coming to rest.

Amber held him in a headlock.

"Okay, okay," Flint gasped. "I won't sell you yet!"

She released him and he turned his head to one side, gasping, spitting grit. A handspan from his head, a small body lay naked in the dirt. A pup, dead several days, he guessed. Pale flesh clung in tatters to its tiny body, where scavengers had feasted.

No: not *body*—*bodies*. A double body, joined from chest to hip; two legs, three arms, two heads—one skull grossly distorted, twice the size of the other.

Sometimes it was easy to distinguish the True from the Lost.

Overhead, vultures soared patiently on a midday thermal.

On the way back down to Trecosann from the Leaving Hill they met the Tallyman.

"Mister Flintreco Eltarn," he said. "Mistress Amberlinetreco Eltarn." He lingered over Amber's fullname, caressing the syllables with his tongue.

The Tallyman was a tall, attenuated figure, stooped under heavy robes, face shaded under a capacious sunhood. There were not many occasions when Flint had to look up to meet someone's gaze, yet the Tallyman, stooped as he was, stood a good handspan taller.

> *The Tallyman comes*
> *in the dead of the night.*
> *When the Tallyman comes*
> *you'd better take fright!*

Children's rhymes, stories told on dark winter evenings, schoolyard rumours and gossip. *Never trust the Tallyman!*

"Tallyman," said Flint, his tone civil. Everyone had their function, he knew. Even tallymen. The Tallyman was a moneylender, a purchaser and collector of debts, a gatherer of favours and promises, used by everyone from Clan Elder to the lowliest bondsman. Universally used, universally despised.

Now, the Tallyman stood in their path where the jungle wrapped its lush green fingers around the base of the Leaving Hill.

Flint took a step down the path, pausing when the Tallyman stood his ground. "We . . ." He gestured along the path, indicating that the Tallyman was in their way. Now he could smell the Tallyman's animal odour, mixing with the damp earthy scents of the forest.

In the shade of the Tallyman's hood, Flint could see the old man's eyes peering out at Amber. Flint was aware again of how much his sister exposed of herself, despite the midday sun: bare arms, bare head, bare legs below the knee.

The Tallyman's eyes roved, lingered.

"We wish to pass," said Flint, his tone more brusque now.

"Do as you like, young sir," said the Tallyman, eyes never leaving Amber. "Be free to leave the young miss with me, though. Me can look after her." The Tallyman spoke in a rough hybrid of pidgin and true speech—for effect, Flint was sure.

"You talk about me as if I'm property . . . livestock," said Amber aggressively.

Again, the Tallyman's eyes roved the length of her body. "What Jesckatreco Elthom says is true," he mused. "This one has spirit, all right."

"Jescka?" asked Flint. "You've spoken with our mother?"

The Tallyman nodded. "A fine woman. Her done ask me to come looking for sir and young miss. Done say they might be up with the bones. Done give me a message for 'em."

Amber was glowering at the Tallyman, but Flint saw clearly that she enjoyed his attention. She was four years younger than Flint, and it was only now, in this instant, that he realised she was on the brink of maturity, feelings both adult and childish at play. For a moment he saw her as the Tallyman must see her, and he felt immediately angry and protective.

"A message?" he asked.

The Tallyman shifted his gaze reluctantly to Flint. "You're to stay with Callumtreco Elthom and his family tonight," he said.

"They need help at the dipping baths, and your mother done offer you out to them."

"Thank you," said Flint stiffly. *Offered out* like mutts . . .

"Tallyman trades favours," said the old man, finally stepping aside. He leered at Amber from beneath his hood. "What favours you got in return, eh?"

"I'm sure Jescka has paid for your services," said Flint frostily. "You can expect nothing from us in return for your message."

"Sir can do as he likes," said the Tallyman, menacingly close as they passed. "But young mistress . . . Young mistress can come with Tallyman, see the world. Tallyman can show young mistress far more than she's ever dreamed."

The two hurried past, Flint squeezing Amber's hand.

Soon the Tallyman was lost behind them in the twists and turns of the track. Maybe he still stood there; maybe he had gone up to the Leaving Hill for whatever nefarious purpose he may have; maybe he was following them, even now.

Amber started to giggle, the child in her winning over the woman. "You're so *straight*, big brother Flint," she said. "You should have seen your *face*."

She pulled free of his grip and used both hands to push her breasts up and together. "You saw where he was looking, didn't you, Flin'? All the time, he was talking to *these*."

Flint felt his cheeks burning. "Come on, little sister," he said. "Let's go to Callum's."

There would be a feast tonight, after the dipping and the cleansing, a gathering of Clan Treco from all around. A time of celebration, a time to rejoice in the gennering arts that made the Clan renowned throughout the region.

It was a time Flint dreaded, a time that haunted his darkest hours.

The track led Flint and Amber through the bellycane paddies, thrumming with chorusing frogs and insects, to the edge of Trecosann.

The town was alive with activity and anticipation. It was the start of the market festival, and many visitors had come from outlying districts. But also, there was a gathering of the clan, a spontaneous and irregular event.

The bazaar was packed, stalls overflowing from the trading square and out into the surrounding streets, lined two or three deep and leaving room only for foot traffic.

Flint recognised many of the faces, traders who only came to Trecosann at market festival time, many of them freemen who lived in protected settlements and enclaves in the wildlands between towns.

He nodded in greeting to Jemmie the old dentist, working away at his foot-powered drill. He waved to Jemmie's daughter, Lizabel, who sold sweet buttered tea to her father's customers—her sugar and pain-killing herbs ensuring a steady trade.

"Maybe you're not so straight, after all," whispered Amber, noticing the direction of Flint's look.

"I am a grown man," he muttered, trying to ignore his sister's raised eyebrow and smirk.

They moved on, into the heart of the market, pausing at stalls as whim took them. Rugs and leatherwork; self-sealing clothing woven from Ritt smartfibres; jewellery made from bones and shells and amber beads; potions and cures and aphrodisiacs brewed from wild herbs— "guaranteed clean."

Amber bought a jaggery stick from a smart mutt child and bit into it, pulling at the stringy pulp with her teeth.

"We should make our way to Callum's," said Flint, as they paused to watch a fiddler play to a pair of dancing crafted dogs. The beasts' hind legs were splayed, giving them better balance as they twisted sinuously upright, front paws describing arcane shapes in the air.

"Dear Flint," said Amber. "My dear, terribly-straight Flint. You need to learn how to enjoy life, darling brother." She blew him a kiss, eyes mad with jaggery rush. "It's market festival, Flin'! Stop worrying about me all the time and learn to relax!"

He turned away. Away from his sister, who he knew was right; away from the two dancing dogs, their morphs crafted beyond their true form. He'd looked out for Amber as they grew up together, stood up and defended her when her behaviour had led to trouble, reassured and protected her when their father had grown drunk and violent, their mother wilful and abusive.

And now she was telling him to relax.

He found a water fountain and drank deeply, then pushed his hood back and splashed water over his face.

Amber often cut straight to the truth of the matter. It was true that he was straight, unwilling to let go. But someone had to be on guard, protecting their interests. It was a role he had adopted from an early age.

He realised he had lost sight of her in the crowd—thronging now, but nothing compared to what it would become when all of the clan and other visitors had arrived.

He rubbed at the moisture on his face, ran his hands through his thick black hair. The ache at the top of his spine was suddenly intense, and he rolled his shoulders, arched his back.

Stepping aside to let Cousin Mallery get to the water, he scanned the crowd. "Hey, Mallery," he said. "Have you seen my little sister? She was watching the dogs a minute ago."

Mallery, a stocky young man with a thick black beard, straightened and shrugged. "Might be at the auction square," he said.

Flint nodded. The auctions were always the heart of any market festival. Mutts would be up for sale there, along with a range of crafted animals, their bodies morphed and remixed in the changing vats. As children, he and Amber had always gravitated towards the auction square, intrigued by the range of livestock on display.

He set off, leaving his cousin to wash at the fountain.

The smell was always intense: a rich, faecal, pheromonal fug that intoxicated, emetised. Stock pens packed close together, low barriers all that were required to keep the lots in bound—in most cases, at any rate.

The livestock knew their place. It was in their breeding, in their bones: a molecular bonding of devotion and duty to the True humans. No matter how far a beast was morphed, the bond was fundamental to its nature; any that deviated from the devotional norm were weeded out rapidly. Humankind was always at the top of the pyramid.

And so the stock stood, squatted, lounged in their pens. The mutts ever-patient, the crafted beasts less so, and occasional fights broke out between goats and hogs and other modified creatures.

Flint strolled through the auction square, pausing to chat with relatives and friends, but he couldn't see Amber. It didn't worry him unduly: she was wilful like her mother, liable to take offence at the most trifling of comments, to head off on her own whenever fancy struck. The festival was always an exciting time: she would make her way to Callum's holding in time for the dipping, he was sure.

He stopped to look at a family of mutts, wondering if his father had sobered himself up enough to come looking yet. Most of the mutt trade here was passing through, mutt dealers pausing at the festival en route to the Tenkan gang-farms in the south, where they were guaranteed sales. Most of the mutts kept in Trecosann were bred locally, but sometimes they would buy in some new blood from the traders.

While crafted beasts were animal stock—twisted and remixed in the vats, bred and interbred to establish new lines—mutts had their origins in the long-lost past in genuine human stock. Many could pass for human at a glance although, equally, many could not.

The family group before Flint now were short and squat, slabs of muscle giving their shoulders a hunched appearance. Their pale skin would be a burden under the dry-season sun—even at a distance, Flint could see pepperings of sun-blisters wherever the skin was not protected by ash-white fleece. They would either be immune to the spreading of the tumours, then, or would require regular healings.

They bred true, though: two young ones clung to the parents' loincloths, equally pale and white coated, already well muscled. The female held a third pup to her left teat—the creature too young yet for Flint to see if it had bred true, although it was likely that it was good, like its older siblings, and would not have to be exposed.

"Hey, you," called Flint, gesturing at the adult male. "You done get name?" All mutts should understand some of the pidgin language they called "Mutter"; most could speak at least a few words.

The male bared long teeth, a nervous expression, possibly a smile. It nodded eagerly. "Done call Shade," it said.

Flint found it hard to make out the beast's words, a combination of its strange accent and the distorting effects of its buck teeth. He gestured. "Walk," he said. "Jump."

Obediently, the mutt walked a tight circle within the confines of its pen, then came to a halt and started to jump on the spot.

"Okay, enough," said Flint. He turned away. The mutt was in good physical shape, but a tracery of silver scars on its back told of past punishments, a rebellious or unruly spirt. This one was bound for the gang-farms, he felt sure.

Trecosann was an old, old settlement, with streets paved in stone and some ancient buildings with walls of granite and roofs of slate.

Cousin Callum's family compound was constructed around one such building, known for generations simply as the Hall, its thunder-grey walls towering high over the street. The roof of this building was a blend of slate and Ritt-fibre sheeting, the new sealing over the imperfections of the ancient.

Although easily three storeys high, the main part of the building was a single hall, echoing now with music and voices. Many of the visiting clan members would camp out in this hall, and as Flint stood on the threshold, he saw the patient activity of mothers erecting screens to provide a modicum of privacy.

Flint liked this building a great deal. It was really only used as a great meeting hall, with the family quarters and stables grafted onto the back, Callum preferring the comfort and flexibility of fibrebuilding construction. But there was something about the old building . . . This hall had stood since the depths of time: touch the stone wall here and you touched something crafted and put in place untold aeons before. The light—floating in through arched, sheet-fibre windows—had a pearlescent quality, a *substance* to it unlike anything Flint had known.

He spotted Petria, Callum's wife. They had been enjoined for three years now. She was a generation younger than Callum, the subject of rumour and public comment when their bond had been announced so soon after the passing of Ann, Callum's first. At the time, Flint had not quite understood the indignation some felt—Ann not yet blended in the vats and Callum was married again. With hindsight and maturity, he saw now what the gossips had implied: that Callum's mourning may not have been sincere, that his relationship with Petria may have predated Ann's illness.

"Petria," he said, approaching her.

She turned, her bellycane-hued face catching the hall's liquid light, a sudden smile erupting.

There was jealousy in people's reactions, too, of course; envy of Callum's good fortune.

"Flint," she said. "Welcome. You're staying over, of course?"

Flint nodded. "What can I do to help?"

Petria looked around, suddenly reminded of her responsibility as host to all these visitors. "I'll be busy here until evening, at least," she said. "Callum may appreciate some assistance in the stockyard."

He nodded. "Is Amber here yet?" he asked. She would probably be out with Callum already—knowing Amber, and knowing Callum.

Petria shook her head. "I haven't seen her. Does she know?"

Flint nodded again. "We both got Jescka's message," he said. "Amber knows to come here. I expect she'll be along later."

She was old enough to look out for herself now, Flint told himself. He turned away from Petria and headed for the big double doors that led onto the compound.

CHAPTER 2

The evening was hot, dry, the open fires and torches serving only to make it more so. The sun, heavy below the Artesian Hills already, daubed the western sky with streamers of blood red.

Flint sucked at a sugar juice and then tossed the empty hull into the flames. He was stripped to his shorts now, his thin torso painted livid orange and red like Callum's and Tarn's and all the other adult men of the clan.

The juice was cold in his belly, and Flint felt rigid with tension. At any moment he might be sick. Sometimes it took him like this.

The Hall loomed, solid behind him, a dark mass against the eastern sky. Granite walls extended from the back of the Hall, flanking a wide stockyard almost as broad as the town's main market square. Fibrehuts adhered to the outsides of these walls, their globular, tumourous shapes contrasting with the straight lines of old.

Maybe half of Clan Treco were here tonight. Perhaps three hundred of the men and women here could claim direct descent from the clan. Twice as many again of those present were attached to the clan in some way: bondsmen and guests and other assorted favourites and hangers-on. Yet more had come from farther afield—some from as far away as the Ritt lands beyond the river Farsam. Flint had rarely seen so many humans together at one time, and then only ever at clan gatherings like this.

Many of the women were dressed in all their finery: smartfibres that changed colour in the firelight; massed feathers of jungle birds; cloaks and shawls of swamp-cotton and pikeskin.

He spotted Jescka, his mother, sitting in state by the changing vats, revelling in the attention. She was covered from head to toe in

18

pink and crimson feathers, interwoven with sparkling fibres. Pale face paint covered the scars on her cheek and forehead.

He approached her. "Mother. Is Amber . . . ?"

His mother was drunk already. "Is she what?" she said.

"I don't know where she is. I haven't seen her since midafternoon."

"You got my message? I said the two of you were to come and help Callum." She met the look of one of the women by her side and rolled her eyes melodramatically. "It wasn't complicated. I'd have thought you could follow it. How did you lose her? You're usually as close as tongue and spit."

Flint tried to steer the conversation. "Where's Father?"

"Lost him too? He's with Callum. Probably lousing up some deal or other." Ever changeable, she added more softly, "Don't rile him in front of the guests, Flint. It's not worth it."

The drumming started then, blue-painted Treco boys pounding on great tympani shells.

Flint left his mother and pushed his way through the crowd. He approached the small group of Elders.

Tarn and Callum were talking, heads close together, arms across shoulders, bellies round and ochred.

"Father," said Flint, stopping by the two.

"Flintreco," said Tarn. Fists and canes were no good in public, so he used words to hurt Flint, taunting him by use of his fullname when all around should call him Flint under such circumstances.

"We have guests," said Callum. "All the way from Clan Ritt." He waved a hand to indicate the group of visitors standing nearby, although the gesture was unnecessary as the outsiders were obvious. There were five of them in this group, all clad in cloaks and trousers woven from the smartfibres for which their clan was renowned. Amongst the feathers and body paint of the Trecosi the Ritts stood out clearly.

One of the visiting men said to Tarn, "You didn't tell me you have a son."

"A daughter, too," said Flint. "But . . ."

"I'm Kymeritt Elkardamy. We're on something of a tour, and we've come to discuss how Trecosi gennering skills might be used in fibre production. Henritt?" He turned to a portly young man of about nineteen or twenty. "This is Flintreco. You were only just saying that there was no one of your own age in our party. Perhaps Flintreco would show you around?"

With the tension of the night and the knowledge of what was to come Flint was in no mood to be playing host, particularly when his guest proved to be just as arrogant and spoilt as he had appeared on first impression.

"I will lead the Ritt delegation to Farsamy Carnival this year," the young man said. "My father has just confirmed this. And you do . . . ?"

"I tend the family fleshfruit plantations," said Flint.

"We have mutts for that kind of thing."

They moved past Tarn and Callum and joined a crowd of younger men by the stock pens. Flint exchanged nods and laughs with those cousins he recognised, but much attention was turned on his fancily clothed guest. "This is Henritt Elkyme," Flint told them. "He travels with his father." Henritt clearly caught the belittling tone of that last remark but was quickly distracted by eager questioning about his travels and the reason for his visit.

Flint studied the crowd, held a short distance back from the changing vats by a line painted on the dirt by Father Grey. None dared cross it.

There was no sign of Amber, even now. Normally she would be there, at the front of the crowd, eager to witness, to see the beasts before and after; late into the night she would be the one waiting by the stock pens, simultaneously intrigued and horrified by the transformations taking place. Some said that with her empathy and intuitive understanding she might have made as good a Crafter as Callum if only she had been born a boy.

Father Grey emerged from the shadows of a smartfibre hut, moving with a rhythmic, shuffling gait. He was a small man, his silver hair tied tightly back in a single braid that reached the small of his back. His bony body was completely naked, painted in a series of swirling hoops of colour that appeared to shift as he moved. A single cord was tied hard around his waist, trapping his penis in place, flaccid but upright.

Nearby, Henritt started to speak but was instantly shushed.

Father Grey's eyes . . . His eyes set deep in their sockets were somehow lit up, the whites brilliant in the evening light. He moved with his arms forward, hanging loose at the elbow, his head rolling, and now he started to sing.

It was a wordless song, a tapestry of tones and sighs and clicks made deep in his throat.

Moving in this way, chanting and singing and shuffling his feet, he completed a full circle around the changing vats, and the crowd stood silent before him.

When he had finished, he gave a sudden shriek, like the cry of a bird, and then threw himself to the ground twitching. Petria and some adolescent girls rushed to him, fanning him, offering him some potent brew to drink, and gradually his twitching subsided and the staring madness departed his eyes.

It was time for the Crafting to begin.

At a signal from Callum, the Clan Elders gathered around the first of the vats and Flint and the other young men flipped the catch of the holding pen and let the gate swing halfway open.

"That one," snapped someone—maybe Mallery, Flint couldn't quite see.

A pole with a looped rope at the end swung across, and the rope closed around the neck of a young goat. The thing bleated and struggled but was dragged free of the pen by two of Flint's cousins.

Callum took the pole from them and unceremoniously directed the animal down a ramp and into the vat. As its hooves came into contact with the acrid golden soup in the vat, the creature bleated and struggled ever more frantically, its every instinct telling it to escape.

Someone slapped its rear with a cane, and Callum dragged it steadily onward into the changing soup, dunking its head under, holding, holding, and then, finally, pulling it clear.

At the far end, he handed the pole to old Tessum and returned to guide the next of the animals through the vat.

Once the goat had passed through, those at the far end handled it with far greater caution, guiding it into another holding pen. When it was safely restrained, they withdrew the pole and dunked it in a cleansing trough.

Flint concealed himself in the depths of the crowd of helpers, part of the event, yet safe from any direct involvement.

The goats and swine and other livestock were only the start, however. The climax of the changing came with the turn of the mutts.

A mother cowered at the back of her holding pen, one pup clinging to her leg, another squashed against her thin, drooping teats.

"Give pups," said one of the youths approaching her, his hands outstretched.

She struggled—the torment in her eyes was clear, as she was torn between two powerful forces: the maternal bond and the ingrained devotion to her human masters.

She gripped the youngest pup around its midriff and held it out as far as her arms would stretch. Immediately the thing started to wail: a pitiful, baby's shriek.

The youth seized the pup and then was momentarily puzzled about how to handle it. He settled for a firm grip on the scruff of its neck, and set off through the crowd, holding it triumphantly at shoulder height.

The second pup still clung to its mother's leg.

"Hey, pup. Come."

Cousin Bellar stood before the pup, hand held out. It stepped forward, took his hand, instinct powerful even in one so young.

The Elders had moved on to the final vat now, the one used for mutts. A short time later Flint found himself standing with Henritt, both squeezed into a space at the front of the crowd, leaning and swaying dangerously over the vat, only two armspans across the gulf from Callum.

His cousin's face was intense, lit up from below in a golden splash of light.

Flint stared downward, his eyes drawn to the glutinous, glowing mass of the changing brew. The stuff looked thick, almost solid, an illusion created partly by its viscous nature and partly by the skin on its surface. The mix wasn't a smooth golden colour, as it first appeared, but rather a swirling, granular pattern of yellow, gold, orange, pink, interspersed with muddy striations. The smell, this close, was sulphurous, astringent.

Callum had spent weeks mixing this brew to an ancient formula, using fluid from beds tended by the Clan for generations.

Now, the crowd unfolded to allow passage for the youth, still holding the youngest pup shoulder-high. Its cries had subsided to a steady whimpering now. Behind them, the second pup walked solemnly, as if hypnotised.

Callum stepped forward and took the youngest of the two. It fell silent as soon as the Elder's hands closed around it.

He turned, and placed it in a fibre basket, suspended from a hook over the vat. Then he started to feed a cord through his hands, lowering the basket. When it met the surface there was a sudden swirling of colour, a belch of steam.

The pup sank below the surface, and Callum held it there for longer than Flint could hold his breath. Then he pulled on the cord, the basket broke the surface, and the pup began to cry again.

Someone hooked the basket with a pole and took it away to be cleansed—no one would touch the thing before the changing mix had been neutralised.

Now it was the older pup's turn.

"Walk," Callum commanded, and it stepped forward from the crowd. It barely hesitated, even when—partway down the ramp—its toes touched the soup. It walked forward until only its head emerged from the changing brew, and then it paused.

Callum took a pole and pushed the pup's head below the surface.

Flint pulled back from his place at the front of the crowd, the press of bodies too intense, a dizziness confusing his senses.

He was breathing rapidly, remembering and not wanting to remember. Memories better suppressed. He edged his way through the crowd, stopping only when he was free, when he could breathe cool air.

Henritt found him by the arched opening in the compound wall that led through to the seed patches and holding pens. "You left," he said.

Flint closed his eyes and remembered the heaving of the crowd, the intensity, the massed, staring faces. He felt dizzy again. He opened his eyes, and Henritt was watching him closely.

"You ran away," said the visitor. "Why? What from? You must have seen a hundred changings. . . ."

"Memories," said Flint. "I ran from my memories."

Jenna was two years older than Flint. Little enough difference, perhaps, but he still saw her as the girl he had grown up seeing as so much older and more worldly, always unattainable.

But even though she was then promised to Shemesh, at the start of the previous wet season she had been the first woman Flint had kissed, a nervous pressing of lips, of tongues, snatched in a rough banana-leaf shelter on the banks of the river Elver.

She had made as if to kiss him again, on that afternoon, but he had been scared, uncertain, and he had fled, sheets of rain drenching him instantly, washing away the heat.

Running then, too, from the past.

Now, she was before him, tonguing stick-spirit, kissing flame. A long feather boa twisted around the gentle curves and slopes of her body, tying dark hair back from her slender face.

Dark eyes flashed at him, and she spat fire into his face.

Stick-spirit flames were white and cold. They stung Flint's skin where they struck, and he turned, bathed in their sterilising whisper.

Jenna spat again, and he felt the pigment fizzing from his skin, leaving him bare, brown. Cleansed.

Cleansing always followed the dipping, cleansing in flame and spirit.

In sudden abandon, Flint held Jenna to him, touched flesh taut beneath feather, smelt stick-spirit so sharp he felt his lungs afire.

She slithered away from him, tongued spirit, kissed fire, spat cleansing flames at someone else.

He felt intoxicated, senses swirling. He made his way over to the bathing trough, peeled his shorts off, and dropped into the cool, scented waters. Others frolicked and splashed, but Flint found a place at the side and let the waters revive him gently.

Later, dressed in long shorts and a tunic, he took another stick of sugar juice from the stall.

He had looked for Amber again, but no luck. He was cross with her now, resentful at his own sense of responsibility for her. This was by no means the first time she had gone off with friends, left him worrying like a fool over what might have happened.

He sucked on the stick.

Jenna.

He would find Jenna. She had broken off from Shemesh recently, so now Flint would have a chance to make an approach, see if she would consider him.

He had rehearsed the words so many times. He knew she liked him. He just needed the courage, the composure.

Out beyond the changing vats and the stock pens, the old stone walls of the Hall ended and a scattering of podhuts had been grown. A lot of them were ordinarily empty, used occasionally for storage and for guests at times like this. Now, fires burnt high in the night, and people were all about in the spaces between the buildings.

A drum band struck interwoven rhythms into the darkness, surging melodies of pitch and pace, the intensity and volume irresistible to the young of Clan Treco.

Flint resisted the urge to sway and shuffle as he walked, the music tugging at his steps. He tipped his head up, saw dancing stars—the clear sky a sure sign that the dry season was now well established.

He saw Jenna, then, still in her feather boa, one end of it draped over her dancing partner's shoulder. Henritt. She was dancing with the visitor from the Ritt clan.

Flint turned away and went to lean against the old fleshfruit tree, leaf-frogs chirruping from the lower boughs.

A short time later, he wandered around the party, exchanging jokes with cousins, asking if anyone had seen Amber. No one had.

He found Mallery and Bellar with a small group by the seed patches, the rough gardens where some of the mutts grew food and fibres to supplement their keep.

"Hey, Flint," murmured Mallery, waving a smouldering headstick at him. "You come join we." He was talking Mutter pidgin, no doubt the effect of alcohol and whatever it was they were burning.

Flint squatted and took the headstick. He knew what to do with it, had tried it once, but the loss of control had disturbed him. He took a sniff, trying not to inhale too deeply, and passed the stick on to eager hands.

He leaned back against a wide tree bole. It felt as if the earth were rolling beneath him.

Much later, he returned to the stock pens, sure that Amber would be there. Fascinated as she was by the dipping ceremonies, she was even more strongly drawn to the changing as it started to take effect afterwards.

Dark figures were silhouetted by a few desultory torches. Callum, Father Grey, Tessum, and Shemesh were gathered around the holding pens set aside for the newly dipped mutts.

Grey was humming, the same tune he had sung more stridently earlier in the evening when he had performed the Dance of the Possessed around the changing vats.

All four were stooped in concentration, barely glancing at Flint as he came to join them.

In the pen before them were the two mutts Flint remembered being dipped earlier. Four others had been dipped, too, this evening, after Flint had withdrawn.

These two now lay unmoving in the straw. Their mother sat against the far wall, knees pulled up defensively, trembling. She was clearly drawn to her offspring, but something at least as powerful was holding her back. The unseen hand of change.

The older pup lay on its back, its spine arched. Its skin was beaded with fever, the fur on its head and shoulders slicked smooth. Every so often a faint, whimpering mewl escaped its lips as Callum concentrated on its changes, muttering prayers and liturgies.

There was hope for this one, Flint saw. It looked fit, and the changes wrought had not distorted it beyond what was viable. Only the years would tell if it would grow into a usable morph and if it then bred true.

Most mutt lines had a tendency to drift towards flawed traits, weakening over generations. It was a constant battle to bring new forms into the breeding lines, new vigour. Most mutts were left undipped, but a few from each generation were offered up for change. The vats held a multiplicity of potential, a soup of traits that could be gennered into malleable recipients. It was for these ancient arts that Clan Treco was so widely renowned.

The changes were not without cost, however.

Tessum, a grey-haired old man, brother of Father Grey, was struggling over the youngest of the pups. He groaned as he fought to master the gennering currents, battling to shape the changes wrought by the dipping.

There were some who dismissed this as mumbo-jumbo, a mystical overlay to a straightforward biological process. Now, watching the old man exert himself so, Flint had no doubt that these men had a grasp of some source of power to which Flint and most others he knew were blind: some way of directing the tiny changing vectors these mutts had absorbed from the vat.

Yet still, despite Tessum's valiant efforts, the youngest pup lay dying in the straw. The skin was stretched tight across its skull, the bones within grossly expanded.

Sometimes it happened like this: the transformations were often beneficial, often benign, but sometimes when they found flawed material to work with the results were like this.

This pup would never have been named even if left undipped, Flint suspected. Its inner flaws would have revealed themselves before it reached naming age, and it would have been exposed on the Leaving Hill.

Flint had long since come to terms with the apparent brutality of this regime. In a world where change and corruption were rife, even human offspring were not regarded as truly human until they were three, by which age most of the traits of the Lost would have revealed themselves.

A soft popping sound drew his attention to the Lost pup before him. The skin across the dome of its swollen head had split, revealing an expanse of white bone beneath, still growing.

Tessum moved away, four more changed pups to deal with.

Flint slept in Callum's family chambers that night.

The outer walls had vented themselves, circulating air on what had become a dry, hot night. He lay and stared out through the slits at the stars pocking the night sky.

His mind was restless in the afterwash of the evening's gathering, disjointed fragments of scenes and voices jostling for attention. Jenna and her feathers, the mutt mother, his father's sneering bonhomie, the smothering scent of Mallery's headstick, the dancing light from the changing vats, Father Grey's possessed twitching as he lay in the dirt.

But there was more than just the aftermath of stimulation that was tying Flint to wakefulness.

There was the steadily growing certainty that something was seriously wrong. Amber had not been seen all evening. Now, when she should be asleep in the cell next to Flint's, the sleeping pallet set aside for her lay empty.

Outside, trees and frogs called in the darkness, and somewhere in the distance he heard the screech of fighting cats.

He sat up on his pallet, pushing the swamp-cotton shawl aside. He rubbed at his face, then stood.

There was a light downstairs, a single oil-candle in a dish in the family cell.

Callum sat at the table, face tired and lined. Petria was at his side, their pup at her breast.

"Still no sign?" asked Callum. He had clearly only just returned from the stock pens.

Flint shook his head. "I thought I might go out and look around," he said.

"And find what? Nothing, in the dead of night, Flint. Nothing but drunks and street rats. Save it until morning when you can see beyond your nose and there are people around to answer questions."

"I couldn't sleep."

"Clearly. Guilty conscience? Did you two have a row or something?"

Flint met Callum's look, resenting the words yet giving them serious thought.

"Not really," he said. No more than usual, at least. But had her teasing of him had more behind it than usual? Her accusations that he was too straight? What undercurrents had he missed in her words? Had she been trying to make more serious accusations about the way he treated her, but only been able to come out with teasing and jokes?

Maybe he was too oppressive, too protective. Maybe she was trying to assert her independence.

"Well . . . maybe," he conceded. "I don't know."

"Go back to bed," said Petria. "Let me talk to her tomorrow to see if I can find out what's wrong."

Grateful, he stood, then left them together.

Back in his sleeping cell he lay down, leaving himself uncovered in the heat of the night.

Outside, a cat screamed again. He did not think it was a good omen.

CHAPTER 3

Dawn brought brief respite before the day's heat, a damp haze clinging to the treetops, screening out the sun.

Flint had seen the sky shade from deep grey to roseate silver, to a weak, golden wash and now to this hazy blue. All around, Trecosann was awakening, groggy after the festivities.

He had been to all their favourite haunts already, called on the families of her friends and questioned those who were awake.

There was no sign of Amber now, and no one had seen her since the previous afternoon.

Passing through the fringes of the bellycane paddy, past the track that led to the town Oracle, he came to the humpy form of the family home. This was one of the oldest fibre buildings in Trecosann, its bulbous form encrusted with vegetation, a self-regulated dwelling that had survived—so it was said—over two hundred human generations. Some claimed even longer.

He went inside.

The only sounds came from Milly the house mutt. She fell silent when she heard him enter, perhaps fearing that he was his father, Tarn. Mutts were inherently of limited intelligence, but what insight they had was specific and sometimes particularly acute.

In any case, it didn't take much insight to grasp the vicious nature of the head of the Eltarn household.

Flint made a brief appearance in the workroom to reassure Milly, and to ask her if she had seen Amber today.

"Milly done see Amber?" she replied, then shook her head. "Just master mistress, eh?"

He went through to the stairwell and climbed the warm,

pliant steps to the sleeping floor. Loud snoring came from his parents' cell.

He pulled the translucent screen aside and stepped into Amber's room. An untidy sleeping pallet with a shawl woven by Aunt Clarel occupied most of one wall—it was impossible to tell if it had been slept in the previous night or not, but Milly would have said if she had been here. Amber's clothes were stowed in the storage space behind the far screen. Alcoves in the walls held a few personal items: an artboard, a pair of weaving screens, a rivershell necklet that matched the bracelet she always wore, some combs, a half-clamshell full of coloured sand.

Nothing appeared to have changed. Nothing appeared to be missing.

He went back down to the family room to wait.

It wasn't long before Tarn appeared, clean-shaven already and dressed in a long cloak.

He nodded at Flint, then said, "You been working? Thought you were at Callum's."

He sounded amenable today. Flint nodded. "I was at Callum's last night," he said. "But I woke early. I didn't come back here to work. I've been looking for Amberline."

Tarn grunted. "Still hiding?"

"I don't know. I'm worried."

"Worried?" Jescka stood in the doorway. Where Tarn was a slack-bodied man, and tall like his son, Jescka was a strongly built woman, with a hard physique softened only by the years.

"Amber," said Flint. "No one has seen her since yesterday."

"But a whole night!" said Jescka. "She's never been gone a whole night before. What's she playing at?"

Tarn stretched. "She'll show up," he said. "Or she won't. She can look after herself."

Flint stared at him. "She could be hurt," he said. "Something could have happened to her." He looked at Jescka, and she, too, looked worried, even scared. A moment of weakness on her part. He felt a sudden sense of empathy with his mother. He couldn't remember the last time he had felt something like that.

"We saw the Tallyman yesterday," he said. "Up by the Leaving Hill. He seemed . . . well . . . *interested* in Amber. We all know what kind of dealings the Tallyman is involved in: what if he's done something? What if he's tempted her away somehow? What if she's been abducted?"

Tarn stood, suddenly menacing. Flint met his glare, fighting the urge to look away. His father leaned towards him and paused, then turned and moved away. Over his shoulder he said, "I'm going to see Callum about some new bellycane grafts. There'll be planting to do if he's ready. I'll expect you here by midmorning, not playing hide-and-seek with your sister."

He found the Tallyman eventually. After asking around Trecosann, he finally came to the brewhouse old Tessum kept by the river.

He was sitting on a shaded bench out front, playing blocks with two of Flint's great-uncles.

Out in the river, gulls followed two haul-boats carrying mutts south, the silver birds crying and mocking as they went.

"Cline. Jambol." Flint greeted his two old relatives, nodding to each in turn.

Then: "Tallyman."

The old debt-trader's face was revealed today, hood pulled back under the shade of the bench's canopy. Flint was reminded of an observation he had made some time ago upon a visit to the Leaving Hill: how clearly, with some people, the skull beneath the face was apparent,

where with most you had to concentrate to see the bones beneath the
surface.

The Tallyman stared at Flint from deep, bony eye sockets. A few
wisps of white beard clung to his jaw. He turned to his two companions. "Think this one buys favours or done give 'em?"

The three cackled, and Flint stood uncertainly, confused by their
innuendo and by the way the Tallyman mixed Mutter pidgin with
everyday speech. "I'm looking for my sister," he said.

The Tallyman nodded. "Amberlinetreco Eltarn," he said. He drank
some of his wild-herb tea, then narrowed his eyes and continued, "A
fit one. Something of the Lost in her, I say. Eh, Jambol? Eh, Cline?"

Cline leaned over the bench. "I always reckoned that," he said. "See
it in her eyes, the taint. 'Something of the Lost' is right, isn't it?
Should have been . . ."

He stopped.

Exposed. That was what he had been about to say.

"Amber's as True as you or I," said Flint. "Her line goes back gen-
erations. She's been ill, yes, but never with the changing fevers—as
Granny Han will certify. Or would you argue with Granny Han,
Great-uncle Clinetreco?"

Cline leaned back again, mumbling under his breath.

Flint turned to the Tallyman again. "Have you seen her since yesterday?" he asked. "When you saw us near the Leaving Hill—you
appeared to be making certain . . . offers to Amber."

"Me been make offers to plenty young ladies," cackled the Tallyman, and his two companions laughed, too. "You be surprised how
come they take one up."

"He's daydreaming again," said Jambol, chuckling.

"Amber?" Flint insisted.

The Tallyman turned and spat green slime into the dirt. "Is a
grown woman," he said. "As can make her own mind. As can make her
own choices."

"Where is she?"

"What should I know?" protested the Tallyman. He turned to his companions. "Why's he bothering me like some dumb mutt?"

Flint ignored the insult. "Have you seen her since we were at the Leaving Hill yesterday?"

Tallyman glared at him. "Lose yourself," he hissed. Another insult, that: as in, *Go and join the Lost.* "Forget her," he went on. "Leave family business to family."

Leave family business to family.

Why had he said that? Why had he put it that way? What had Amber's disappearance to do with the family, with the clan?

He found them in the yard, out at the back of the old Hall. Jescka lecturing Petria on something or other, Callum and Tarn watching over the newly changed stock and haggling over cane grafts.

"No sign?" asked Callum. He looked as if he was about to go on, then stopped, sensing Flint's mood.

"I've been speaking to the Tallyman," said Flint, squaring up to his father. "He told me I should keep out of family business. What kind of business have you been doing, Father? What's happened to Amber?"

There was violence in Tarn's eyes, a rage he was trying hard to suppress. His public face.

"What do you mean?" demanded Jescka. "What are you talking about?"

"You've always treated her differently," said Flint. "Always singled her out. She used to tell me you treated her worse than a mutt sometimes. And now she's missing and what are you all doing to find her? So tell me: how much did you get for her?"

He ducked under Tarn's swinging fist, and before he could stop himself he lunged upwards.

Tarn was off balance, tipping forward, and Flint's shoulder came up under his armpit.

The older man grunted and staggered back, clutching at his shoulder.

Flint was crouching low, arms spread, waiting for the next move.

And then it started to sink in. . . .

He had never stood his ground like this before. He had always accepted the punishment, had always believed that somehow he really deserved it.

He waited for his father's next move, and it was not long coming.

Overcoming his initial surprise, Tarn feinted to swing another blow but instead stepped forward and kicked Flint in the knee.

The joint exploded in agony, and Flint fell to the ground.

Had that animal screech really been his own?

Eyes squeezed shut in pain, he didn't see the next blow, couldn't be sure if it was a boot or a fist that slammed into his face and turned his world briefly dark.

He learned later that it was Callum who stopped Tarn, stepping between the two of them, perhaps saving Flint's life.

Sitting in the dirt with his back against the bathing trough, Flint looked up at his cousin. There were many branches of lineage separating Flint from Callum, yet his older cousin had always been someone he trusted and turned to.

Now, Callum thrust a wad of dampened sapwool at him. "Tarn has gone," he said. "Clean yourself up, boy."

He seemed shaken by the fight, shocked at the public display of violence. "And then you can tell me what you think you've found out."

Flint pressed the wool to his face. When it came away it was dark red. The pain was dull, remote: his knee pulsing steadily; his face pulped and numb. It would get worse, he knew. It always did, before it got better.

Normally, it was Amber who would look after him in the aftermath of Tarn's rage. But now she had gone.

He spoke, past the swelling. "They've always treated her differently. Father, especially. Ever since she was ill, even though Granny Han said it wasn't changing fever and she was still True. Amber knew it."

"Amber's their daughter," said Callum, taking the wad of sapwool and rinsing it. "She's family."

Flint looked at him. "Family can become Lost," he said. "Family can be born Lost"—he remembered that gruesome pup's body with three arms and two heads on the Leaving Hill—"and the fevers can change you."

"Amber wasn't Lost."

"Did Tarn believe that? Did Jescka?"

"What makes you think they've done something to her?"

"The Tallyman. He said it was family business. Why would he say that? That choice of words means he knows something he's not telling. Why are they dealing with the Tallyman?"

He recalled their encounter at the foot of the Leaving Hill. The Tallyman's appraising eyes, wandering up and down Amber's body.

At the time both he and Amber had thought it was lust in the old man's eyes, but now Flint saw that it was not lust but greed. The Tallyman had been pricing her up.

When a human baby shows signs of the taint—when it reveals itself as one of the Lost—it was taken and exposed on the Leaving Hill. Until they were old enough to have demonstrated their Trueness they were not even named, not regarded as fully human, but merely *pups*.

But some forms of corruption can take longer to emerge, and yet others can be acquired through the changing fevers. Those too old to expose on the Leaving Hill were banished into the wildlands between settlements or, more commonly, sold as bondsmen or even into the mutt trade. Flint knew of one family where this had happened only a year ago—they had even argued that poor, flawed Thom would have a better life as a bonded labourer. Perhaps they had even believed it to be true.

"The Tallyman has many functions," said Callum uncertainly.

But one of his most lucrative was as the town's agent for the mutt trade.

Oracle bulged grossly, a swollen, fleshy mass embedded in the heart of the bellycane swamp. It stood as high and half again as Flint, although who knows how far its anchoring smartfibres extended into the mud? Purple veins crept across its surface, interlocking, clumping in naevoid knots. Tumorous polyps attached by pulpy cords floated in the swamp water as if, after thousands of years, the thing had finally learnt how to multiply by division.

Oracle would know he was coming. Its sensory fibres would feel his footfalls on the raised path it maintained to connect it to Trecosann. It would know him from the rhythm of his steps. It would taste his mood on the breeze, hear his breathing and the pulsing of his blood as he approached, even from some considerable distance.

Already, as he came near, a bulbous sphincter had relaxed, awaiting him.

"Flintreco Eltarn," it sighed, as he clambered inside.

Sweet smells: newly split fleshfruit, sliced bellycane, many that he knew well yet couldn't quite place. Oracle was playing on his senses. Soothing him. Plying its pherotropic arts in order to ease him into lucid-trance.

He lay back in Oracle's warm embrace. The pain in his knee—so sharp, after walking here from the Hall!—began to subside, and breathing through his broken nose started to ease.

"Tell me of the world," said Oracle. "Tell me of my clan."

Oracle always spoke like this, as if it was somehow one of the True. Perhaps at some time in the far past there had, indeed, been something human in Oracle and its kind.

"The world is unchanged and the clan prospers." Reassuring platitudes. Flint closed his eyes.

"Your injuries will heal," Oracle told him. "Although the damage to your nose means that it will never return to its former shape."

"Amber's gone. She disappeared yesterday. Missed a changing festival, a clan gathering. I think she's been taken, traded."

"Tell me." Soft, enveloping tones, almost too low to hear. Flint felt himself floating free, reluctantly releasing his hold on his senses. The all-encompassing security within Oracle scared him every time, as he lost his grip on his body and its pain: a transient fear, before he was submerged.

He relived their visit to the Leaving Hill, Amber's questions about the nature of the Lost. *What if I were not human? What if you were not human? Do you think that ever happens?*

And then, their encounter with the Tallyman and his assessing gaze; Flint's trek around Trecosann, asking questions of everyone he met, seeking out all their childhood haunts and hiding places, of which there were many, for they had many reasons to hide. And his fight with Tarn, of course.

. . . every step hurt, his back sore from a caning, but he kept going, determined not to let it show. This was young Flint's eleventh dry season, and he had long since learnt how to cope with the discomforts of life.

It was a lesson Amber had still to learn. She had run from the family home this morning. Showing her weakness and fear.

. . . he was lucid-dreaming, a part of his mind told him, still clinging to consciousness, to control. Oracle had cast him back into childhood, tapping buried memories.

Now he watched himself from a short distance. Thin and tall for a ten-year-old, black hair flopping in the breeze, skin the colour of the finest golden sugar. And such a solemn look in his eyes!

The boy trod the path from Trecosann to the Leaving Hill. There had been a row, a fight, and Amber had fled.

He remembered Aunt Clarel, now: once a regular visitor to her brother's house, but no more. Clarel had been there, that morning, had glimpsed Flint's pain even if she had not understood its source—had *blinded* herself to its source.

And now, the boy emerged from the last fringe of the forest. From this point you could look out across the tops of the trees, down to the cleft that marked the winding route of the river Elver, the waters hidden by vegetation. Monkeys chattered from somewhere nearby, no doubt gathered around an outgrowth of fleshfruit somewhere in the canopy.

Flint jumped, stretching high, and then jumped again. The second time, he managed to pluck a trumpet flower from the drooping bough of a dawn oak. He sucked the nectar from its meaty pod, then held the purple petals tight across his mouth and blew. The resulting note was pitched high, a nasal buzz, the sound the trees made to lure pollinators.

He blew again and surveyed the hill for signs of movement, but there were none.

The boy discarded the broken flower and trudged resolutely up the hill, following a path that wound up the slope across open ground littered with the white fragments of the Lost.

At one point a black vulture sat watching him, its wings spread defensively over a recent corpse, its bare face slick, reddened. It lifted heavily, struggled for height, soared with its head hung low, watching, waiting.

At the crest of the hill there was a low wall, carved from the bedrock, forming a rough circle. Flint paused in the narrow entrance, the threshold between Lost mutt pups and Lost human pups.

Within, the bones were more sparsely distributed, yet still dense enough to impress on the ten-year-old the frequency of change within the womb even amongst the True.

In the middle of the circle, a naked brown girl lay curled like a pup, knees drawn up. She was crying, he could see that much. She hurt too, in her own way.

He went to her, and she twisted fearfully until she saw that it was Flint.

"I'll kill him," he said softly, a promise he had made on many occasions.

She dipped her head again, but she had stopped crying.

He found her clothes nearby and dropped them where she could reach. "You won't die of exposure like this," he told her. "You'll just get stiff and sore."

"I belong here," she said.

"You hate this place. You told me."

"They hate me. Father says I'm worse than a mutt. They're going to make me sleep in the stock sheds. I belong up here, with the spirits of the Lost. They should have exposed me."

"You're too old to expose," said Flint, watching the crows in the treetops. "And if they tried I'd stop them."

"You always look for me, darling brother. You always know where to find me."

Flint looked at her now, as she finally reached for her tattered vest. "Only because you're so bad at hiding," he assured her.

. . . only because you're so bad at hiding. Now, drifting in lucid-trance, those words hung around him.

"If you're so bad at hiding, then why can I not find you now?"

"Amberline is older now. Her ways are more sophisticated. Also, it is easier to find someone when they want to be found."

There was usually reason behind Oracle's ramblings, Flint knew.

"Amber was more disturbed than I realised, wasn't she? Yesterday, on the hill and in the market. Is she hiding, then? Somewhere I haven't looked?"

Oracle's silence was answer enough. He had looked everywhere she might hide, asked everyone she might be with. He had failed. He had protected her for so long—they had protected each other, in truth—but now he was powerless.

She might have run away; he would believe that of her. She might even have been foolish enough to take the Tallyman up on his offer of travel and adventure.

The stupid child did not understand the dangers beyond the safe confines of Trecosann.

Or perhaps she did. He remembered her as a young girl, curled up and naked at the summit of the Leaving Hill, trying to find a place with the spirits of the Lost.

Perhaps she understood the dangers all too clearly.

CHAPTER 4

He came to the decision without really thinking much about it. Without Amber what else was there for him in Trecosann? A drunken and violent father. A mother so self-obsessed that he might as well not exist for her. His work on the holding—his father could just as well buy another mutt. . . .

He spent the rest of the morning revisiting their old haunts and hiding places, asking relatives and friends if they had seen her, making absolutely sure that she had gone.

And then he set out to follow her.

Whatever was out there—on the road, in the wilds between settlements—Flint was certain that it would be worse for Amber, a child who had barely set foot outside her hometown before now. He, at least, had travelled and had some idea what he was getting himself into.

And so, now, he stood on the jetty close to Tessum's brewhouse, having filled his belly with flatcake and fleshfruit. Leda's ferry would be in soon, and he would be on his way.

She could, he knew, have set out in any direction from Trecosann, but there was a logic behind his decision to cross the river Elver and head east.

Not only had Oracle shown him that Amber may well have been more disturbed than he had realised—enough so to run away, perhaps—but Oracle had also reminded him of a time when Aunt Clarel had been a regular visitor, always a calming influence in the family home, always a favourite, in particular, of young Amber.

If Amber had, indeed, decided to run away, leaving the only place she had ever known, then her most likely destination would be the home of someone she trusted, someone she loved. Clarel lived two days east of Trecosann in the Treco settlement of Greenwater: distant enough to be safe, yet near enough to be a sensible goal.

It was Oracle's way to reveal truths obliquely like this, and Flint felt certain that it had drawn his attention to Clarel for a reason. He wondered if Amber had gone to Oracle, too, if Oracle had shown her Clarel, hinted at refuge with a loved relative. . . .

Or was he clutching at false hopes?

Another reason to head east was simply that, for part of the way, the road to Greenwater coincided with one of the main trade routes heading south: it would be an obvious way out of Trecosann, and he might find someone who had seen her.

And if she had been taken—or sold—into the mutt trade, then there were two main routes: if she was on a haul-boat on the river then he had no hope of finding her; but the other way was along the main trade road, heading east and then south to Farsamy and beyond.

Leda's ferry ground into the soft cane rings protecting the jetty, its bladderpump engines sighing and farting as the canespirit feed constricted. Instantly the waiting crowd flowed on board. The direction of traffic was almost entirely one-way today: traders leaving the market early before the festival ended tonight, business done for another month.

Flint edged forward, his pack slung over one shoulder. He had not set out unprepared: he had a pouch of money tucked away inside his tunic; and in his pack he had a sleeping roll, spare clothes, a water bladder, and some more flatcakes. In his belt he carried a sheathed knife—although judging by the assorted long knives, arrows, and other weaponry casually on display, he had come out underarmed, reminding him again of what he was venturing into.

At the edge of the jetty now, he reached out for the grab to steady himself and climbed onto the boat.

Leda himself was taking payment from the travellers, a fat money belt slung diagonally across chest and shoulder. Flint handed him a dime and said, "Cousin, have you seen Cousin Amber recently?"

Leda pursed his lips as he took in Flint's battered features, and then he shook his head. "I heard she's missing," he said. "No luck yet?"

Flint sighed. "No," he said. "None yet." He was familiar with disappointment by now.

Leda's was not the only boat that plied these waters, he told himself—particularly at festival time. Amber might even have disguised herself and crossed the river unnoticed—not hard with so many strangers in town.

"Will you watch out for her, Cousin?" he asked. "She's not been seen for two days now."

Leda nodded, and Flint yielded to the pressure of the crowd and moved towards the fore of the boat.

The waters of the Elver were grey with silt. Flint stared at the swirling patterns of mud and then looked back at the retreating jetty, the bulbous podhuts clustered around the waterside.

He wondered if he would see Trecosann again.

He wondered if Amber had seen a similar sight, and what thoughts had been passing through her head. Nervous triumph at her escape . . . anger, perhaps, at the way her family treated her. Or fear?

He recognised the man next to him, a leatherworker from one of the forest settlements. "Cousin," said Flint, conferring clan status on the man regardless of whether it was rightfully his.

He found it hard to talk, the vibration and passage of air hurting his broken nose. He persisted, though. "I'm looking for my sister, Amber. She is about so high"—he held a hand flat across his chest— "and she has thick, chestnut hair down to her shoulders. The whites of her eyes are yellowed by childhood jaundice. She is a True daughter of Clan Treco."

The man shook his head. "I know her, from your description," he said. "I've probably sold her leatherwear at market. But I don't think I've seen her this festival. Sorry, Cousin."

Flint moved on. There were perhaps thirty passengers on Leda's ferry, and he only had a short time before they landed and the travellers dispersed.

". . . about so high, and she has thick, chestnut hair . . ."

"Sorry, Cousin."

". . . the whites of her eyes . . ."

Heads shaking, sympathy in their eyes.

". . . a True daughter of Clan Treco."

"I saw you together a day or two ago—was that her? I remember her laughing. Haven't seen her since, though."

The ground on the far side of the Elver seemed little different, the same hard-packed, grey mud that would turn slick and ankle-deep in places in the depths of the wet season.

There were two podhuts here, and beyond, the jungle had been razed for a distance of easily forty paces, with only low scrub and grasses growing in that space.

The wilds started here.

The forest surrounding Trecosann on the other side of the river was managed by the clan, regular cleansing purges keeping down incursions of the truly wild morphs, protecting the citizens and their crops and livestock from the wilds. The forest here on the east side of the Elver, however, was not husbanded so conscientiously.

Flint pulled his hood forward over his head and went over to the nearest hut. Inside, a moustachioed man sat back in a bucket seat, chewing on a jaggery stick. "Cousin," said Flint. He asked about Amber, asked if the man had seen anyone fitting her description passing through yesterday or, perhaps, earlier today. The man shook his head.

When he emerged, most of the travellers had already dispersed.

Two tracks led away from this docking post. One headed south, along the riverbank. There were three Treco villages in that direction. Flint considered following that track, and asking in the villages. But if Amber had shown up in one of these villages, the Elders would have sent word back to Trecosann.

The second track cut across the stripped buffer zone between river and jungle, heading east towards both Greenwater and the trading route called Farsamy Way.

Already, those travellers who had not headed down the riverside trail were on the far side of the clear area, heading into the jungle. There were a dozen or more of them, carrying high packs on their shoulders, pushing handcarts and guiding a single mutt-drawn wagon. Flint settled his pack across his shoulders and hurried to catch up.

After a short distance, he was struggling. Heading steadily uphill, his knee ached with every stride and his breathing rasped painfully through the swollen passages of his damaged nose. He would have to pace himself carefully on this journey, and so he slowed to a rate that would still, eventually, bring him level with the group ahead of him. He had no wish to travel alone just yet.

The jungle here seemed little different to that on the west bank of the Elver. He recognised the trees, familiar from their leaf shapes and calls: dawn oaks clustered together, reaching dark for the sky and cooing softly in the breeze; assorted forest ferns stood as tall as some of the trees, their great fronds casting deep shadow beneath; occasional whitewoods stood ghostly and skeletal in the thick growth; nut palms, clemmies and softspines, packed tight. Lianas and drape moss hung from boughs bejewelled with flowers and fruit.

All so familiar and yet . . . in the wildlands, nothing was to be trusted. What might appear familiar on the surface may easily be corrupt within, with the changing vectors rife in the unmanaged lands between settlements. Creatures too small for the eye to see, attacking the signature within the body, shifting, distorting, pulling traits across species at will so that human became not-human, animal not-animal, plant not-plant.

The trees had closed in over the track as Flint walked, and now his rhythm was broken by the sudden shriek of some forest creature from the canopy above.

Again, he wondered at Amber's thoughts if she had taken this route. Had this dark cornucopia entranced or frightened her?

All the time as he walked, he studied the jungle to either side. Much of the time it presented an impenetrable barrier, a screen of lush greenery fighting for sunlight where the trail cut through the jungle.

But there were gaps, spaces, little clefts in the darkness where animals must pass.

No sensible person would leave the trail when they were out in the wilds like this, but what of Amber? Young, confused, upset—might she find the shady refuge beneath the trees a temptation?

Perhaps a hiding place from other travellers.

If that was the case, then her chances of survival—alone in the wilds—were slim, and Flint's chances of finding her even slimmer.

All he could do was hope that his deductions were correct and that he was on her trail.

He steadied his painful breathing and increased his pace, despite the discomfort in his knee.

"Here—chew on some of these. It'll help."

Flint squinted at the fold of green leaves Lizabel held out towards him, not wishing to appear ungrateful.

"It's okay," she assured him. "They loosen the swelling. I need 'em a lot when Pa's not so good."

Her smile only went up one side of her face, and Flint wondered if she had been struck down with some kind of seizure at some time, a healer unable to fully cure herself.

He nodded. Lizabel's father, Jemmie, was pushing his cart a few paces ahead of them on the track. It was widely known that people only used the old man's dentistry service because the pain could be soothed by Lizabel's healing herbal teas.

He took one of the leaves and chewed on it. The bitter sap released by his chewing took rapid effect, greatly easing his breathing.

"See?"

Flint had caught up with the small group of travellers some time before. All were heading for the Farsamy Way. All knew of Amber's disappearance, and none had any information for Flint.

"It's brave of you to come out looking for her like this," said Lizabel.

"You people travel these routes regularly," said Flint. Lizabel and her father were freemen with no particular clan affiliations, no particular home. "Anyway, clan-folk travel the wildlands too. I've been this way before. I've been to Treco settlements along the river, and out as far as Greenwater. I've even been south as far as Beshusa."

He fell silent, realising that he sounded too defensive. Walking at Lizabel's side, he couldn't see if she was smiling on the other side of her face or not.

"You let me have a look at you, will you, young sir?"

Jemmie pulled at Flint's lips, prising his jaws apart.

"You tell me you fell over? Hit your face on the ground an' your leg on a rock?"

Flint grunted, dribbling, unable to answer while the dentist had his fingers rammed into his mouth.

Just as Flint was about to retch, Jemmie released him, rocking back on his heels, pushing his wide-brimmed hat back on his head.

Flint turned away, tasting dirt in his mouth. He took his water bladder and drank deeply.

They had stopped to rest in a roadside clearing, with a good deal more travel to do before breaking for the night.

"Nothing's bust," said Jemmie. "Your teeth are fine. It's just your nose was bust when you 'fell.'"

"Thank you," said Flint.

"You keep your hands off my Lizabel, you hear?" The tone of the old man's voice had not changed. For some reason that made his threat seem even graver to Flint.

Flint looked at him. "I . . ."

"I'm not making no accusations, mind, but I know how you clan-types treat your mutts. I know what your father treats 'em like, too."

Mutts? He thought of Lizabel, of how she could appear both wise and childishly innocent, with no transition between the two, of her damaged face, relic of an old illness, he had thought.

The man nodded. "Not always so obvious, is it? She changed when she was twelve. The fevers took her ma, an' left Liz with something missing"—he tapped his head—"an' something extra. So now we travel an' we never go home to where people know, to where people will treat my daughter like little above a street rat. D'you understand, young sir?"

"No," said Flint. "I don't understand why you're telling me when it's clearly a secret you hold close."

"Your sister," said the old dentist. "You know what the possibilities are. Maybe run away, maybe lost, maybe sold into the trade and fucked senseless already by the scum who run the mutt lines. Why I'm telling you is you got to be realistic and to be aware of what's likely to have happened, if you're ever going to cope.

"And more, young sir: you got to hold onto your hope. You're out here for her, and I respect that a lot when there's not much I'll respect other people for any more. You're all she's got. And you got to remember that whatever may have happened to her by the time you get to her, whatever may have changed in her, there are some things that hold true through it all.

"When the changing fevers came, eleven years ago, they took a lot of what Lizabel was, but they never took it all. You got to hold on to what you can, young sir. You hear me?"

There was a growth of podhuts ahead of them in the gloom. Flint had not expected that. He couldn't remember if they had been there when he had come this way as a boy, on a family visit to Clarel and dry-season work on the bladderpump farm.

The huts were empty, sealed against incursions from the wildlands, popping themselves open only when they sensed humans in the clearing.

This was a well-used road, Flint knew—that was, after all, one reason he had chosen this route. It made sense, then, to grow accommodation for travellers here, a day from Trecosann.

"How's the travel suiting you?" asked an itinerant labourer called Alal. The group sat around a low fire, eating supplies of flatcake and fruit, and drinking sweetwater from a podhut bladder.

"It's all bigger than I'd expected," said Flint. He had been walking for most of the day, and still they were climbing Spinster's Spine, the chain of hills separating the vales of Eels and Farsam. The name was appropriate, for the hills were like great vertebrae, locked together below a skin of soil and rock and tree. A sleeping giant.

"We've been walking all day," he explained, "and yet we've travelled so little." He had realised, during the course of the day, his own inadequate sense of geography. He knew the surrounding lands; he had some kind of grasp of the general directions and travel times to the main settlements of Farsamy, Beshusa, Coltar and Ritteney; and yet . . . so little idea of what lay beyond. Humankind interacted on a local scale, it seemed, each settlement the centre of its own world, of an interlocking network of settlements scattered across the wildlands.

To find one person in such vastness!

Alal, a man of much muscle and slow, careful thought, paused a long time in the golden half-light before saying, "I wouldn't have it any smaller. The world. I've been in big towns, where people live crammed together. I worked in Farsamy once. People so close together ain't the same kind of people."

"Plenty of work for a dentist, mind," said Jemmie, cackling.

Flint shared a hut with Alal, grateful for the big man's human noises in the long hours of the night.

Not long into the morning's trek, they parted company. The trail they had been following, a tight-packed mud road flanked by dense jungle, came to a crossing point where it cut straight across a wide road crafted from some dark stone that was flecked white and pitted with a tracery of fine cracks and clefts.

A wooden board lay flat at the side of the junction, its surface etched with arrows, words, directions. You had to stand right over it to read the words. The board indicated the directions and travel times to Farsamy, Greenwater, Trecosann, and Berenwai. A fifth arrow pointed off into the heart of the jungle and was labelled, simply, HELL, NOT FAR.

Flint eyed his travel companions. He had names for all fifteen, now, although many were still strangers; Alal, Jemmie and Lizabel, however, had become more than mere acquaintances in so short a time.

He realised that he had nothing with which to repay these people their kindnesses.

"Stick to the path, young sir," Jemmie told him again. "Hide yourself from travellers unless you are certain of their nature." He didn't try again to persuade Flint not to travel to Greenwater alone, that argument already settled earlier this morning.

The dentist reached for his belt and released the long sheath that held his machete. He handed it to Flint. "Protect yourself," he said. "May you have the Lord's luck in finding your sister."

Flint stood silently, knowing not to protest. He watched the group depart, Jemmie pulling his little cart, Alal and the others guiding their mutt-drawn wagon along the stone road, heading south.

Then he turned away. He studied Jemmie's gift, and then attached it to his own belt. He drew the machete. Its blade was dull, the length of his upper arm; its double cutting edge was marked from use. He returned it to its sheath.

If Amber had left Trecosann of her own choice, then she had almost certainly passed this way. But now Flint realised that his journey would present ever-greater choices where his path might diverge from that of his sister. It was, indeed, most likely that she would head for Aunt Clarel's home in Greenwater, so Flint's choice of route was a sensible one. But she may easily have reached this point and—even if her intention had been to head for Greenwater—decided instead to head south, drawn to the excitement of Farsamy and beyond. He knew that she would find the prospect of travelling to the big town tempting. She could easily have fallen in with a group of travellers, as Flint had, and *then* decided—or been persuaded—to stay with them on their journey to the south.

Or to the north. He turned, narrowed his eyes against the warm breeze, and studied the stop-start, humpback progress of the road heading north up Spinster's Spine. The town of Berenwai was several days' trek away. It was possible, he conceded, although they had no relatives or friends there and, Clan Beren traditionally being regarded as impoverished neighbours, there would be little to draw Amber in that direction.

On sudden impulse, he took a fist-sized flint nodule from the ground and struck it against another. Again, and on the third blow it cleft in two: newly cut flint, the best he could do to signal that he had passed. He placed both halves neatly on the arrow pointing to Greenwater. And then he strode across the Farsamy Way, seeking the trail where it plunged into the jungle once again.

Soon, he realised that the track was heading steadily downhill. He must have passed over the crest of Spinster's Spine without realising: where distance gave the hills a definite profile, in reality they were little more than a gentle ripple in the landscape.

Trecosann behind him, he was on his way to Greenwater.

As he had yesterday, he eyed the surrounding jungle while he walked. There were still trees and other plants he recognised, but also many that were new to him.

With Jemmie's advice fresh in his mind, he wondered if Amber would have acted similarly: hiding from any travellers she encountered. Sensible advice, where you might just as easily encounter bandits and other lawless itinerants as well as the Lost—changed people and mutts cast out or escaped.

The clear implication, though, was that she might easily hide from Flint—particularly earlier when he had been part of a group.

So as he walked, he studied the undergrowth, the entrances to animal tracks, the gaps between scrubby thornbushes, hoping against all odds that he would see her hiding there.

He thought of old Jemmie's words. *You're out here for her, and I respect that a lot when there's not much I'll respect other people for any more. You're all she's got.* Was he really all she had? If she was out here on her own, then maybe that showed that she didn't need him to be looking out for her any more. Was he out here for her or for himself, then? A chance to break free.

Perhaps.

What did remain true was that there was nothing for him to stay in Trecosann for. And if Amber *hadn't* left out of choice, then he was the only one trying to help her.

It was the uncertainty as much as anything, he realised: he had to find out what had become of her. A selfish reason perhaps, then, after all. He looked around himself again at the forbidding walls of the jungle. He did not regret his decision to come after her, not for an instant.

By the middle of the day, with the sun high over his hooded head, Flint was thirsty. He had long since drained the last of the podhut's sweetwater with which he had replenished his water bladder. Earlier, with the sun lower and the trees affording shade, it had not been so bad, but as the heat had increased he had drunk too greedily.

He checked the water bladder again, but it had not miraculously been refilled.

He moved to the side of the trail, under the shelter of a great claw-leaved tree fern. He pulled his hood back, and felt the heat recede just a little. He studied the fern's scaly trunk for signs of infestation before squatting and leaning back against it. He had seen many long lines of army ants today, memories of childhood stings increasing his awareness of the hazards of even everyday things.

There were sounds all around. Insects hummed and creaked and pipped; birds cried high in the canopy; other creatures—rats, lizards, more birds, perhaps—snuffled and scuffled on the forest floor.

He straightened his leg, the injured knee supported now by bindings and a poultice prepared by Lizabel.

The inherent respect for True humans was widespread in the wilds, too, Flint knew, but clearly it did not extend to the biting insects. Where the backs of his hands had been exposed they were covered in pink welts. What if vectors of the changing fevers could be transmitted by these tiny creatures, he wondered, scratching all around the most recent bite?

He blocked the thought, aware that he was spooking himself.

Eyes adjusted to the shade now, he saw that the forest thinned a short way in, and in the pool of light he saw bulbous clusters of flesh-fruit hanging low.

He studied the ground carefully, head full of children's terror tales of snakes and venomous spiders the size of a grown man's head, of mantrap plants that would close around the legs of the unsuspecting and slowly suck their victims deeper into the dissolving digestive juices held in bladders beneath the ground.

There was just a thick layer of dead leaves, twigs, a scampering black beetle as long and narrow as Flint's little finger.

Tree and fern trunks stood vertical, and little else grew in the shade of the forest floor.

Flint moved farther from the trail, passing through the forest to where another screen of vegetation thickened at the edge of the clearing.

He drew the machete and swept it down once through the greenery, and then again. Several small moths erupted from the leaves, whirring into the sunlight.

He stepped through.

Fleshfruit hung, fat and purple, paired side by side in a bunch as long as Flint's arm.

So tempting, but he knew he wouldn't dare eat from this bunch, wouldn't risk even a taste of their sweet, meaty juices. There was so much richness in this biological wonderland between settlements, so much diversity and fecundity. And yet the abundance was illusory: all this richness, and so much of it could easily be corrupt, tainted within. He would have to be foolish, or desperate indeed, to risk eating or drinking anything he found in the wildlands.

Some of the riper fruit had already come away from the top of the bunch, but there was no sign of them on the ground. The insects and rats would take care of such fallings, but there could easily be larger beasts here.

Flint looked around, remembering Jemmie's advice that he should never leave the trail.

He stepped back through the opening he had hacked and then paused to get his bearings. It would be so easy to lose one's way in the jungle.

It was only a matter of paces across the bare forest floor to the tree fern where he had sheltered from the sun on the edge of the trail to Greenwater.

He hesitated under the grasping fronds of the fern.

Ahead, on the trail, was a small figure. A woman, or a girl, with long dark hair and downy, fleecy clothing.

Flint stepped out, broke into a run, and then stopped and called aloud. "Amber!"

Please, let it be Amber!

CHAPTER 5

Only twenty paces separated them when the creature—yes, creature!—stopped and half turned.

The thing was naked, he saw now: what he had mistaken for thick, fleecy leggings and jacket were instead its heavy fur, merging, tangled across its shoulders with the dark strands of hair on its head. Hair too dark to be Amber's chestnut tresses, even in the spreading shade of the forest trail.

Its face was simian, thrusting jaws and flattened nose bare and pink, its human lineage only really evident in its eyes.

"Stop!"

But it did not. The thing was no mutt, or at least it was no longer a domestic variety—it either had no understanding of language, or it had lost the deep-seated obedience that was in all mutts.

It parted its lips and gave a little snarl, catlike, and then it darted into the trees, vanishing instantly from his sight.

The fleshfruit, he realised: they had not fallen, they had been harvested, taken neatly in pairs as they came ripe. There was intelligence, then, in this creature, or in its kind. He thought of the seed patches some of the mutts kept in Trecosann when their owners allowed it. Perhaps horticulture was instinctive for some mutts, giving them a special intimacy with the earth and its produce.

He turned, fearful.

A face peered at him from the shadows, barely spitting distance away from him.

And then it was gone.

The same dark hair as the female, but this one was broader of face, squarer, and Flint guessed it to be male.

He felt for Jemmie's machete and let his hand rest on its well-worn grip. To draw it would be an act of aggression, but it would also prepare him better for any hostility on their part. He already felt himself to be surrounded, imagining untold hordes of the creatures waiting in the trees all about, drooling over the flesh of the True, over the various forms of torment they could put him through before he expired at their hands.

He turned slowly on the spot but saw no more faces, no sudden movements in the shade. Perhaps they had fled. Perhaps they watched him still, waiting their moment or unable to attack him because of ingrained respect for the True.

"Me master out of Trecosann," he said. "You speak? You been know me words?"

No response. Was he just talking to trees? Talking to illusions?

"Me been look for mistress outta Trecosann. Her got red in hair, yellow in eye, she high like this." He held his hand level with his chest, struggling not to laugh aloud from panic, from the ludicrousness of him describing his sister to the jungle. "If an' you see her you treat her plenty good. You been know me words? Her find me Greenwater." He gestured along the trail.

He turned slowly again. No sign of them, but he felt sure he was being observed.

He set off towards Greenwater, holding himself tall, keeping his pace slow, fighting the urge to keep looking, searching, all around.

You treat her good, he thought. Treat her good.

Some time later, he was alone. He just knew it. He stopped, turned a full circle, felt sudden sweat prickling his forehead.

And then he fell to his knees and vomited into the dirt, retching over and over, as panic belatedly overtook him.

Later, sitting on the trail, knees up to his chin, he rocked back and forth. Eventually, he made himself climb to his feet and resume his trek.

He recognised this bit of the trail, he suddenly realised: a crook in the path where one last screen of tree ferns shielded the view from a traveller's eyes.

A few more paces and then a panorama unfolded before him. The trail here wound lazily down a steep scarp slope to the flood basin of the river Transom. The waters of the river were still high from the wet season, still extending out across the forest floor, making it more like a lake with scattered trees emerging.

There, spreading out below, was the town of Greenwater, very much living up to its name, with as much as half of the land within the town's stockades submerged in placid, leaf-green water.

The stockade itself formed a gently curving arc enclosing the town on the west and north; the other two boundaries would normally be marked by the snaking meander of the river, which was now only discernible as an area of slow-moving water not broken by emergent trees and huts.

The northern end of the stockade was completely clear of the water, the land raised to form an island. As the ground fell away from there, the stockade followed its contours until its mud and timber construction formed a dyke enclosing the flooded part of the town.

Within the defences, walkways raised on pontoons connected the dwellings, narrow thoroughfares dipping and bobbing on the water. The podhuts themselves were supported by inflated bladders, anchored in place to great stakes that had been driven into the ground.

Flint had never seen Greenwater in flood, had never quite been able to envisage it like this, despite the tales of Clarel, Mesteb, and the others. He wondered at the mentality of a people—his relatives!—who lived with this annual inundation.

Even at this distance, he saw the figures of people in the town, on precarious walkways, in boats and rafts, passing along the top of the stockade, and out in the open streets in the dry sector of town.

And already, he felt his pulse quickening, wondering if Amber was here ahead of him, if it really could be as simple as all that. He prayed fervently that it could.

With one last glance over his shoulder, he started to walk down the track to Greenwater.

"I am Flintreco Eltarn," he said again, his voice raised to carry across the water. "I have come to visit my Aunt Clareltreco Elphelim."

The boy atop the stockade still stared, still kept his wall-mounted crossbow directed towards Flint. The boy was barely into adolescence, and his grubby features and tattered clothing—and that mad stare—made Flint suddenly fearful of what he would find in Greenwater. Had they all been struck by the changing plague? Had they been taken over by some degenerate subhuman mob?

The boy glanced to one side as a man came to join him. "Flintreco?" he said. "Travelling alone?"

Flint thought he recognised this man as an occasional visitor to Trecosann. He nodded. "It is a matter of urgency," he said. "My sister, Amberline, is in danger. I'm looking for her. Can I come in?"

The man nodded. "I know him," he said to the boy with the crossbow. He reached down and did something behind the wall, and suddenly great eructations of gas popped from the water before Flint as a series of bladders inflated, thrusting a walkway above the surface.

He stepped onto the bridge, more stable than he had expected. Ahead of him, a gate opened outwards, welcoming him, finally, to Greenwater.

"Petertreco," said Flint, stopping before the man, just inside the Greenwater gates. The name had come to him as he traversed the walkway, waters thick with green algal scum lapping tamely to either side. "Thank you for allowing me to enter."

Peter stood nonchalantly, a small-axe hanging loosely from one hand. "It must be urgent indeed for you to travel alone through the wilds," he said. His eyes were calculating, assessing Flint for threat, for signs of change.

"I travelled in a group as far as Farsamy Way," said Flint. "I came directly here when my friends headed south. My sister Amber disappeared before the changing festival. Despite our searches, we have not found her. She has quite clearly left Trecosann and, if she travels voluntarily, then her most likely destination is Greenwater."

The two of them stood on a narrow wedge of raised land behind the stockade. Above, the boy and some other young men stood on the town's defences, leaning precariously down to hear what was said.

It was only when he saw how poorly these people dressed that he recalled his impressions of this place from his earlier visit as a boy: of people who had to work hard merely to carve an existence out of the jungle, a meaner, leaner level of subsistence than he knew from Trecosann.

"Your sister isn't here, Flint," said Peter gruffly. "I'm sorry to let you down."

They were the words Flint had anticipated. If she were here then they would have been far quicker to tell him so.

Flint looked away. The ground here had been submerged until recently, and its surface was slick with green slime. He wondered again at how they could live like this.

They climbed the mud slope to the top of the stockade. Its exterior surface fell away vertically to the frothy waters. Flint saw that the walkway was deflating and sinking again. He looked back towards the fringe of the jungle.

"Your defences are impressive," he told Peter. His words masked an unspoken question: *What have I just passed through to get here?*

"The wilds," Peter said simply.

"I saw . . . humanoids, in the jungle," said Flint. "Mutts, perhaps. Only a few minutes' walk back to the west."

Peter nodded. "If we had the resources we'd purge the wilds around Greenwater," he said. "There are mutts, as you describe, and there are all kinds of changed beasts out there. They're getting closer all the time, getting bolder, too. A lot of them are reasonably harmless: the subservience to the True is ingrained deeply even in the wild stock."

"But . . . ?"

"You can never be certain. Sometimes the changing fevers can remove the shackles, although thank the Lord we don't see that often. It's not just mutts out there, though: the humans are the worst. Some of them are Lost—"

Victims of the changing fever, Flint thought, chilled by dark memories, dark fears.

"—and some of them are just bad to the marrow. You're lucky you got here in one piece, Cousin Flint, lucky you got here at all."

The hard lines of Aunt Clarel's face made him think of his father. He flinched as her hand brushed against his face, but it was a gentle touch, a sympathetic gesture. The bruising on his nose and jaw was still evident.

"It's okay," he said. And indeed his breathing had been easier today, the healing speeded by Lizabel's therapeutic herbs. "My nose will never be straight again," he added, softening his words with a smile.

He saw in her eyes that she knew that it was her brother who had inflicted Flint's injuries.

"Whatever possessed you to come all this way?" she asked.

Flint had been mulling this over throughout his journey. Love for his sister, yes: for years they had been there for each other. He had spent much of his life looking out for her, and now she might need him more than ever. But also it was less noble than that. It was an opportunity, a chance to seize the freedom he so fervently still hoped that Amber had seized.

"Can I stay for a while?" he asked. If he had passed Amber en route—if she had, as he had suspected, hidden herself off the track whenever she encountered other travellers—then she might still be on her way to Greenwater. He could head back, he knew, but if he did so he might just as easily miss her again.

Clarel tutted somewhere deep in her throat. "You think I'm going to turn you away do you, you silly young bugger?"

She turned and headed back along the narrow walkway in the direction from which she had come.

Flint shouldered his pack and followed.

The small raft maintained its position on the water, despite the steady tug of the Transom's current. A fibre net trailed behind it, steadily filling and swelling with green scum. According to Clarel's partner, Chendreth, the locals called this process "skinning the river."

The algal blooms at the end of the wet season were rich in minerals from the Elphine Hills. Rich, too, in a particular strain of changing vector. Fed into the bladderplant nursery beds at this time of year, the scum instigated vigorous growth, and a promiscuous exchange of traits between varieties. Many of the resulting sports would be useless, the changes too extreme and damaging—like that young mutt pup that had died after its dipping in the changing vats in Trecosann. But many would be promising enough to be maintained, nurtured, and perhaps propagated and grown for trade.

Mastery of the changing arts was Clan Treco's greatest achievement, something they did better than anyone else, with the skills passed down through the generations.

"Yes, I do think Tarn would sell Amber," said Flint in answer to Chendreth's question. "If not into the mutt trade, then as a bondsman. He has always treated her as little better than a mutt—she always said that."

Chendreth worked at winding her cord, hauling the nets in behind the raft. She kept her head turned slightly away from Flint's gaze. Barely a year or two older than him, but yet he was struck by a gulf between them: Flint awkward, unsure of himself; Chendreth a woman comfortable with herself and with her role in Greenwater life.

"I have never met your father," she said now. "Clarel talks of him sometimes. . . . She won't go to Trecosann any more."

Flint knew that Clarel had stopped visiting, but nothing had ever been said and so there had been no finality to it.

Over in the settlement, there were voices, and Flint spotted a small group passing through the stockade. There were at least six people, and they had a wagon being hauled by a team of four mutts. He wondered how they had manoeuvred it over that inflatable walkway.

"Mesteb," said Flint. The trading party was back from the market festival at Trecosann. There would be news! Clarel had been urging Flint to wait for Mesteb's return, assuring him that he would bring news of Amber, news that she had shown up at home, after all.

At a nod from Chendreth, Flint squeezed a valve on the bladder-pump engine and the raft surged gently for shore.

In his five days at Greenwater, he had spent long hours at the stockade, staring into the wilds for any sign that Amber was out there, always disappointed at the end of his long vigils.

In that time the waters had receded a long way, but many of the riverside streets were still awash, the anchored podhuts still connected by walkways suspended across bladderplant pontoons.

Now, he guided the raft past the normal landing jetty and through the centre of Greenwater. A short time later they bumped against the pontoon that abutted Clarel's podhut.

One of Clarel's mutts reached down and secured the raft with a loop of cord, and Flint and Chendreth clambered up onto the walkway. Instantly, the mutt jumped down onto the raft and started to gather up the skinning nets, deftly trapping the harvested scum in a floating cane basket.

Flint trotted along the walkway, almost missing his footing at one point and plunging headlong into the thick, scummy water.

Soon he was in a street slick with the green froth of the algae.

Mesteb and his party were still by the gates, chatting with Peter and some of the other townsfolk.

Clarel was there, too—so calm on the surface yet here she was, eager to find out what news Mesteb brought.

Mesteb was a tall, broad-shouldered man, unhooded despite the sun's glare, his long hair threaded with silver, tied back from his face. His eyes had the look of someone who had lost much, betraying his normally jovial nature.

He spotted Flint and instantly gave a slight shake of his head. "Clarel tells me you're looking for your sister," he said. "The two of you are the talk of Trecosann: the runaways. Everyone knows what a bastard Tarn is." He glanced briefly at Clarel, then, as if only just remembering that Tarn was her brother.

"She didn't run away," said Flint. It was a conclusion he was finally starting to believe. "She took nothing with her. I checked her room and nothing was gone. Amber's impulsive, but she's not stupid: she wouldn't just go off with nothing. And if she had fled she would have come here."

She might never have made it this far, of course.

Or she might never have left Trecosann voluntarily in the first place.

He remembered play-fighting on the Leaving Hill. *We'd just sell you to the mutt trade*, he had teased her. And he remembered the Tallyman's appraising eyes, putting a price on Amberlinetreco Eltarn.

He peered at his aunt from under the wide-brimmed hat she had given him. His presence made her uncomfortable, he knew, but she tried hard to hide it.

She had followed him out here to a rocky promontory that cut straight out into the Transom's flow. Great rubber trees hung out over the river. Lines of land anemones clung to the underside of the trees' boughs, feathery tentacles trailing down to the water, trapping moths, birds, fish in their downy grip.

Flint held a long, arching cane across the water, its tip raking the current, accumulating a knot of algae: glistening, glutinous stuff.

"What will you do, Flintreco?"

Where Tarn used his fullname as a weapon, distancing himself from his own son with inappropriate formality, Clarel used it to draw him in: Flint of Clan Treco—he belonged. People cared.

It was a calculating use of his fullname, too: a deliberate gesture. Warmth and spontaneity were hard for Clarel. Flint had seen it often in Chendreth's looks, the hurt at the distance Clarel maintained even from her lover. The affection between the two of them was so brittle, he was impressed that it endured.

He raised the cane, watched water dripping from the captured algae, then dipped it again.

"She may be dead," he said. "In which case I am wasting my time. She may have run away and I have simply got it wrong that she would head here—maybe she has gone to Farsamy, after all. She may have run away and fallen into the hands of traders, or she may have been sold directly into the trade.

"If she is still alive out there, then all that I can do is spread word. You told me yourself that Clan Treco is more dispersed than most: there are Trecosi in most of the major settlements of the region. I even know some of these people from their visits to Trecosann.

"I'm a free man, Aunt Clareltreco. I intend to travel and ask people to watch out for a foolish girl with chestnut hair and jaundiced eyes."

"Your mother . . ."

Clarel stopped, and Flint waited for her to go on.

"Your mother is a difficult woman," she said. "I don't defend my

brother—I was glad when Mesteb told you that the people of Trecosann are finally seeing him for the beast that he is. No, I don't defend
him. But I do think that he and Jescka deserve one another. He's
devoted to her, despite everything: that's why Amber's presence
affected him so . . . so adversely."

"What do you mean? What are you telling me?"

"If Tarn never treated Amber like a daughter, it was because he had
good reason," said Clarel.

Hindsight. A lens that sharpens recollection, reshapes memories.

"My mother took lovers?" He had known. But he hadn't made the
connection. He had known that she had a lover, once, but that was
more recent than Clarel implied.

Clarel nodded. "Mesteb has been one," she said. "But there have been
others, too. Mesteb confessed to me last year, when he was sick with the
gripes and scared it might be changing fever. He wanted to off-load his
guilt while he could. So he told me. And he told me why he stopped
seeing her. He couldn't stomach her visits to the seed patch."

Flint moaned, turned away. He knew the euphemism: visit the
seed patch and that's where you find the mutts.

He had always thought Tarn's cruel jibes at Amber's nature related
to her illness as a child, not to her parentage!

If Clarel's claims were true, then the only wonder was that Amber
had not been exposed on the Leaving Hill as a pup, or that Tarn had
not sold her into the trade at his first opportunity. Only Jescka could
have stopped him, he realised.

CHAPTER 6
DINAH'S STORY

Dinah sniffed. She tasted change on the pretwilight air. She knew that was not usually a good thing to taste.

She returned to her work, sluicing the swill buckets in a stream of brown water channelled through bamboo pipes direct from the river Elver.

She hummed herself a little tune. It was one her mother had taught her when she was not much more than a pup. An insect buzzed in her ear. Quick as a striking whipsnake, she enclosed it in one of her fleshy fists and slipped it into her mouth. It tasted of blood.

She stacked the last of the collapsible buckets by the outflow and wiped her hands on her frayed, off-white pinafore.

Flies and change. Strange tastes. She would remember this day as the day of flies and change.

Dinah was smart like that. Mutts could be blessed in many ways, but memory was not usually one of them. Old Ellis at the leisure house in Beshusa had taught her the trick of remembering things by hanging them on labels in your head. Already the day of flies and change was the day when two pups had died in the pens; when Nico had given her a white flower from the swamp trees; and now it was the day when Mas' Torbern had returned—she could smell his sweet sweaty smell above all the other approaching scents on the air—with Mas' Enchebern and a group of many visitors for Dinah to attend to. *Many*, for Dinah, was a number greater than the number of fingers on both hands.

Dinah didn't apply labels to all the days she passed through, but only to those she felt to be important in some way. Today, for instance, she only chose to mark as significant when she tasted her returning master.

He had been away since the previous morning. That meant that Dinah had been able to get on with her chores without too much hindrance or hurt, but now that she knew he was returning, she felt her heart hastening with pleasure and pride.

She emerged from the work cabin into the fading light of the day. Maddy was there already, shifting her weight from foot to foot in the dusty square. The poor thing didn't know what was happening, only that *something* was happening, confusion clear on her apelike features.

Dinah hugged her, holding her friend's head to her soft breasts. "Masters coming," she said, explaining to the poor, feeble-minded creature. "Me done smell masters coming home."

She took Maddy's hand and led her to where a series of wooden rungs were lashed to the stockade wall. She led the way up the ladder, climbing to the walkway from where the two could look out from the transit camp.

They were standing on the side of the morning sun, which meant that they could look out across the overgrown waters of the Little Elver. This part of the river was a wide, shallow channel that cut through a meander formed by the main river, separating Stopover Island from the mainland. A short way downstream, Dinah could see the thick green ridge of the causeway that joined her home to the mainland.

Yes! There, where the trees and vegetation thinned and the causeway fell away to be replaced by a slender living wood bridge, she saw a line of people and mutts. Too far away to identify the individuals, but she knew her master Torbern was there. She clutched Maddy's hairy arm in anticipation and love and dread.

Dinah and Maddy scampered through the camp to make preparations for their master's arrival. Stopover was a big camp, as large as any in the Ten, she had once been told. There were many masters in Stopover and, although Dinah was quite naturally in the thrall of them all, her bond to her own master was the most intense. She knew that her devotion to Mas' Torbern was something bonded deep in the matter of her body, a gut thing—she was, after all, a clever mutt: she understood far more than most, far more than she would ever let on. Knowledge did not—*could* not—alter her ingrained devotion to her master, though. She loved Mas' Torbern more than she could love a pup of her own.

All around the two of them, a fug of animal smells blanketed the dry air. The dirt track they followed was one of many that formed a grid pattern in this part of the camp, the paths bounding sunken holding pens set chest-deep in the ground. Each pen was enclosed by a picket fence made from slender wooden poles interwoven with smart-fibres and roofed in with fibre netting. Hands gripped the poles, and faces peered out at the two hurrying mutts.

As Dinah and Maddy went on their way, the two of them sang old songs of family and devotion and Harmony—Dinah singing the words and Maddy humming the tunes in her gravelly, surging contralto.

And around them, voices rose from the holding pens, joining their song.

"Drink for our guests, mutt! You done listen?"

Dinah ducked her head, cowed by the violence in her master's voice. Love hurt, she knew, but she was a good mutt and she could only do as he bid.

She took a mug thrust at her by one of her master's guests. He was a big man, muscle softened by good living, his square face rounded by a thick growth of dark beard. She dipped her ladle in the urn of mulled herbal wine and filled the mug. The man took it from her, his look sliding uneasily across her face.

Dinah smiled inwardly and took another mug to fill. They did not keep her here for her looks, she knew. She was heavily built—a perk from working in the transit camp's slop-house—and her face bore the scars of past mistreatment.

Dinah had spent her early years in Lady Leder's leisure house in Beshusa. Running errands from room to room, she had quickly learnt what kind of leisure it was that the masters enjoyed with her mother and the other mutts and humans owned by the fearsome Lady Leder. The physical contortions sometimes seemed funny to her, but the intensity was unmistakable: her mother was often hurt by the customers, but the power they had over her was an awesome thing. It was the normal devotion of mutt to master taken to an extreme level. In later years, Dinah had known mutts addicted to jaggery residue, and she had seen that it was a similar thing: her mother hooked on the masters and the things they did to her.

Dinah had so wanted to be like her mother. But, regardless, the day had come when Lady Leder had sold her to an architect-grower across town, dismissing her distress with a surprised, "But you're fat and you're ugly and you're far too clever for my clientele, my dear thing."

"Lights!"

Dinah hurried around the big, gloomy verandah where Mas' Torbern was entertaining his guests. Roofed over with great banana leaves and livermoss, the verandah was rapidly filling with darkness as evening took hold. Threaded through the walls were translucent tubes filled with Artesian glow-water. Dinah stroked them into action, and the area pooled with warm light.

As she did so, she stole surreptitious glances at the masters around her. Four of them were outsiders, guests in Stopover. She recognised them from previous visits. They came often to do business with Mas' Torbern and the other mutt traders. The big bearded man was Mesteb from Clan Treco, and now he was talking with Mas' Torbern and Mas' Enchebern.

Her own master, Torbern, was dwarfed by Mesteb. Dressed in a side-pinned cloak and long trousers that hung loosely from his wiry frame, Torbern had shaggy black hair, a thin beard, and narrow eyes set deep in an angular face. Every movement of his, every gesture and expression, had an air of command and confidence to it. It was natural enough that Dinah should think such a thing, but she saw that he had this effect on the True humans around him, too. They deferred to him, almost as mutt deferred to master.

Just then a chattering sound rose from the holding pens just beyond the verandah, where Maddy was fussing over the new arrivals.

Dinah hurried across and dropped through a gate into the low-level pen. Maddy had spilt most of a bucket of water onto the dusty ground, and now she muttered curses at the new stock.

Dinah put a hand briefly on her friend's back and felt the poor thing trembling, fearing punishment for the mishap.

The new stock had been split into single-sex groups and put in a number of holding pens upon their arrival. There were four different varieties of mutts in eight pens to Dinah's left, and two more in four pens to her right.

This was the pen for the female Lost, and now they crowded around Dinah and Maddy—curious, more than anything, Dinah decided. There were five of them. Three were True humans who must have been changed at some time in their lives. Most likely they had fallen victim to one of the changing plagues that occasionally spread through the human population.

The remaining two were harder to categorise. One was a child of maybe ten summers, tall and slim and staring blank-faced at Dinah. The other was older, almost into womanhood, full-figured, dark-haired, and the most striking thing about her was the golden tint in the whites of her eyes.

Both these two had the air of the True about them, and Dinah felt immediately subservient to them. And yet she knew that both must be corrupt in some subtle way. Many children of the True were born with deviations from the norm, in many various ways. Where their flaws were obvious they were exposed to the elements as pups—better that than let them live. But sometimes the deviations were more subtle and only emerged in later life. Dinah had seen many like these two: raised and nurtured among the True and later disowned. Some were turned out into the wilds, but most were sold into the mutt trade. They were usually trouble, their upbringing making it hard for them to adapt to their new circumstances. Their natures had to be subdued and shackled if they were to adjust.

Dinah looked at the two, and wondered how much of a fight they would put up.

From Maddy's snuffling curses, she guessed that one of the two had snatched at the water, causing her to spill it. She remembered tasting change on the air, and now she realised that it may have been trouble, too, that she had anticipated.

Mas' Torbern led them around the holding pens, gesturing expansively down at the mutts. "Finest cages you could find," he said to his guests.

Dinah followed at a safe distance, ready to respond to her master's commands. Unlike most mutts, she could follow the full speech of the True, as long as they did not speak too fast or have particularly strange accents, as some of the guests had.

Mas' Torbern's words were true—the holding pens were, indeed, well constructed—but he was simplifying things for his audience.

All mutts talked of freedom, of living in a place they called Harmony where they were in charge of their own destinies. In Harmony everyone had a place, their strengths respected, their weaknesses supported. In Harmony, diversity was embraced, not feared, and humankind took many directions.

Most mutts, however, would never consider actually *trying* to escape to Harmony from even the poorest conditions. Their ingrained devotion to True humans was enough to keep them in place. So, to a large extent, these pens were overkill.

But in some mutts the devotion was not so strong and, in some, changing illnesses had weakened it so much that they would be willing to try to escape. And then there were the fallen humans, the Lost, in whom the devotion was not inherent: they learnt subservience at the hand of masters like Torbern. The Lost learnt to obey through fear and discipline, not love, and it was in these fallen humans that the desire to escape was strongest.

And so the holding pens of Stopover had been built to contain the keenest escapees. Even the nimblest of mutties—midget mutts destined to work high in the fleshfruit trees—would be secure in the holding pens of Stopover.

"Finest cages," Mas' Torbern repeated. "Keep 'em all in their place. None of 'em get out of Stopover, 'cept on a haul-boat."

"Why the mutthounds, then?" asked one of the guests.

The pens were secure, but Dinah knew that most escapes took place elsewhere in Stopover: from the exercise yards, from the fields and fleshfruit groves, from the haul-boats moored at the docks. The mutthounds were used to track them down.

Mas' Torbern gave a high, drawn-out whistle between fingers and teeth, and immediately the hounds started barking and howling from their kennels by the causeway.

And in instant response, all chatterings and murmurings from the mutt pens fell silent.

Mas' Torbern grinned, teeth white in the spreading gloom. "Scares the shit out of 'em," he said softly.

They stopped by the pen that held the five Lost females and, for some reason, Dinah felt her pulse quickening. She prided herself on understanding the workings of her mind and body, but she did not know why she should feel nervous now.

Overhead, clouds of tiny bats swirled in the darkening air. Dinah watched their twitchy flight, then looked away.

She saw that Mas' Torbern was watching one of the females. The pretty one with the golden tint in her eyes.

Dinah looked away again, across the ranked cage-tops to the dark fringe of the enclosing stockade and the towering trees beyond.

When she looked back, her master was still watching the pretty one, and leaning across to exchange words with Mas' Enchebern.

Enchebern opened the pen's gate and leaned in, over the heads of the enclosed females. He pointed at the pretty one, and said, "You. Come here to me. You hear me?"

Pretty one pretended not to understand, but one of the older females nudged her and hissed a few words of Mutter close to her face. Relieved, no doubt, that it wasn't her they summoned.

Reluctant, the pretty one edged forward and, at another gesture from Enchebern, climbed out of the pen.

She was wearing a thin tunic and loose trousers. Fine clothes for one in such a position. She held herself proudly, too.

"Get this one a drink," said Mas' Torbern, and Dinah hurried over to the urn to draw a small mug of mulled wine.

When she returned she stopped uncertainly, holding the drink out before her.

Mas' Torbern held the pretty one's chin between thumb and finger, tipping her face up so that it was illuminated by the silvery light of the near-full moon.

"Mestebtreco," said Torbern. "One of yours, no?"

The big bearded man nodded.

"Maybe we should keep this one, eh, Mesteb?" Mas' Torbern's hand moved down to the pretty one's breasts and then pulled at the clasp of her tunic, splitting it open at the front. He cupped a breast with the hand. "What do you say, Mesteb?"

The big man stood awkwardly. "She's a cousin," he said finally.

"But Lost, of course," said Mas' Torbern. "Or you wouldn't have taken our money for her."

Mesteb nodded. "You can see the change in her eyes," he said. "And in her nature."

All the time as they spoke, Mas' Torbern's thumb worked in circles around the pretty one's exposed nipple. Dinah felt sickened, angered, and—she recognised it, even as she felt she should repress it—triumphant. The pretty ones always got more attention. Sometimes it served them right.

She still stood uncertainly with the mug of mulled wine. Now she raised it, as if to remind Mas' Torbern that he had commanded her to fetch it, to remind him that she was here, waiting, unsure.

Distracted, he reached for it.

The pretty one, who had until now been standing stiff as a tree, lashed out with her left hand and knocked the mug from Dinah's— from Mas' Torbern's—grip.

Hot wine splashed over the master, and the mug rattled away into the darkness.

He cursed, rubbed at his face, and the pretty one took a pace backwards, away from him.

He stepped towards her and pushed, and she tumbled back through the open gateway into the holding pen. "Later," he growled. "I'll teach you some manners."

From this level it was quite a fall into the pen, and there was a dull thud and a gasp of pain when she landed.

Mas' Torbern turned on Dinah, and somewhere in the shadows she heard dear Maddy chattering nervously, fearing for the safety of her friend.

He seized Dinah's wrist and pulled her towards him, his face lowered so that the hot stench of his breath was damp on her wet cheeks. "You clumsy little shit!" he yelled at her, and then the back of his free hand smashed into the side of her head, sending her reeling, leaving her in a crumpled pile on the ground.

It sounded like bells clanging in her ears, only a more constant sound. She tasted blood and remembered catching a fly and eating it and tasting blood then, too.

He came for her again, and she knew he didn't care that his guests were watching, knew that he enjoyed having an audience, was excited by them, roused by them.

He hit her again, and then she felt his hands pulling at her clothing and she heard Maddy chattering, the sound more distant now, more muffled. Heard Mas' Torbern's voice, barking and snuffling sounds that were more animal than human, laughter and triumph and anger.

She cried out now, and then, merely, cried. And all the time she loved him so much, her master, the man who could do to her what he chose and always she would be his devoted slave.

She loved him and she hurt and she knew that this day of flies and change had been too long already.

She woke in the cabin, smells of damp wood and bodily odours thick in the air. Shafts of light slotted the lean-to walls, low and bright. Early-morning light.

She shifted, realised that her head was raised on a folded coat, her treasured sleeping blanket pulled up across her body. Maddy must have looked after her last night, brought her here and settled her to sleep.

Many mutts slept in this cabin, a mosaic of bodies arranged across the dirt and leaf-litter floor, occupying all available space and yet most not even touching. Dinah saw that Granny Di was awake, sitting on her haunches. The old matriarch rocked back and forth with little nervous motions, working her toothless jaws as if chewing. Granny's eyes were unfocused, and did not see Dinah as she raised herself stiffly from the floor.

Maddy slept nearby, her compact body secure in the ladle of big Han's. Dinah folded her blanket and stowed it with her coat on top of a low beam.

She left the cabin.

Of all the times of the day, this was the one Dinah treasured most. Dawn newly broken, there was something about the light that seemed fresh and untarnished. Peace spread across the massed ranks of holding pens, only occasional mutterings and groans breaking through.

She had tried explaining her feelings to Maddy once. "We done sing about love of the Big Mas'," she told her friend, referring to the mutt songs they were all taught as pups. Songs about the Lord who had made them long ago in the shadow of man. "Done sing about Harmony." A place of freedom, a place of release. "This time make Harmony here," she concluded, pressing one hand to the side of her head and the other to her chest.

Maddy had grinned and muttered, and maybe somewhere in her heart she had grasped the sense of Dinah's words.

Dinah passed through the holding pens, taking a route that wound through the sector controlled by Mas' Torbern. All sleeping, or quiet at least.

At the moment there were many hands worth of holding pens occupied by Mas' Torbern's stock—many more than Dinah could ever hope to count. He bought some of them from haulers who passed down the river, and along the Farsamy Way. Later he would trade them on to dealers in the big market auctions. Others he had not bought but instead held on behalf of his regular clients, taking a portion of their sale price in return for housing and breaking them.

The holding pens of Stopover had filled steadily in recent days in readiness for the big auctions at Farsamy Carnival. Dinah had a good sense of time, an understanding of the shapes of events in the general flow from wet season to dry and back again. She remembered the build-up of tension and anticipation in the days before Carnival from early in the previous dry season.

She stopped by a pen occupied by eight pale, smooth-skinned males, and she enjoyed the sex musk on the air. Two were awake, and she savoured their interest. One pushed a hand deep into his loincloth and started to stroke himself, eyes slitting, rolling. They had water in their bucket, slops and bread in their trough. She moved on.

The mutties in the next pen were all sleeping, bundled up in a heap in one corner. They were small creatures that would barely reach her waist when standing upright. Their prehensile tails and dark fur made them look more like monkeys than mutts, but miniature, bald heads with human features gave away their true nature. Dinah had worked with mutties in the fruit groves at Arrabesh for one long dry season. All day long she had fetched and carried as the mutties worked high in the trees, and she had rapidly become enchanted by their chattering version of Mutter pidgin and their fantastical tales of the wilds.

She came to the pen where they had put the five fallen women.

Four slept, one sat upright, back to the mud and stone wall, knees drawn up to her chest, hugging her legs. Pretty one's yellowed eyes stared wide above her scabbed knees. They were focused somewhere else entirely, another world, and Dinah thought of old Granny Di in the cabin, rocking back and forth on her haunches and staring into another place.

Their bucket was empty. Maybe it hadn't even been replenished after Maddy had spilt it the previous evening. Dinah reached down and hooked it out.

Returning with the bucket full, she squeezed the gate's release, smartfibres relaxing at her touch. The gate flipped open, and she climbed down into the pen.

She hung the bucket in place and looked around the pen. The three older females slept together, the child a little apart from them, her face twitching to some dream or other. Dinah squatted in front of the pretty one.

Pretty one's tunic hung open at the front, where Mas' Torbern had split it the previous evening.

Dinah swept mid-brown hair away from the pretty one's eyes and saw bruising and swelling on the girl's face.

Not so pretty today.

"Pretty one?" said Dinah softly, stroking the girl's brow. "Pretty one done got name? Done call me Dinah."

Now, pretty one looked at her, a puzzled expression on her face.

The gold in her eyes was a rich honeyed brown this morning. "Tan eyes," said Dinah. "Done call pretty one Taneyes."

Dinah dipped a corner of her pinafore in the water bucket, squeezed it, and then came back to the female she called Taneyes. Gently, she eased the girl's head up, clear of her knees, and saw that she had a swollen, split lip, blood on her chin, bruising across all of one cheek. Gingerly, she dabbed at the blood.

It would make little difference, for now. Dinah was smart, and sometimes she was able to understand things in new ways, understandings that startled her when they happened. Now she saw that it was different for this poor thing. For Dinah, love would overcome all, but it was not the same for Taneyes because Taneyes did not have the kind of deep-seated love for Mas' Torbern that she did. Even when she came to love him it would only be through fear, not the gut-love that true mutts like Dinah were born with.

For those like Taneyes the pain must be so much *more*. . . .

Just then, the pretty one flinched. Dinah must have accidentally found a tender point.

Taneyes reached up, took the damp corner of pinafore, and put it in her mouth. Dinah went to the bucket and scooped a handful of water out. She brought it back and let the girl sip awkwardly.

When she had finished, Taneyes looked up at her. "I hurt him," she said, baring her teeth like an animal. "He . . . I bit . . ."

Dinah stroked the girl's hair. *He will always hurt you more*, she thought, but said nothing.

She came to the stockade and climbed to the top, wincing at an old pain in her right hip.

A path led along the foot of the stockade, separated from the Little Elver by a tangle of low vegetation. It was hard to tell where dry land ended and river began, as the thick growths extended across the shallows, slender, fleshy tree trunks bursting from the greenery to form a sparse copse across the water. Up in the canopy, hummingbirds dipped pollen-dusted heads deep into buzzing and whistling bell flowers.

Dinah hummed a song of her own, her head filled with half-formed words that she knew did not even come close to the wonder she felt at times like this.

Soon, the stockade curved sharply to her left and the transit camp was behind her. Forest enfolded her in its lush embrace. Here, she tasted tree marten and fruit bat on the cool air; overripe meat-melons cloyingly sweetened the breeze; and the peaky, salty tang of fish, of course.

She quickened her stride, wondering if Nico had tasted her as she had already tasted his briny scent.

At its northernmost end, the island of Stopover curled partway across the mouth of the Little Elver like a fish hook. Nico had told Dinah once that it was because of the hard rocks here: they formed great crags and cliffs that were three or four times her height, and they stood strong against the scouring actions of the Elver's waters. Nico explained things well, but still Dinah had difficulty in seeing how water could wash away rock. . . . She believed him, though. Sometimes being smart meant knowing when to accept the truths of others without fully understanding why.

In the small bay tucked behind the northern hook of the island, the fisherfolk had made their home.

It was a precarious existence: a colony of mutts living in virtual freedom on an island that was at the heart of the mutt trade. Nico told Dinah that there were several such colonies, scattered along the banks of the Elver and Farsam, home to his race of semiaquatic mutts. The niche they occupied was so specialised and their adaptations so particular that they were easier tolerated than enslaved.

She came to the gravel beach and pulled at the ties of her pinafore. Naked, she plunged into the still waters, gasping at the chill.

Dinah shared some of the privileges of the fisherfolk, for she was trusted as one of the go-betweens, passing messages and supplies between them and the masters of the transit camp.

Sudden turbulence, silky, flowing touch of body against body, and Nico burst through the surface at her side.

Laughing, she pushed him away, and stroked backwards towards the rocks. She pulled herself out and waited for him to join her in her element.

He popped out of the water and landed in a squat, feet and a hand giving him tripod balance.

He was beautiful.

Dense fur grew in swirls across his shoulders and down his body, giving him a warmth and bouyancy in the water she could never match. Wide shoulders and chest gave his body a wedgelike profile, tapering to narrow hips and legs, then fanning out in wide, paddlelike feet. Adjusting to the air, his tiny nostrils flared, breathing slits sealing over.

"Dinah," he said, his voice as always reminding her of a child's. "Blessings upon us."

She asked of his mother, who had gone down with a high fever a few days earlier.

Nico looked down at the water. "Big Mas' done take her," he said. He tried to say more, but faltered.

Dinah studied his tight features, pained to see her friend struck by such clumsy inarticulacy. Words should be easier to find, but the masters always hated a mutt with education. Give a mutt words and you give it the tools to craft ideas, Old Ellis had once told her.

"Tell me what done happen in camp," said Nico quickly.

She always told him about events at the camp. "Many haul-boats in docks," she told him. Nico would pass word, and fisherfolk would go to defoul the propulsion bladders and screws, a regular job for them at this time of year.

"Higgs done tell me ask for more shellfish and diggies," she went on. Supplies for the visitors: the best fish for the masters' guests, everything else ground up into the mutts' swill.

Nico nodded, absorbing the information. He reached across and touched Dinah's brow. "What be hurt in here?" he asked.

"Mas' Torbern done come back," she said, the words and distress scents enough for Nico. She knew he was jealous of her love for the master, but she was helpless to change anything. Her love for Nico was a head thing, not a gut thing. It was her own choice, but it could never be greater than her love for Mas' Torbern.

"Mas' done bring some Lost," she went on. "One pretty one. Me done call her Taneyes. Mas' done teaching her to obey. Taneyes fight too much. Mas' for give big teachings to break Taneyes."

Nico would know what *big teachings* meant: the changing vats. Those who wouldn't be broken sometimes had to be wiped clean in the changing brew. Most years there were some like Taneyes.

Nico leaned over her, dripping water onto her face. "Be want Taneyes on Highway?" he asked.

She shook her head. Until now that had been exactly what she had wanted, but now she knew it was too risky. "No, Nico," she said. "Taneyes done hurt Mas' Torbern—Mas' been want for teach her." There was no way they could get Taneyes onto Harmony Highway when she was getting special attention from Mas' Torbern.

"You have friends," pleaded Taneyes. "I need your help!"

Dinah recoiled from the pretty one. She had marked this one down for trouble from the start, and now she knew she had been right.

She remembered the words of Old Ellis. Some mutts were naturally clever, and some scraped together an education. Some had an advantage because they had good blood in them, as she was convinced Dinah had—by good blood, she meant blood of the True; she meant that Dinah was the product of one of her mother's liaisons with human men at Lady Leder's leisure house.

But the cleverest mutts of all were those who concealed their intelligence, for humans never trusted a mutt who could think.

"Please, mas'?" Dinah said now, doing her best to look confused by Taneyes' words.

"I don't belong here. It's all a mistake!"

Today was the day of smoke and flight, and of all days Dinah did not want the pretty one causing trouble today. She knew this when she had seen the wisps of smoke curling up from the northern end of the island shortly after the day's first light.

"We all looking for Harmony," said Dinah, the sudden change in her tone silencing Taneyes. "Ain't all of us able to find it, you hear me?"

"What can I do?" Softer now.

"You don't cause trouble for the others, you hear?" Dinah was talking true talk now, breaking out of Mutter to get through to the pretty one. "You keep your thinking head together, you keep yourself ready for whatever happens, but you don't ever do anything to cause trouble. You hear?"

Taneyes nodded, and suddenly Dinah felt a great rush of fear that for the first time in her life she had committed too far, given her trust to someone who now held her life in her hands.

The timing was all wrong.

Dinah looked around and knew that there was no way she could get warning to anyone. She remembered her words for Taneyes: *You keep your thinking head together, you keep yourself ready for whatever happens.*

That was all she could do.

She ducked her head and followed the small group: the masters, Torbern, Enchebern, Caltreco, Bereshbern, and Treebesh; the mutts, Maddy, Tender, and Wake; and the Lost, Taneyes and the girl, Lariss.

They followed the track at the foot of the stockade on the morning sun side of camp, Little Elver to their left, the causeway a short distance behind them. Here, the waters of the small river formed a wide swampy area between the island and the jungle. Great pools of sediment and slime were separated by ridges of wood and silt. Looking down from the stockade it was apparent that the pools were a human construction, a channelling and concentration of the tools of nature.

It was here that Stopover's changing vats had been formed: clay-walled troughs, their sides lined with smartfibre, an armspan wide and deep enough to submerge someone of Dinah's stature. Or Taneyes'.

Mas' Torbern had decided to dip the two Lost females, just as Dinah had anticipated. "One too sullen to be any good," Dinah had heard him say this afternoon. "Just like her mother. And the other too damned spiteful." Wipe them clean now and they might still be ready in time for sale at Farsamy Carnival.

But the timing!

Today was the day of smoke and flight, and the changing vats were only a short distance from what the fisherfolk called the Widdy Gates, where the mangrove swamp was at its thickest, where cover was best.

Dinah had seen the wisp of smoke scratching the upriver sky earlier today. A sign. On her rounds she had sung as usual, but today her song had been of Harmony and freedom and readiness, her Mutter pidgin little different to the masters' ears but loaded with meaning for a small number of those in the holding pens.

Mas' Torbern drank from a bladder he had been carrying slung from a cord loop at his wrist. "Right," he said. "Time for a fresh start for you!"

He gestured, and Tender stepped over to Lariss and took the girl by the arm. Tender was bulky and almost hairless, bred for hard labour. His hand easily encircled the girl's upper arm.

Dinah watched, horrified as ever at this spectacle, at the ease with which the masters would do such a thing. The changing brew they used here was distilled with the help of expertise from Clan Treco: changing vectors would subdue and subvert anyone exposed to them, leaving them pliant and malleable, putty to be re-formed and reshaped at will.

At a signal from Mas' Torbern, Tender moved towards the changing vat, and the girl shuffled along at his side. Enchebern took her now, and Torbern took her other arm. Between them they guided her to the top of the steps that led down into the changing brew.

Torbern pushed, and the girl teetered forward and placed a foot in the brew. Her expression never changed from one of blank incomprehension. Dinah wondered what horrors she had endured already: perhaps the change could be a blessing for some, she mused.

Taneyes was watching her, terror in her stained eyes.

Dinah went to her, offered her a drink of sweetwater from a bladder. It was her role to offer comfort and care, both before and after.

She wanted to look away, but didn't. "We be no-powered under the Big Mas'," she said, hoping her words conveyed her inability to offer more than comfort.

Taneyes swallowed, then looked across Dinah's shoulder to where the girl was now knee-deep in the brew. "Before the little masters, too," she said.

Dinah pictured, somewhere within the stockade, hands on smart-fibre locks, the fibres relaxing in response to the touch. Holding pens opening. And later: questions and beatings, investigations to find who had accidentally left the four pens unsealed.

She looked away, down towards the thickening screen of trees, where mangroves clustered together. Some said the trees concealed convoluted ribbons of raised ground, paths that twisted through the swamp, away from Stopover Island. Dinah had never been closer than this before, had never had the chance, but she knew the stories to be true. She knew the paths through the swamps were the first stage on the Highway to Harmony, the path to liberty for those few mutts who were free of the gut-love for True humans that bound Dinah and her kind into service.

She looked up at the stockade, expecting at any moment to see fig-ures there, voices raised, all going wrong because Mas' Torbern had chosen this precise time to dip two recalcitrant Losts.

Nothing. Not yet.

"Make you brave," Dinah murmured to Taneyes. "Me be look after you."

The girl: waist-deep, pausing, turning her head to look at Mas' Torbern, Mas' Enchebern, and the others. The same blank stare, not even accusation in her eyes.

"I feel it," she said—the first words Dinah had heard pass the child's lips. "Will it hurt, Daddy?"

Mas' Torbern prodded her between the shoulder blades with a mutt stick and the girl plunged forward, facedown in the vat.

He held her below the slick green surface for the space of several breaths, and Dinah imagined the changing bugs filling the child's nose and mouth, surging deeper into her body. And then he released her. She floated to the surface, limp at first. Then she shuddered. Her arms broke free, a hand found the edge of the vat, and she pulled herself upright.

Mas' Torbern turned away from her, and wiped his mouth with the back of a hand. "Right," he said. "The other one. Let's get this finished."

The two big mutts, Tender and Wake, came and took a hold of Taneyes' arms. Expecting trouble, Dinah supposed.

Instead, Taneyes shook her head, and their hands fell away from her.

She stepped forward, her stride slow, measured, precise. She stopped and faced Mas' Torbern. "I am True," she said. "You have no right to do this to me. I will remember."

Mas' Torbern's upper lip curled up to one side, and then he stepped towards her and spat in her face.

She flinched, made as if to wipe her face, and then stopped herself. Straightening, she stepped forward.

Mas' Torbern waved away the two mutts and seized Taneyes' arm himself. Dinah saw whiteness spreading where he gripped her bare flesh, so tightly did he hold her.

By the steps to the dipping vat they stopped and he released her. "Say good-bye to yourself, bitch," he said.

Just then, Dinah saw movement down by the mangroves. She shifted from foot to foot, spilling the sweetwater she carried. No more movement, but she knew it was all happening now, all likely to go wrong.

Mas' Torbern pushed Taneyes, and she set foot in the changing vat. "I feel it," she taunted him, repeating the words uttered by the girl who had called him *Daddy*. "I will remember you."

Dinah saw a sudden change in Taneyes' expression, a movement of the eyes, an unspoken *Oh*. Dinah turned and saw figures down by the mangroves, just as Taneyes had seen.

Taneyes looked at Dinah now, questioning.

And Mas' Torbern sensed that something was wrong. He glanced over his shoulder at Enchebern and the other masters. At any moment he would see what was happening by the mangroves and the alarm would be raised.

Taneyes' arm snaked out and caught Mas' Torbern's clothes at the waist.

Both hands now, gripping his clothing, tugging, pulling in crude parody of his own clawing hands the night before.

She leaned back and he fell with her, arms flailing, mutt stick flying off into the swamp.

The other masters shrank back as a great spray of changing brew splashed up out of the vat and then fell back, enfolding the two bodies entwined like lovers in the sickly brew.

Silence.

Long silence.

Then a sudden burst of confused exclamations.

And then the sound of moist partings, of bodies pulling clear of the thick, slimy brew. Two figures emerged, dripping the goo into the dirt. One lashed out, struck the other, and Dinah saw Taneyes sprawling on the ground.

The one who had struck out now stood in a low crouch, legs apart, arms spread.

"Well?" he screeched. "What are you waiting for? Someone get some water and *wash me off!*"

The masters huddled, keeping their distance. Then Mas' Enchebern gestured, and Wake hurried up the path to comply.

Dinah looked back towards the mangroves and saw only a dark tongue of jungle, spreading out across the swamp, silent and undisturbed.

None of them would go within a few paces of the two when they emerged from the changing vat.

Treebesh, the visiting master from Beshusa, berated the others. "You have that fine whipping post, don't you?" he said. "Time we used it."

"She's changing," Mas' Enchebern pointed out, his voice calm, reasonable. He gestured at Taneyes, now kneeling, holding her head and groaning. "She's gone already. She's a blank. What is left to punish? Whipping's only going to spoil stock." Taneyes would fetch a better price at market if she left here in good condition.

Wake returned sloshing a bucket full of water. Mas' Torbern took it and doused himself with the brown water, scrubbing manically at his hair with clawed hands. "It's okay," he gasped, as he did so. "I'm clean. It's okay."

Some time later, they walked back along the path at the foot of the stockade, the other masters keeping apart from Mas' Torbern. They spoke little, but it was clear to Dinah that communication was taking place: an understanding shared.

Eventually, Torbern slowed, clutching at his head. Mas' Enchebern gestured at Wake and Tender, and the two mutts went to help their master.

"No," he groaned. "Away." He tried to straighten. "I'm okay."

Wake and Tender backed off, and the other masters continued on their way, unwilling to meet Torbern's staring eyes.

A short time later, he staggered forward and almost fell. This time he didn't object when the two mutts went to support him.

Back at the holding pens, a commotion was being raised. Men hurried about, calling and gesticulating. Mutts jabbered and chattered from their pens, excited and confused.

Amid the disarray, the party stopped by an empty pen.

Enchebern pointed at the pen. "In there with them," he said. Lariss and Taneyes stumbled into its shade and slumped to the floor.

The two mutts holding Torbern hesitated. Enchebern gestured again. "All three of them," he said. "Go on."

By now, Torbern was too feeble to resist. "Let me out," he gasped as Wake and Tender backed out of the pen.

Enchebern merely stared at him.

"You have changed," the master said. "Or, at least, you are in the process of changing. You belong with the Lost now, Tor."

Just *Tor*—Enchebern had quite deliberately stripped the clan affiliation from the fallen master's name.

The changed were tended in their holding pen by Dinah.

Through the night, the sounds of mutthounds came from beyond the stockade. The hunt was on for the escapees, but trails were hard to follow through the mangrove swamp, even for the hounds, and Dinah knew they had a good start on the Highway to Harmony. Once across the Little Elver it was unlikely they would be caught.

Dinah had more immediate concerns, though, as she sat with the three.

Of all of them, it was the girl, Lariss, who seemed most mildly affected by the change. She sat quietly, much as she had before. Occasionally, she spoke in a little girl voice. "Daddy?" she said, many times during the night. "Is that you, Daddy?"

Both her father, Tor, and Taneyes spent the night wracked with high fevers, crying out at sudden internal pains and traumas as the changing vectors worked on them.

So sudden and abrupt! Dinah heard cracking sounds as the bones in Tor's skull shifted, his forehead doming outwards and then receding. Dinah had seen such drastic shifts before, and on each occasion the victim had died from the trauma; but somehow Tor pulled through and in the morning lay quietly, shivering and sobbing.

Taneyes curled into a ball, her head resting on Dinah's lap. Dinah stroked her hair and cooed soothing songs and words into her ear. "You be okay," she told her repeatedly. "You keep you in you head, baby Taneyes. You hear me? You hold onto you'self. Dinah help you know who you are, you hear?"

Over a period of several days the three stabilised. And slowly, Dinah realised that her love for Tor was dying. Changed, he was no longer her master, and the gut thing had faded away. She felt no pangs of loss when time came for him to be shipped downriver to market.

They stood on the dock, the same group as the one that had set out for the dipping a few days before: the masters, Enchebern, Caltreco, Bereshbern, and Treebesh; the mutts, Dinah, Maddy, Tender, and Wake; and the changed, Taneyes, Lariss, and Tor.

The haul-boat was full, only three more places to fill.

The masters stood a little apart, talking among themselves. They were fascinated by Tor, drawn to him and repelled by him. It was as if they were making sure that this was actually happening. Tor watched them, too, blankness in his eyes.

It really had gone. Dinah was certain now. The gut-love of mutt for master had died as the changes wracked his body, and now he was nothing to her. He had his daughter, after all. Lariss remembered some things from before, as many changed could remember some things from before. The things that made a big impression, the things that hurt.

"Mama done live Sedgetress," Lariss had told Dinah, referring to a settlement upriver. The girl had learnt quickly to talk Mutter and play dumb, absorbing Dinah's advice with a wisdom beyond her years. For some, the change was a release, and Dinah hoped it was so for Lariss.

"You remember you papa?"

Lariss had nodded grimly. "Remember well. Things Papa done . . . Remember well."

And now, as the three moved towards the haul-boat, Lariss smiled back at Dinah, a little hand on her father's back, guiding him to the boat. "Bye, Dinah. Lariss done remember. Lariss make to look after Papa, you hear?"

And Dinah wondered what, exactly, the girl meant by that.

Taneyes went, too. A changed woman, she had retained her self-contained bearing, but Dinah had little idea of how much else she had clung on to. She was stable, at least, the changes complete.

As the three were guided into their holding pen on the boat, Dinah noticed something. All around, it was as if the normal routines of the day had been suspended and everyone had stopped what they were doing. The masters on the quayside; the mutts labouring on the docks and on the clutch of six or seven boats; in the dusty road that led from dock to the main settlement small groups had paused en route. In the water, even, heads were bobbing: the fisherfolk, pausing in their work of unfouling bladderpumps and screws.

All stopped to watch the departure of the fallen master.

Dinah turned away. The moment was gone, and normal activities resumed. When she looked back, the haul-boat was edging out into the river, and the fisherfolk were not to be seen.

She hadn't given this day a label, a hook to hang it on in her head. She didn't like farewells.

She went back through the stockade and cut across the transit camp, heading for the track to the fisherfolks' settlement. Nico would be there before her, waiting in the waters of their meeting place. More haul-boats were expected, and Mas' Enchebern had given her instructions to pass on to the water-mutts. She had the gut thing for Mas' Enchebern now, and he was a kinder master than Tor had ever been. But the love in her head for Nico was something of her own—*their* own—making.

She started to hum a tune; a song of Harmony, a song of love.

CHAPTER 7

Here at the aft of the haul-boat the stench from the mutt pens was little short of overpowering. Little wonder that the crew quarters were at the fore of the boat. There must have been a hundred of the creatures crammed into a line of pens in the bowels of the boat. The pens were half above deck and half below, shaded from the harsh sun only by a scattering of banana leaves weighted in place by rocks.

Flint settled back against the side-boarding and chewed on half a flatcake, trying to hold his breath as he ate in order to keep the food palatable.

Trader Gillambern would not feed him from the boat's supplies— he had made that much clear—despite the money they had taken from Clarel to pay for Flint's passage to Farsamy.

It was midafternoon now, and Greenwater was lost far upstream in the great meanders of the river Transom. By morning they would have reached the river Farsam, well on the way to the city of Farsamy itself.

He finished the flatcake and sipped from his water bladder, filled from the rainwater reservoir at the front of the boat. Gillam grudgingly allowed Flint water, at least.

It was four days now since Mesteb had returned from Trecosann with word only that Amber was still missing, and that both she and Flint were widely assumed to have run away from their father's brutality.

"How will you get there?" Clarel had asked, again, the previous day. No longer did she ask what he intended; no longer did she try to dissuade him from continuing his search for Amber in the backstreets and mutt auctions of Farsamy; no longer did she try to persuade him to settle here in Greenwater.

"Farsamy Way is a well-travelled route," he told her. "Chances are that I will fall in with another group heading south."

"Chances," she said dismissively. "You shouldn't take chances in the wilds."

Flint gestured with a hand: the still-receding floodwater with the cargo of river algae and the changing vectors it carried; the elypsian tree that grew from the water by the jetty, and the bulbous, diseased growths that had erupted overnight from its silver trunk; the kaleido-scope swarms of moths drawn to the corpses of fish stranded by the falling waters, attracted by the salt on their skin. "Risk is all around," he said. "Chance. You can't hide from it. I accept the risks of my journey to Farsamy."

"It is Carnival soon."

Flint nodded. Clans from all around would send delegations to Farsamy for Carnival, the greatest gathering of the year. Deals would be negotiated between clans that would bind them in trade for the year to come and beyond. Disputes would be settled, too. Clan Elders would debate matters that could not be settled locally. And, of course, the cit-izens of Farsamy would put on the biggest party they could manage.

"Mesteb travels to Carnival via Trecosann," said Flint. "I will not travel with him. I will not return to Trecosann. I've asked him to pass on word of my good health to Cousin Callum." A thought occurred to him then: "How about the haul-boats?" he said. "They go downriver to Farsamy."

Clarel nodded. "I could arrange passage for you," she said. "Clan Beren depend on us for bladderpumps for their boats. I know the traders. They would take you far quicker than you would manage on foot. If Amber really is heading there you could well arrive before her."

And so he found himself here, lurking at the back of one of the great haul-boats that plied the rivers Transom, Elver, and Farsam, thankful that he had some meagre supplies of food in his pack and short and long knives at his belt.

Lisebern paused atop the mutt pens partway down the boat, interrupting one of her occasional forays from the forecabin. She pulled at
her cloak, raising it above her hips, squatting to expose great slablike
buttocks to the air. Flint saw a dark gash, a tangled pubic shadow, and
then a stream of yellow liquid stabbed down through the roof of the
pen. A squeal came from below, a nervous chattering.

All the time, Lise stared at Flint, smiling at his discomfort.

Flint had never seen such calculating cruelty in another person's eyes
as there was in Lise's. He had never felt such an inner chill in the presence
of another. She made her trading mate, Gillam, seem meek by comparison.

"You seen something you like, have you?" she said, approaching
him casually, her long cane rattling the pen roofs behind her.

Now, she stood above him on the last of the pens, Flint still down
on the ribbed deck at the rear of the haul-boat. She gripped her crotch
and squeezed through the coarse swamp-cotton cloak. "It's all Gill's,
see? You touch me, he'll have you. If an' he even catches you looking
he'll be feeding your balls to the snapping turtles."

Flint looked away, skin burning.

"That's right. You don't look at what you can't have."

There was a sudden pained yelp, and Flint looked back again to see
Lise withdrawing her cane from between the pen's bars. He saw one of
the mutts cowering against the far side of the pen, others milling
around it and eyeing the woman above them fearfully.

Lise laughed, turned with a wiggle of the hips, and made her way
slowly forward.

Flint refused to walk over the tops of the cages as Gillam and Lise did. He
had never really considered how mutts were treated, partly because their

mistreatment was outside his experience: it was simple good husbandry to look after your mutts. Seeing them in these conditions, though . . .

To traverse the length of the haul-boat he walked along the narrow gangway at the side, hanging onto the pens with one hand to help balance. There was no barrier to catch him if he slipped, and underfoot there was only the yielding, leathery surface of the decking. It would be easy to go overboard.

The waters of the Transom here were thick with silt, much of it scoured out from flooded vales and swamps in the aftermath of the wet season.

Now he paused and settled on his haunches, hanging on with both hands. He thought of the snapping turtles that followed the boat, his backside hanging out over the water in this position. . . .

The level of the gangway was halfway up the pen's side, so he had to look down into the interior. Within, in a space perhaps five paces across and as many long, there were fifteen mutts.

The smell seemed muted to him now, as evening settled. His senses had dulled to it after a time. Body odour, sweet manure, urine-soaked rushes, and the ancient, oiled tubers from which the haul-boat had been grown combined in a smell quite unlike anything Flint had known before.

These mutts were more humanoid than many on the haul-boat. Probably only shoulder-high to Flint, they were powerful-looking creatures. They were all naked, but for filthy shorts, but their bodies were well protected by their thick, fleecy hides. Their faces were narrow—doglike, in a way.

Nearby, two of the creatures were grooming: one stood patiently as the other ran fingers through its coat, picking out bugs and small pieces of broken rush and other debris.

"Listen up," said Flint, interrupting their peace. All fifteen faces turned towards him immediately, their ingrained obedience to True humankind running deep.

"Me master outta Trecosann," he said. "You speak Mutter? You been know me words? Me been look for mistress outta Trecosann. Her got red in hair, yellow in eye, she high like this." He held his hand level with his chest. "If an' you see her you treat her plenty good. You been know me words? Her find me Farsamy."

He moved on, tried again.

There was a great diversity of mutts, even on this one haul-boat. Many were only distinguishable from humans by their general demeanours, by subtle differences in physique and, of course, by their inability to speak anything other than Mutter. Lise had said earlier that these beasts had "good blood in them," laughing again at his shocked reaction to her crude references to human-mutt interbreeding. She could not know that it made him think of his own mother, his own sister. He studied these mutts closely, but there was nothing in them that recalled Amber to his eyes: his sister was True, he was certain, even if her father might not be Tarn. Others of the mutts on the haul-boat were far more animal in form, moving about apelike on foot and knuckle, little more than pack animals.

And in among them were the Lost.

The pen near to the forecabin held at least four mutts that were different. Flint came to that pen now, and told them all to listen up. Ten turned instantly, rapt in attention; four turned sullenly, slowly—suspicious and fearful.

Sometimes, when the changing fevers strike, there is left behind the empty shell of a human being: a blank with no memory, no desires, no spirit. A human become animal, a human become no more than a mutt, only fit to be traded.

Flint stared at the four blank faces, compelled by the thought of the individuals who had once lived in those bodies, the lives and memories lost forever.

"Me master outta Trecosann," he went on. "You been know me words?"

As he spoke, he was aware that he was being observed with amusement by Gillam and Lise, but he went on to the end and, as ever, the only response was a few mutters, an enthusiastic nodding of heads, the mutts ever eager to please a True human.

"You gonna ask me if I seen you mistress outta Trecosann, are you?"

Flint turned to meet Gillam's look. The trader was sitting in a fold of his cabin wall. The whole forecabin was a podhut grown in situ, fleshy walls merging with the haul-boat's deck in an interlocking of tiny fibres.

"Have you seen her?" asked Flint. The trader had already heard his description of Amber.

Gillam shook his head. "She pretty?"

Flint shrugged.

"She is an' she'll fetch a good price." Gillam cackled, and somewhere from the cabin Lise laughed too.

Flint turned.

"You wasting your time with the mutts," said Gillam, more gently now. "They ain't none of them so bright. Ain't no one want to buy a brainy mutt."

The haul-boat lay anchored for the night at the mouth of the river Transom. The waters were strangely calm here, before the turbulence where the Transom joined the great river Farsam.

Flint lay on his sleeping rug at the rear of the boat. Despite the day's heat, the nights were cold, and he savoured the slight warmth emanating from the deck. Now that they were no longer in motion, the smells from the mutt pens were not wafted back to him so intensely, and instead he smelt sweet nectar from the trees overhanging the water.

He couldn't get the four Lost out of his mind. He wondered how they had been so afflicted. The fevers, perhaps. Or punishment for heinous crimes—Flint knew only too well that such punishments were sometimes inflicted.

He turned onto his side.

Who might have changed them? he wondered. It was not only Clan Treco that had mastered the changing arts, after all. He remembered childhood tales of bogeymen—tallymen!—who kidnapped children and adults and changed them so that they could be traded as mutts.

He wondered again—as he had ever since the moment Greenwater had disappeared around a bend in the Transom—at the wisdom of travelling on a haul-boat, trusting his safe passage to the traders.

He woke to sudden turbulence. He scrambled to his feet and saw that they were under way already, the haul-boat kicking and bucking as it bore out from the mouth of the Transom and into the river Farsam. Looking up along the length of the boat, he could see that the craft itself was twisting in the waves, yielding to conflicting pressures.

Gulls screamed in a massed flock overhead, wheeling and swooping and darting down at the rough water for scraps of food. Flint had no idea what it was that they might be finding to eat.

He pulled the hat onto his head, the morning's light interrupted by feathery clouds scudding across the face of the sun. He fastened his hat and cloak against the wind and pulled himself along the gangway—treading carefully—to join Gillam and Lise on the foredeck.

He had intended to ask if he could help in any way, but as soon as he reached the foredeck, Gillam turned from the boat's wheel and snarled, "Keep out of the way, or I'll pen you with the mutts."

Lise wasn't here. She must either be in the forecabin or somewhere back with the mutts.

Flint retreated, deciding to brave the gangway again and return to the rear of the boat. He would bide out the rest of the journey there, he decided.

Lise was in one of the pens, about a third of the way back along the haul-boat. The gate was open, but none of the mutts tried to escape. Instead, they cowered flat against the cage sides, trying in vain to retreat from Lise.

As Flint watched, she raised her cane. Too cramped in the pen to draw it all the way back, instead she used the broad base as a club and smashed it into the temple of one of the mutts.

The creature whimpered and dropped to its knees.

Lise realised she was being watched and turned, smiling. "You leave them be," she said. "They're mine."

"Okay," said Flint, raising his free hand. "I'm just going past."

But why was she treating them like that? Mutts couldn't help but be obedient. She didn't have to beat them to get their obedience.

Flint resumed his journey, but then paused as the mutt on its knees tried to get back to its feet and Lise snapped, "Don't move!" She raised her cane again.

The mutts eyed her and the cane and fell still.

Flint stared at Lise. The mutts obeyed her because they feared her and not because they recognised her as a True human who must naturally be obeyed.

He had always thought it obvious: the difference between True and Lost. He stared at Lise in shock and wondered how much of the river trade was controlled by her kind, by outcasts from the world of the True—by those who had lost what it was that made them human. The very idea offended every rule of civilisation he had grown up with.

"What is it?"

He raised both hands this time. "Nothing. Nothing. I'm just . . ."

She seemed to recognise the understanding in his eyes. She raised her cane and advanced on him, but he had the advantage of height and position.

"Stop her," he commanded and, instinctive obedience overcoming fear, the mutts stepped in front of Lise, forming a protective wall.

She swung the cane, beating at them.

Flint stepped back and slammed the gate down on the pen's side, bolting it home. He had no idea what he would do, could not even think what might be his options.

He turned, and saw Gillam advancing along the top of the pens, another whipping cane in his hand, a look like thunder on his face.

Immediately Lise started to yell and wail, her little dark hands clutching at the bars of the pen, trying to force the gate open from within.

Flint worked his way sidestep along the gangway, but Gillam was making rapid progress.

Flint glanced over his shoulder into the fierce waters of the Farsam. And then he stepped over the side, plunging into water, opaque and brown and chill as the mountaintops from where it came.

CHAPTER 8

He thought he would never even break the surface, and he thought, too, that maybe that would be for the best.

He opened his eyes to darkness—stinging, muddy water scouring his eyeballs instantly. His senses were numbed by the utter cold, and his limbs hung loose, dragged only by the surging of the current, tugged this way and that, that way and this. He had no sense of his position in the water, his depth; no sense of whether he was rising or sinking, or merely suspended in a current at some indeterminate depth.

It was the fiery pain in his lungs that prevented him from succumbing to the river's cold embrace. More and more, all he wanted to do was inhale, fill his lungs, and yet he knew that if he did so the river's hold on him would be final, its cold, silty fingers penetrating his lungs, stilling his raging heart.

He had never wanted anything so intensely! He felt his head filling with madness, voices urging him to breathe, *breathe, breathe!*

Something snagged around his ankle, coiling up his lower leg.

The voices stilled and he jacknifed his body, flapped his arms, and a hand brushed against a warm fibre wrapped around his shin.

He remembered the land anemones anchored to the trees overhanging the Transom at Greenwater, long tentacles trailing into the water. For an instant, he believed he could pull himself up to the surface along one of these tentacles.

But no . . . he thought that the thing had come from below, not above. It had been reaching up from the riverbed. He was getting his bearings.

He fumbled at his belt, found the machete. He couldn't swing it— the waters were too thick, too resistant to sudden movement.

He stabbed down, sluggishly. Felt the blade's flat side strike his knee.

He felt his senses starting to darken, knew he did not have long. Did the tentacles carry some kind of numbing poison, or was it just the lack of air finally finishing him?

The grip eased. The blade must have struck home.

The coils fell away from his leg, and Flint felt the machete handle slip from his grasp . . . lost.

He arched his back and pushed with his feet against the water. Arms above his head, cupped hands pulling down in a clumsy parody of swimming.

He broke the surface, drew air, lungs afire. Slumped back in the water, head just above the surface, coughing and retching, wishing that he was dead.

Eventually—the passage of time meant nothing to him now—he rolled onto his front and started to kick. The shore was a distant green fringe, the river violent and cold. He knew there were many snapping turtles in the river here, athough most were too small to attack a grown man, but he didn't know what else might lurk in the depths. He remembered the wheeling flock of gulls, where the rivers met: there was clearly food for scavengers here, and probably food for predators, too.

He fought the urge to swim harder. He was not a strong swimmer: he must pace himself if he ever wanted to set foot on dry land.

The shore loomed forbiddingly.

He had swum so far, his strokes mechanical and repetitive like the instinctive movements of a bladderplant, and now . . .

The shore of the river Elver at Trecosann consisted of gentle, muddy shelves lined with swamp grasses and rushes—so benign a shore that the clan had had to excavate a berthing channel for the town's docking facilities.

As he swam he had held dear the prospect of crawling ashore onto a shingle beach, or pulling himself through the soft clutches of river grass.

Yet now he trod choppy water, staring up at the rocks. A mass of stained white boulders huddled by the river, grey foam smashing against their flanks.

The current tugged him in towards the vortices at the foot of the cliffs, and he allowed himself to be drawn towards the rocks.

A glancing blow knocked the air from his lungs, but his instinct, by now, was refined by desperation. The fingers of one hand wedged themselves into a cleft in the rock, skin tearing, but still his grip held.

Another hand found a crack between two boulders, and he hauled himself up so that his chest was clear, his hips, and then a foot found purchase and he pushed up.

He lay naked in the sun.

All children were taught at an early age that they should not expose themselves to the dry-season sun, for at this time of year it was easy to burn. Those vulnerable would come out in crops of sun-blisters: little brown growths of skin cells that would have to be excised and sealed before they could spread.

But Flint was cold, right through to the bone. His boots and clothes, heavy with chill water, lay spread out on the rocks to dry.

The sun felt good, dry heat tingling across skin sensitised by the scouring of the thick, gritty water.

Finally, he sat up, hugging his knees to his chest. His left leg was a livid pink up to the knee where it had been gripped beneath the river. He studied his left hand, raw and bloody from the rocks. He remembered Lizabel, the dentist's daughter. She would have had something to heal his torn and injured skin.

He stared out across the waters of the Farsam, which looked so deceptively benign from this elevation.

There was no sign of the haul-boat now.

He was on his own. All he had were his clothes and the short knife he had brought from Trecosann. All else—money, food, clothing, machete—was either on the haul-boat or lost in the depths of the river.

Behind him, the jungle was thick and forbidding.

In a cluster of chalk boulders nearby he found a fist-sized lump, almost a perfect sphere. He raised it with his good hand and smashed it against the side of a bigger rock. It split into two, with a few small fragments flying off under the shock of the impact. River flint. He placed the two pieces where he had rested, and then he retreated to the shade of an umbrella tree that grew from a crack between the rocks. The gesture was meaningless, but it comforted him to have left his signature in this small way.

He struggled in his head to sort out the geography. All the settlements, within Clan Treco territory and beyond, were connected by traditional routes through the wilds. He had a vague, patchwork understanding of the layout of the land: two days' trek east of Trecosann lay Greenwater; one day east and then six days north up the Farsamy Way lay Berenwai. He knew of the three rivers: the Elver, the Transom, and the Farsam. But it was hard to put it all together in his head.

He was on the east bank of the Farsam, at the point where the great river was fed by the Transom. If he could head south along this bank, he would eventually reach a crossing to Beshusa, he thought; and farther downriver, Farsamy itself.

He would have to travel through the jungle, though, for it grew right down to—and, indeed, *into*—the river where the terrain allowed.

He would never survive such a journey without eating and drinking from the jungle—food and drink that could easily be loaded with changing vectors and other poisons. Such a journey would kill him. Or, worse, *change* him.

The nearest settlement to the point where the rivers met—at least to Flint's inadequate grasp of geography—was Restitution, home of the Riverwalkers.

The Riverwalkers were not a clan in the conventional sense of the term: a gathering of family groups of the True, bound by blood and history. The Riverwalkers formed a scattered community made up from many different clans. They boasted the finest engineers of the True, many of them joining other clans as bondsmen, trading on their skills and understanding. Many of them travelled, too, visiting settlements to preach and proselytise.

The only Riverwalker Flint had ever met was an old man who called himself—some said self-deprecatingly, others said arrogantly—Knowsbetter. Grey and frail, Knowsbetter travelled alone from town to town, staying for a few days here, a few days there. He charmed adults with his gentle insight and good manners; he intrigued children with tales of adventure in which the God-fearing Riverwalkers always found a peaceful end and all others died in manners both horrible and darkly funny.

The detail of his stories now escaped Flint, belying the Elders' fears that the old man had been brainwashing the young, but one thing Knowsbetter had said had stuck: he had described his home among the Riverwalkers as "north of where the rivers meet . . . you can hear the roar of the waters from the Communary."

Flint did not know if the Riverwalkers' settlement was on the east or west shore of the Farsam, but he could hear the roar of the rivers meeting loud in his ears, so it could not be far.

As long as the old preacher had been telling the truth, of course.

For a time he was able to head north in the open, scrambling over the rocks that formed a low cliff above the river. Soon, however, the scat-

tered trees—umbrellas and squat oaks and others he did not know—
grew thicker.

Finally the rocky outcrop retreated and he was walking on spongy
mud, matted with moss and grasses, which gave softly with every step.
Soon even this ran out and he was confronted with thick, oozing mud and
water, scattered trees even growing up from the waters of the river itself.

This was probably still the effect of wet-season flooding, he realised,
and in a few weeks this would be dry ground, but now it was impassable.

He had to head inland, away from the Farsam.

It would be so easy to lose himself in the jungle.

Through occasional gaps in the canopy, he made sure the sun was
at his back. Still heading north.

This was no longer just a matter of looking for his sister, he knew.
It was a simple matter of survival. All else was secondary.

Now the sun was at its greatest height.

He had been walking for most of the morning.

The jungle was patchy here. The forest floor was rocky and bare in
places, and in others it was choked by growth of tangleweed and thornbushes, with trailing brushes of moss hanging from the trees.

Midday.

Flint realised something was wrong only moments before his knees
buckled and he slumped to all fours, vomiting dark liquid onto the leaf
litter that lay thick here.

He stared at the dark stain, fascinated. Instantly, beetles and other
small creatures swarmed over his ejecta, craving its moisture, its nutrients.

His guts tightened and he retched again, dumping a smaller quan-
tity of bileous dark scum onto the unsuspecting insects.

Dizzy, muddled, he slumped. Rolled onto his side. Drew his knees
up, shivering and hot at the same time.

He woke to snuffling sounds, damp probings of his face.

He moved, and a small animal chittered in alarm and scurried away.

He sat, peering around in the twilight gloom.

His brief glimpse of the animal had suggested it was some kind of rodent, something like the street rats that kept human settlements clean. That might explain why it had been puzzled by him, why it had done nothing to harm him: street rats, like mutts and many other species, could do nothing to harm a True human. Even out here in the wilds, subservience to humankind went deep, it seemed.

The sickness must have been a delayed reaction to his near-drowning in the Farsam. Or at least, that was what he hoped. The alternative—that he had picked up some jungle illness or fever—was too disturbing.

He felt okay now. Strong enough to move on.

The light was poor, but he could still see where he was going. He thought it wise to at least look for some kind of shelter for the night—not that he expected to sleep.

Darkness made him stop some time later, his only shelter a rocky, waist-high ridge that cut straight through the forest. He could hear a gentle background roar when he stopped moving, and he felt comforted when he realised that it was the sound of the river somewhere nearby.

His back to the flat stone of the ridge, he saw out a lonely vigil. The sounds of the jungle at night were different to those of the daytime: a lesser volume of animal noise, a steady hum that must be insect in origin, the cooing of oak flowers in the breeze, occasional shrieks and booms of night animals and birds.

He dozed occasionally, waking with a start each time, disoriented, confused, frightened.

The rocky ridge was the remains of a wall, he now saw. Morning light slanted through the trees, picking out skipping butterflies and scarlet bucket-flowers hanging from great, trailing lianas. Nearby, half submerged by tangled growths of forest-floor scrub, there were other walls and fallen buildings.

A long-abandoned settlement. Was this all that remained of Restitution?

He remembered Knowsbetter's words: yes, he could hear the river's waters from here, although not the sound of the meeting rivers as the preacher had implied.

He followed the long wall that had provided shelter in the night. At its end there was a thinning in the jungle and great bunches of fleshfruit hung, bulbous and purple.

He was hungry and thirsty, and yet he knew all too well that you should never eat the fruit of the wilds.

He turned away.

He found a clump of bell flowers. Moisture gathered in the cuplike bracts around the base of each flower. He knew he would not get far without at least something to drink, and so he tipped one of the flowers up and supped at its sweet water.

The hunger did not go, but it eased.

He thought he could manage another day, drinking only water, but if he was still alone in the jungle after that he would have to find something to eat, relying only on his judgement to find food that was palatable and not corrupt.

He was walking, he realised, although he could not remember deciding to set out again.

Survival instinct, he decided.

Ahead, there was a thick screen of lianas, beaded with scarlet flowers. He had to get through.

His heart was racing, his head muzzy.

Oracle. He had to get to Oracle.

He tasted it on the air, the sweet pherotropic blanket descending on him, soothing his muddled thoughts.

Lucid-trance smothered him, even as he was out here in the jungle and not safely enfolded in Oracle.

Wrong, he realised.

Oracle doesn't call. Oracle doesn't reach out through the jungle to haul you in. . . .

A great globular mass of flesh nestled in the clearing, as if dropped from a great height. Oracle's skin was thick and encrusted with foul growths, dead white flakes lifting and settling with its inner heavings. Dark veins pulsed across its surface; melonlike tumours clustered around its girth; fissures and sphincters opened and closed at many points on its slick, greasy hide.

And the air was heavy with Oracle's secretions, far more intense than any Flint had ever experienced at Trecosann's Oracle.

"Master," a soft, seductive voice said. Oracle knew he was here. It had sensed him coming, had tasted his scent on the air.

"Master. Oh, Master! Tell me . . . of . . . tell me of . . . the wooooorld."

Its voice soft, its voice breathless and unpractised, Oracle spoke to him, soothed him.

"Master . . . tell me . . ."

Oracle sat in a quagmire of its own making, a shiny green swamp surrounding it, its smartfibre filaments reaching out through the marshy groundwater, down into the bedrock itself. Oracle sat at the centre of its swampy home, Flint realised, and although he had not entered Oracle, he was already surrounded by it, engulfed by it.

That slick around Oracle's base . . . It reminded Flint of the changing vats Callum tended at Trecosann. Oracle was mad, Oracle was corrupt—Oracle was *changed*.

And Oracle wanted him.

Dark forms around Oracle's base. Not cancerous eruptions as he had first thought, not distorted polyps.

They were bodies.

Human, perhaps. Some smaller: children, or mutts, or beasts from the wilds.

All drawn in by Oracle.

He wondered how long ago this settlement had died, how long its Oracle had sat here, deprived of company, deprived of the input its kind so craved. Driven mad by loneliness and change, sole survivor of an ancient settlement.

And even as he wondered this, he was on his knees, crawling over the swamp grass towards Oracle.

He couldn't stop. His will . . . his flesh . . . too weak to resist Oracle's pull.

It was the sound of voices that saved him. A steady chant breaking through the cloak of madness Oracle had cast over him.

He tottered on the brink of the glowing pool that surrounded Oracle.

"Tell meeee . . ." the thing urged him. "Tell me . . . of the world!"

Leaning forward, supported on all fours, almost falling, he heard the chanting.

The slumped shapes of the fallen clustered around Oracle's flanks. Bodies. Flesh darkened and collapsed around bones, skin crisped and husklike, and yet the things were still alive, or at least animated in some way!

Slowly, a head turned towards him. Sunken eyes studied him, a skeleton mouth grinned, a narrow tongue flicked across tightly stretched lips.

Another lump moved, almost completely covered in encrustations of some kind of fungus. Eyes stared.

"Tell me . . ."

The chanting came from farther away.

Conscious again, he realised that he was blanking out for long intervals, giving himself up to Oracle's chemical inducements.

He looked down and saw his green reflection in the striated surface of the pool, smelt the familiar sweet sulphur smell of the changing vats. He was leaning so far forward that he might easily topple.

It would be so easy to give himself, to become, to join . . . Oracle.

The chanting. Voices.

He pushed himself back from the brink, sat back on his heels, teetering, dizzy.

Back, he twisted, caught himself, started to crawl away, hating himself for doing so, hating himself for wanting to stay with Oracle.

He came to a broken wall and pulled himself to his feet, gasping for breath.

Oracle was some way back now, lost to sight behind the trees and the undergrowth, and still its pull was intense.

There was light ahead, a thinning of the trees.

He staggered in that direction, brushing aside drapes of moss and realising as he did so that only days before the thought of merely touching a forest growth like this would have chilled him to the core. Now, it was in his way so he pushed it aside.

He emerged on a narrow rocky shore and looked out across the grey waters of the river Farsam.

Out in the middle of the channel, a line of people—no: golden-fleeced mutts, he realised—were walking on the water, taking great, exaggerated strides and chanting to keep themselves in time with each other.

The mutts were walking against the current.

Flint stared.

It was a low boat, he saw now. Two humans sat at the rear of the craft, heads close together, talking to each other. The mutts were driving the boat somehow, the energy from their tread giving the boat the power to fight the river's current.

He had found the Riverwalkers, he realised.

"Hey!" he called out, waving his arms. "Hey! Over here!"

But they didn't hear him, didn't see him.

Soon they were lost to sight.

They had been a figment of his fevered imagination, he thought, as he worked his tortuous way through the jungle, staying as close to the river as he could manage. A vision conjured up by the mind-altering scents with which the mad Oracle had filled the air.

And then he heard the chanting again, in the distance.

Moments later, he emerged into a clearing where the trees and undergrowth had been cleared, a buffer zone between the wilds of the jungle and the home of the Riverwalkers.

A tall wooden stockade lay ahead of him, and as he approached he saw faces peering out of window slits, and figures gathering on the top of the wall, pointing and gesturing.

He looked down at himself. His clothing was filthy with mud and debris from the forest. He staggered into the open, limping heavily on the leg that had been injured by Tarn and then seized by some river creature. He clutched his injured hand to his chest.

If the madness in his eyes reflected the madness in his head, then he must look a deranged sight indeed.

"Knowsbetter?" he gasped. "Is Knowsbetter here?"

Some distance short of the stockade he stopped, convinced that they would not let him in and that they could not be blamed for turning him away.

He dropped to his knees.

"Knowsbetter . . . ?" he gasped, and then fell forward onto his face.

CHAPTER 9

He opened his eyes and they were all around him. The sky was near white with glare from the morning sun, and so it was hard to distinguish details in the silhouetted forms looming over him. There were six or seven of them: the men with thick beards and all with some kind of ornamentation—dangling beads and other odd shapes—tied into their hair.

The Riverwalkers had found him.

Rock grated against his cheek as he stirred.

"Knowsbetter?" he gasped. "Is Knowsbetter here? Is this Restitution?"

There was a low rumble of voices, heads turning, hands gesturing. They carried spears, he saw, held ready to strike.

Something tapped his cheek and he turned his head, saw that it was the blunt end of a spear. A man looked down at him. "Wha' make you ask for Knowsbetter?" the man said.

They were talking to him in Mutter, Flint realised. It was understandable, given his rough appearance and the strange manner of his arrival.

He tried to concentrate. Tried to fight the exhaustion that smothered his reasoning.

"I . . . I . . ."

He tried to push himself upright, but immediately the spear butt swung low, struck his wrist, and he collapsed facedown on the dusty ground.

More angry exchanges, words impossible to distinguish. Darkness at the edges of his vision.

They made him stand, gesturing and prodding with spears and mutt sticks.

Upright, he swayed vertiginously. A sharp prod in his left buttock set him moving. It took all his concentration simply to walk at first.

Sparse grasses and thornbush grew in the cleared area between jungle and stockade, and a profusion of tiny green lizards skittered out at every footfall. He found himself fascinated by the tiny details. He shuddered. He decided that he must be suffering the aftereffects of his sickness, or of the mad Oracle's chemical attractants and hallucinogens.

In the periphery of his vision he saw his captors, their hair tied in long tails down their backs. All had smartfibre chains around their heads, threaded through tiny carved bones and beads that changed colour continually. They wore long, plain cloaks under which he knew they would be barefoot.

The stockade was taller than the one at Greenwater, faced with smooth planking that would make it hard to climb. High gates retracted as they approached, sliding smoothly into the wall itself.

His foot struck a rock and he stumbled.

Instantly a spear prodded at him. "Up on you feet," a young woman snapped.

They passed through the stockade and entered a grove of cultivated fleshfruit trees. Instantly, Flint's stomach clamoured to be filled. He looked all about, dizzy.

Figures from the top of the stockade looked down, voices jabbered, sticks thrust.

He staggered on.

The settlement was a short distance farther. He narrowed his eyes against the glare and saw the bulbous shapes of podhuts, lined up in rows. Some were caged in bamboo scaffolding, new compartments being grown, shaped by the exoskeleton of cane. Restitution seemed a healthy place, a growing town.

They came to the first of the podhuts, at last, and people emerged to look at the small procession, to stare at the sorry creature their neighbours were driving into town.

Flint's breath rasped painfully now, his steady progress maintained by frequent prods from behind.

More faces, staring. Wide eyes, the whites almost luminous against dark skin. The people wore simple cloaks, men and women alike. Few wore hats or hoods, he saw. He remembered that Knowsbetter had disdained protection from the sun, too. Differing constitutions and immunity, perhaps, or simply different attitudes to risk.

They came to a small square, and by now a sizable crowd had gathered around them. Sticks and staring faces . . . Flint felt dizzy again, confused. Suddenly he was back in Trecosann. A boy, barely nine years old. Staring faces. A mutt stick in his hand, its surface smooth in his small grip, its point specially sharpened for the occasion. Pointing and thrusting. Flint and others guiding the beasts into the changing vats.

"No!" he cried out, panic suddenly ripping loose. He twisted, saw looks of sudden alarm on the faces of those guiding him.

Sticks raised to thrust, spears raised to strike home.

Flint flailed his arms, backing away from them.

He came to a wall and pressed against it, felt the podhut's pulse deep within. Steady, ceaseless, comforting.

He slid down the wall until his chin came to rest on his knees, and around him the Riverwalkers closed in.

"My name is Flintreco Eltarn," he said. His throat was raw and painful, but he was determined to talk clearly in order to communicate to them that he was a True human, despite what they might think. "I come from Trecosann. Knowsbetter visited Trecosann several years ago and told us all about Restitution. Is he here?"

He was in the centre of a square, somewhere in the settlement he believed to be Restitution. Banana leaves arched overhead, a canopy quickly constructed by young boys to protect him from the midday sun.

Twist-woven loops of smartfibres coiled around both of his ankles. They anchored him to the bedrock softly but securely, tightening only when he struggled.

Before him now, a short man of middle years squatted on his haunches, his greying beard forming a curtain that swept across his knees. Beads and small white figurines had been tied throughout his thick hair. He studied Flint closely, head angled slightly, something like amusement in his eyes.

"Cherry said he'd found a monkey," the man said now, in a voice as high and soft as a young woman's. "If you hadn't called for Knowsbetter you'd probably have been left to the Lord's judgement." He reached into the bag slung from his shoulder, produced a bladder and handed it to Flint. The water it held was sweet and cool.

There were real monkeys in the jungle, but Flint knew that this man used it in the sense more commonly used as an insult: a distorted, changed creature bearing some human traits, lower than a mutt or even a common domestic beast.

"I am a True human," said Flint. "I understand why your people should doubt me, but I am True. I was lost in the jungle. What can I do to prove myself?"

The man smiled now. "Oh, you'll get your opportunity," he said. "We live in a time of trials. We must all prove ourselves in the eyes of the Lord."

Flint sat in his shelter, knees drawn up to his chest, biding his time. He took comfort in the fact that they had taken him within their stockade and provided him with water and a few wedges of fleshfruit.

As the afternoon passed, he had slept uncomfortably and fitfully, had watched hawks soaring high on thermals, watched ranks of children practising martial arts in the street, swinging legs and clubs with disturbing synchrony of movement, unified by high-pitched chanting. People had passed, all turning to stare at him: the freak, the monkey.

The sun was swollen and orange in the western sky now, floating lazy above the treetops. The dry, menacing heat in the air was beginning to ebb away, much as the aches and pains in his body were finally starting to subside.

Flint felt more at ease now than at any time since he had left Trecosann.

He waited, and finally they came.

There were four of them, including the one who had been tending to him during the day.

They stood before him and bowed their heads, hands held out before them in some gesture akin to supplication. Some kind of formal greeting, Flint decided.

The one with neat ranks of narrow bones hanging from the quick-fibre band across his forehead spoke first. "Welcome to Restitution," he said. "I apologise for your quarantine, but you arrived under somewhat peculiar circumstances. We trust in the Lord, but our fellow men must earn our trust." He smiled at this, and Flint suspected that his words were some kind of play on a catechism or saying.

Something in his voice suddenly penetrated Flint's consciousness. "Knowsbetter?" he asked, staring at the man's evenly sculpted features. He should have been older than this, Flint thought, but then memory can be misleading sometimes.

The man shook his head. "My uncle," he said. "I have not seen him in fifteen years, since he took to the road. I heard last year that he had found his judgement on the road to Rittasan."

Dead, Flint assumed, from the finality of the man's choice of words. Decoding these people's words was like trying to follow Mutter, he thought: familiar words used in different ways, with subtly different meanings.

"My name is given as Seesthroughlies," the man continued. He held a hand out to indicate his three companions. "My brothers' names are given as Judgesothers, Teller, and Tallofmind." The last was the short man who had tended to Flint during the day.

Flint wondered suddenly if these names were those they used among themselves, or names created just for his use. He recalled Knowsbetter's fondness for word games, and the debates in Trecosann about what was to be inferred from the old preacher's choice of name.

"My name is Flintreco Eltarn—"

"He gives himself a name!" Judgesothers interrupted.

"Before the eyes of the Lord!"

"He is not a Riverwalker," Seesthroughlies reminded them.

He turned to Flint. "Flint of Clan Treco, child of Tarn, Brother Cherrytree tells us you are a monkey, a facsimile of the human form put in our midst by the good Lord to test us. Brother Tallofmind here tells us that you claim to be a True human, fallen on unfortunate circumstances, that you turned to the Riverwalkers in the hope of the Lord's mercy. Which of my brothers should I believe?"

"I am True," said Flint simply. "I come from Trecosann, where my family is long-established. My sister, Amberline, disappeared, and so I set out to find her. Whether she has run away or been abducted, I intend to find her."

He drank from the bladder Tallofmind had brought. "My cousins bought me passage on a haul-boat to Farsamy, but the crew . . . Both were Lost, and when I learned this they turned on me. I was lucky to escape from them, even if it landed me on the bank of the river Farsam with no food, water, or money.

"I worked out that I was several days' travel through dense jungle from Beshusa and even farther from Farsamy. But I recalled the time, many years ago, when your uncle, Knowsbetter, came to Trecosann. His stories were popular with the children, and he stayed for several days."

He paused again and drank more sweetwater. "I remembered his description of Restitution: a short way north of where the Transom and the Farsam meet—not far from where I found myself stranded. I travelled north, staying close to the river where possible."

"You found us easily enough?" asked Seesthroughlies. "You passed through the jungle without problem?"

Flint recalled the mad Oracle. "There was an Oracle," he said. "One that has changed. . . . It tried to lure me with its siren scents."

"The Lost wisdom machine is a danger to all who travel south of here," said Seesthroughlies. "It shields us from that direction—many of the Lost and the fallen go to their judgement there—but it is a grave trial for any of us who stray near."

Flint thought of the perverted corpses, their desiccated flesh melded into the swollen walls of what Seesthroughlies called the Lost wisdom machine. "There were bodies," he said. "Joined to the Oracle with smartfibres. They moved. They watched me, as if they were being kept alive by the thing."

"Alive or dead," said Teller. "They fell before the Lord."

"Their judgement has found them," agreed Seesthroughlies. He looked at Flint now with a measuring gaze. "You must have been close to the wisdom machine to see what you report," he said.

Flint met the Riverwalker's look. "I have been through a lot," he said. "I am not easily defeated."

He realised that his words were true, and as he spoke he became suddenly aware of the gulf that had opened up between himself and the naive young man who had left Trecosann only a matter of days before.

Night in his makeshift shelter was cold, a steady breeze cutting through the clearing from the direction of the river Farsam.

Flint sat, huddled up, shivering. The jungle sounds were distant, only a few strange shrieks and cries carrying above the background buzz of insects and trees. Closer to, he heard the insistent rush of water. He realised that he may have misinterpreted old Knowsbetter's words: "north of where the rivers meet . . . you can hear the roar of the waters from the Communary." He had thought that meant that you could hear the sound of the rivers meeting but the preacher could simply have meant that you could hear the sound of one of the rivers, as Flint now could.

He had been lucky, then, he realised, as he sat in the cold, anchored to the ground by the intimate ankle-embrace of twisted cords of smartfibres.

Later, someone—a woman, moving with hurried, apologetic movements—brought him a blanket. She scampered away immediately, not responding to his words of gratitude. The blanket was made of a coarse fibre, an animal wool, Flint thought. It smelt damp and mouldy, but then so too, in all probability, did Flint. It was a long thing, and he was able to wrap himself twice in it.

Soon, he was less chilled. He lay on his side, head raised on a fold of the coarse blanket, and managed to sleep.

The slow, insistent beat of a gong woke him when the sky was still dark, a red stain spreading up from the eastern horizon, limning the peaks of the distant hills with a golden halo.

His ankle bonds stretched far enough for him to shuffle behind the small shelter and piss in the dirt. Stomach cramps took him, and he had to drop his breeches and let loose a jet of diarrhoea. He wiped himself with his left hand—the traveller's way—and rinsed with what remained of the previous day's sweetwater. When he looked back, he saw that three scrawny street rats had emerged to clean up after him.

When Tallofmind came with the woman a short time later, carrying between them a new bladder of water, a Riverwalker cloak, and some food wrapped in a vine leaf, Flint said, "I think I may be ill."

Tallofmind glanced at the woman. In the golden light of dawn, Flint saw that she was young and slim to the point of emaciation. He realised that her staring eyes were unseeing, and yet she was so attentive—turning her face in response to those around her. Following by sound and scent, he supposed.

She reached forward, and her rough little hands touched his face, his brow, felt the contours of his skull.

"Blind Jewel is a healer," said Tallofmind, watching the woman's face intently. She gave a small twitch of the head and he continued, "You may be sick, but you need not worry yet. You do not have one of the diabolic fevers. You told us yesterday that you have swallowed river water and passed through the jungle to the south. From the teachings we learn that there are many tiny machines and animalcules so small as to be invisible, each with a purpose in the Lord's scheme. When they take refuge in our bodies they cause us to be ill."

Flint felt another stomach cramp. "Can you heal me, Blind Jewel?"

She handed him the vine leaf wrap she had brought. He unfolded the soft green leaf and found two slabs of some kind of unleavened bread.

"Eat the bread," said Tallofmind. "And the leaf, too. After she brought your blanket in the night, Blind Jewel told us you were unwell and asked Brother Seesthroughlies to give his blessing to help you."

Flint did not feel like eating, but he raised a piece of bread and bit off a small piece. There were herbs in it, but he didn't recognise their flavours. He took a larger piece and chewed.

"Eat well," said Tallofmind. "For this evening is the time of your trial."

The day passed in a sequence of confusing, disconnected images. In his more lucid moments Flint wondered if he had been drugged or was, in truth, more ill than Blind Jewel had appreciated.

There was a period when he lay paralysed while all around him was a blur of motion. It was as if he had been bound up so tightly that not a muscle could move against its constraints. It was as if time itself were flowing around him, distorting like reflections in a rain-rippled pool: the world speeding by, motion folding around him, and yet Flint unable to respond.

Later—or earlier? or at the same time?—his mother, Jescka, came to him. She was beautiful, he realised, and he understood that this was not Jescka as he knew her, but Jescka as she may once have been, when her hold over the men of Trecosann had been that of a hand within a glove. The power of sexual attraction was great indeed, he understood. She had never been slim, but now the curves of her body folded into each other with the beauty of a winding river, the purest creation of nature. Skin like the finest Ritt linen, smooth and flawless. No scars marked her features yet, no bitterness in her eyes.

But then her face changed before him: her lower lip split open, one eye closed up with swelling, the eyebrow gashed above it. Vivid red blood smeared her perfect skin, plastering her fine black hair to her scalp.

"You've been a bad boy," she slurred, through broken mouth. "Now you're in big trouble. You'd better do as I say, do you hear?"

Another time: the clearing around him filled with sudden noise and movement. Children's voices raised high, singing and chanting. He sat shivering, wrapped in his night blanket, chin on knees, and watched as the children marched and pranced all around the square, all in perfect time to the irregular beat of a small hand drum, played with both ends of a small bone by a fierce woman with strips of raw flesh woven into her hair. He remembered seeing children practising martial arts the previous day, and saw in this display many of the same synchronised movements: high kicks and chops, and fantastically gymnastic leaps and twists through the ever-changing spaces between fast-swinging clubs and spears.

Another time: he was alone on the peak of a hill, ankles fastened to the rocks by a twist of quickfibre. All around him lay bones, some still draped with ribbons of skin, hair, leathered flesh. Rats crept through the bones, always tidying, always cleaning. Vultures soared above, and landed to scramble higgledy-piggledy over the corpses on the ground—untidy gentlemen of the dead, as he recalled Amber once calling them. They were waiting for him, he knew. Waiting for his time to come.

The Riverwalkers came for him as the sun hung low in the sky. Tallofmind and the one called Teller led a small group of men, women, and children, faces solemn, reverential.

In response to Tallofmind's signal, Flint stood. An old woman stepped forward and stooped to do something at his feet, and he felt the sudden release as the quickfibre anklets fell away.

Another gesture. The cloak Tallofmind had brought this morning still lay on the ground in Flint's small shelter.

"What is this?" asked Flint. "Why must I stand trial? What is happening?"

"We live in a time of trials," said Tallofmind. "The Lord has answers for us all. Undress and then put the cloak on."

Flint pulled at his tunic, dropped it in the dirt. His shirt followed, and then his breeches and shorts. At a signal from Tallofmind, he kicked off his sandals, too. Naked before them, he bent at the knees to gather the cloak, and then he dressed himself in the clothes of the Riverwalkers.

They led him across the clearing to a street that passed near to the great river. The ground was hard beneath his bare feet, and he trod gingerly over the sharp stones, struggling to keep up. Passing through clustered podhuts, they came to a larger building made from wood and stone, some kind of hall. Others were gathered here, and immediately Flint saw that they were outsiders: young men and women dressed in the same simple cloaks. There were a dozen—no, fourteen, he counted—standing in the small square by the building. Some talked nervously to each other; most were silent, looking scared and excited and eerily calm.

"Welcome to the Communary of the Noviciate," said Tallofmind. "Join the other trialists, Flint. Your time is nearly here."

"What is this?" he said in a low tone to a pale young woman standing a little apart from the others.

She turned her gaze in his direction. "The time of trials," she said simply.

The blankness in her eyes made him wonder again if he had been drugged, if they had all been drugged. He found it impossible to put an age on her now: at first he had thought her young, but there was something ancient in her look.

"I am Flintreco Eltarn," he said. "I don't know what all this is about."

"Another Trecosi," said the woman.

Flint looked at her. "You are Trecosi, too?" he asked, trying to place her.

She nodded. "Once," she said. "No more."

"Who are you?" he asked. "Where are you from?"

"We are nameless before the Lord," she told him.

A gong rang out again, like the one that had woken Flint this morning. It came from somewhere high on the Communary building, but he could not see where.

Seesthroughlies emerged from the high arched doorway. In his hand, an oil lamp burnt bright in the fading evening light, its smoke coloured and softly fragrant.

Without word, he strode past the gathered novices and passed through a space between two tall stones. The novices followed.

Flint hesitated, but when Tallofmind gestured at him he decided to follow, not knowing what other option he had.

Podhuts clustered to the right; a dark barrier of thicket oaks lined the left of the path, trunks squashed shoulder to shoulder in thick clumps. He smelt nectar on the evening air, and the musty scent of damp forest floor. He was aware of the procession falling in behind Seesthroughlies and the group of novices.

They came to a ravine, with the sound of a stream somewhere below in the shadows. A precarious rope bridge spanned the gap, and they proceeded across. The rope felt rough beneath his raw feet.

On the far side they came within sight of the northern span of the defensive stockade, and Flint saw an array of low fires, people moving about.

A soft glow came in patches from the ground, and Flint knew that they had come to a series of lagoons of a type he had only heard about. Much like the changing vats in Trecosann, these lagoons were filled with a thick brew of changing vectors, but these were natural formations whereas the vats were artificial.

Seesthroughlies stopped and turned, his head backlit by the glow from the deadly changing pools. He raised his hands, palms outwards, his scented oil lamp suspended from a loop of fibre around the fingers of one hand.

"Novices of the Restitution," he said, "your time of trial is close."

Flint felt damp warmth run down his thigh, but his shame at losing control was nothing to the terror that now engulfed him.

CHAPTER 10

"**T**he last years of man are a time of trial for us all," intoned Seesthroughlies. "We are nothing before the Lord until he chooses us, until he seals us within the faith. In these dying times only the chosen ones will rise to paradise. All others find eternal damnation. The faith has chosen you, children of the Lord, and you have chosen the faith. Tonight your faith will be sealed."

Flint stood silent, isolated in the group of novices. He wondered how much they understood. Those who showed fear, perhaps, but many showed excitement and eagerness, all of their faces lit by the intense glow from the changing lagoon only a few paces distant.

Now, Seesthroughlies lowered his lamp and pulled at his cloak, opening it, discarding it.

He turned and stepped out into the changing lagoon.

Flint gasped, half raised his hands in fear, and then he stopped, stared, felt even more confused than he had during the day when he had been overcome by successive deranged visions.

Seesthroughlies walked on the surface of the changing brew, his hurried, nimble strides taking him rapidly across to the far side, feet touching the surface for mere instants.

He stood on firm ground, spun on his heels, and let loose a tremendous roar of triumph. He stood in a half stoop, fist raised, his swarthy body glowing with sweat picked out by the lagoon's fearsome glow, eyes wide and staring.

People started to sing from nearby, the steady rhythmic song-chant that was now familiar to Flint. Seesthroughlies moved over to where someone had ignited a tray of stick-spirit. He stepped into it, white flames lapping up his legs, and then stepped out of the fire, cleansed.

A child hurried round to Seesthroughlies and offered him his cloak. He dressed and returned to stand before the novices.

"Trust in the Lord," he said softly, a great weariness suddenly in his tone.

Just as Flint began to suspect some kind of trickery, Seesthroughlies squatted and picked up a stone. He lobbed it into the pool and it sank instantly.

"If the faith has truly chosen you, then the Lord is your guardian," he said.

The bladder of frenzy wine was passed to him, and he drank deeply, savouring the fizz on his tongue, the burning in his throat. He needed the strength it gave him.

Slightly disoriented, he studied the faces of those around him. He saw Tallofmind, barely chest-high to him. "Tallofmind," he said, approaching the Riverwalker. "You have to stop this! These novices have chosen to be here—they all want to be Riverwalkers. They've chosen your faith and prepared for this, but I haven't! I don't want any of it."

Tallofmind placed a hand on his arm. "You should seek calm," he said. "We live in a time of trials, and your greatest trial approaches. Tread softly," he added. "And do not hesitate."

The first of the novices approached the pool and dropped his cloak to reveal a body still loose with adolescent puppy fat. He looked slowly around as if savouring the moment and then set out across the changing brew. His small, rapid steps carried him across to the far side, where he collapsed into the arms of two waiting attendants.

Another two crossed, each adopting the light tread of Seesthroughlies, each slumping gratefully into waiting arms on the far bank, each then guided through the cleansing flames.

Closer now, Flint stood one back from the changing lagoon. The novice ahead of him was the young Trecosi woman he had questioned at the Communary. He looked beyond her to the pool. There was a layer of scum across the surface, he saw now. Something like the blanketweed that grew across the swamp pools back in Trecosann. He wondered again if there was trickery involved, and he allowed the thought to calm him a little.

The novice in front of him stepped forward, and now Flint was intensely aware of the glare from the pool and the insistent chanting song rising from all around. The frenzy wine had a hold of his senses, he realised, and it was both a comfort and an antagonist: calming his core yet intensifying all sensation.

She paused, loosened her cloak, and let it fall so that all she wore was a slender bracelet on her left wrist. Flint stared at her nakedness, so close and pale, so strangely sexless.

She stepped out onto the pool, little nimble steps taking her halfway across before the blanketweed appeared to be folding itself around her feet, her ankles, slowing her, sucking her down.

She tried to keep going, but she had broken through the surface layer and now she was up to her knees, her thighs. Arms windmilling, she somehow managed to keep moving, but the stuff was over her hips now.

She gave a little cry as she tipped forward, and yet still she managed to keep pushing herself on through the goo.

At the far side she emerged on all fours, sobbing softly. The waiting helpers backed away.

The singing continued, not faltering, as one of the helpers—at last!—threw a blanket over the fallen novice and helped her clear.

Three had crossed; one had fallen. Now Flint stood at the front of the small crowd of novices, his turn arrived.

He drank more frenzy wine, felt its fizz, felt its burn.

The atmosphere had subtly changed now. Not so much because of the fallen novice, but because they sensed Flint's reluctance. He was no normal novice: he was suffering this trial to prove his humanity, his worthiness to survive, he realised. They could easily have left him to die, but instead they had chosen to give him this chance before their Lord.

He saw men with spears and sharpened mutt sticks, ready to encourage him if his reluctance lasted much longer.

He stared at them, suddenly overcome again with memories of being nine years old, having a mutt stick thrust into his hand. "Go on, Flint. It's your duty. It's your justice." The stick, heavy in his hand, its surface smooth in his small grip, its point specially sharpened for the occasion.

He remembered jabbing with the stick, Flint and others guiding the beasts into the changing vats.

But no, not mutts and livestock: pointing and thrusting at a man, Flint and Jescka and Tarn each jabbing at the cowed figure, goading him forward and down the ramp into the changing vat.

Justice, they had said.

He remembered the man's look of resignation as he stepped forward into the vat, faced with no other choice. Jescka and Tarn goading him, Flint copying, angry and scared and proud to be taking part in the retribution. The changing brew engulfing the man as it had engulfed the novice just now.

The man was a criminal, found guilty, his sentence to be changed at the hands of his victims and to be banished, his legacy destined to haunt and torment Flint with fear and guilt and anguish forever after. Guilt, more than anything. Something to be submerged, repressed, something to be forgotten.

Justice, he thought, and guilt. Was there a balance?

He stepped forward.

His clumsy fingers fumbled at the tie of his cloak, then found the cord and pulled it loose. The garment fell to the ground, and he turned to survey the eager faces of the crowd.

Even the chanting had fallen silent now.

Calm, he turned full circle until he faced the pool again.

He moved forward to the edge, smelt sulphur, smelt salt and decay and something he could not define.

He stepped out onto the pool, and the surface yielded gently beneath his weight.

A second step, a third.

Small strides, contact kept to a minimum.

He had expected heat, wetness, but instead there was a cool, leathery surface beneath the raw soles of his feet.

A surface skin, the layer of blanketweed, was all that supported him. Wetness would signal a rupture, a weakness, an inevitable descent into the changing brew.

He stared at the changing pool, shutting out the world. He felt himself part-blinded by its malevolent glow, coiling patterns surging just below the surface.

How long? How far?

He seemed to have been walking forever, and yet he was barely halfway across.

No going back now.

The crowd was chanting again, but the sound, despite its insistence, was distant to him, hardly registering.

This was where the previous novice had hesitated, sensed the enfolding clutches of the lagoon.

He didn't let his stride break. He fastened onto Tallofmind's words: *Tread softly, and do not hesitate.*

Harsh grit on his feet, stinging. Arms folding around him, preventing him from stumbling back into the pool.

He had crossed to the far side. He was safe.

"Blessed one, blessed one. Child of the Lord."

The helpers were mumbling, chanting as they embraced him. He felt a rush of panic, of elation, of confusion. They were tugging at his arms, jostling and directing him. He staggered on, felt the tingle of cool spirit flames caressing his feet, calves, shins. Removing any traces of the changing brew that may have adhered to his feet. He stepped out, the soles of his feet newly sensitised to the abrasive surface of the rocky ground. He felt his arms being guided into the sleeves of a cloak, a cord tightening around his waist. A smartfibre chain tightening itself around his head, the knobbly indentations of beads along its length against his skin.

"Flintheart," said a voice, a man's voice.

Seesthroughlies was guiding him away from the pool. "The Lord has chosen you. The faith has found you. The Lord has given you a name."

Flintheart. Strong, but liable to fracture. It felt right. No clan affiliation, no paternal assignation, just Flintheart. He liked it. They had given his name back, both more and less, and it fit.

"You do this the wrong way round, Flintheart," Tallofmind told him a short time later in that long night.

They sat in the shelter of a small outcrop of rock, a quiet spot amid the frantic intensity of the Riverwalkers' celebrations. Of fifteen novices only four had fallen, the ratio far better than they could rightly expect, apparently.

"How so?"

"Most novices spend many days in retreat, learning the techniques of inner control, coming to their own understandings of the ways of the Lord in the dying years. Only then do they face their trial in the faithwalking ceremony."

"I did not choose this," said Flint. "I was not given a say in the matter."

"The faith chose you. Circumstances put you among us and gave you the opportunity to find faith and the ways of faith."

"I'm looking for my sister, not faith."

"Maybe faith will find her, too, before judgement finds her."

He could agree with the small Riverwalker on that. Judgement: death and change to these people were all the Lord's judgement. He nodded.

Tallofmind was studying him in the gloom. Flint shrugged, and said, "What is it?"

"You are a Riverwalker now, brother Flintheart. You should stay in the Communary and learn the ways of faith."

Flint rubbed at the soft stubble on his chin. "Give this time to grow, eh?" he said, pointing at Tallofmind's great thicket of beard. "You saved my life," he went on. "I am honoured that finally you welcome me into your community. But I do not have the time to devote to the kind of learning you talk of. Amber's out there somewhere. I need to get to Farsamy, Tallofmind. My chances of finding my sister are slim, but they are greater in Farsamy than elsewhere. Do hauliers pass through here? Would it be possible for me to arrange passage?"

Flint spread his hands. "I have nothing," he added. "I would not ask if there was any other way."

"I will ask Sees," said Tallofmind. "You will always have a dirt floor to sleep on in Restitution," he said, grinning.

"The man, he says don't do this, don't do that. Don't eat fruit from the wild fruit tree. Don't drink the sweetwater from the wild pretty sap flowers. You'll be *changed*, he say. You'll become what you're not now, he say!"

Frenzy wine splashed Flint's face as Teller strode around the small clearing, knees kicking high, waving his arms and swinging his wine bladder with abandon. Normally subdued—or at least, that was how Flint would have described him—tonight Teller was a man possessed.

He drank deeply and stood forward, hands on hips, bladder hanging from a loop of twine around one wrist, body tilting precariously over his rapt audience.

"Don't listen to what the man says," he told them, his voice suddenly soft, purring. "When the Lord is in your heart you *know*—you don't need to be told. Monkey come out from the jungle"—suddenly Flint felt eyes on him—"monkey scratching in the dirt, monkey making animal sounds. Lord in your heart and you *know*. Ain't no monkey: that's a fellow brother of the river. Brother Flintheart's in the Lord's eyes like you and me."

Teller leaned even farther over the seated listeners and thrust the wine bladder at Flint.

Flint took it, drank, wiped his mouth on the back of his hand.

Teller pulled away, yanking the wine from Flint's hand by its length of twine. He spun on his heels, arms flailing, wine spraying. "We're living in the end times," he said. "The last trump, it sounded many many years ago, I tell you. The last trump sounded, and Biogiddeon shook the man who says this, the man who says that.

"We're living in the end times, brothers, sisters. We have risen up to face our judgement. When the last calling comes and the Lord chooses, He chooses those with faith in their hearts, those who have proved their trust in the Lord beyond doubt. You, me, brothers and sisters: we seen some fine faithwalking tonight, but we're all faithwalking every breath we take.

"It's so easy to fall, brothers and sisters, but you don't know when the Lord is watching, when the Lord is testing. You don't know—*I* don't know—when the final call will come, when each and every one of us will be judged before the Lord. But I tell you one thing: we sure will know when it happens. . . ."

The faithwalking ceremony had become a party, in which much frenzy wine and jaggery tea was drunk, but now the gongs were sounding and Flint felt their insistence echoed in the pulsing deep in his aching skull.

Flintheart the Riverwalker. It seemed both appropriate and incredibly alien to him, but he knew he had become more Flintheart than Flintreco Eltarn.

The faithwalkers carried between them the four who had fallen, none of them being fit to walk. Flint walked with someone's legs across his shoulder, separated from changed, still-changing, flesh by only a few folds of rough fabric.

At the ravine they were reduced to single file, and suddenly the legs were a terrible burden. Shocks and tremors passed back along the rope bridge from Walkedfar before him, and he felt that with each step his foot would go through the bridge into emptiness.

The wine lent confidence to his movements, though, and they reached the far side without mishap. Once there, Flint gratefully allowed another of the walkers to take the load from his shoulder, and he walked, lightheaded and slightly apart from the others, back up the rock path to the Communary.

He was to spend the night there, he realised. This night and how many more before he could be on his way? He was free, he knew. Having proved himself before these people's Lord, he was their equal, their guest. But when would he have the opportunity to leave?

He followed his fellow walkers into the cool interior of the Communary.

The building reminded him of the Hall at Trecosann where Callum and Petria tended the changing vats. A deep sense of age hung in the dry air, and moonlight pooled under tall windows with coloured, pearlescent glass.

Someone lit a line of oil lamps, and Flint saw that the floor consisted of compacted mud and rushes. Sleeping rolls were removed from
a shelf near the door and spread on the ground, and the four fallen were
eased onto them.

Flint stood, uncertain. There seemed to be an understanding
between the other faithwalkers to which he was not privy. They had
been together for some time before this night, he knew, studying and
training in preparation for their trial of faith.

A hand, light on his arm. "Brother Flintheart."

It was the youngster, Walkedfar. "We must tend to the fallen," he
said. "I will sit with Rendel—will you join me?" He indicated the Trecosi woman Flint had helped carry back to the Communary—the one
who had refused to give her name when he had first encountered her.
It struck him then as incredibly sad that he should only learn her name
after she had fallen.

He nodded. "Thank you . . . Brother Walkedfar."

They sat, legs crossed, either side of Rendel.

"She was of Clan Treco," said Walkedfar, after a protracted silence,
broken only by murmured voices from elsewhere in the Communary.
"She came from a place called Tremellen."

Flint nodded. Tremellen was one of the small clan settlements
strung out along the river Elver to the south of Trecosann, little more
than a jetty and a cluster of podhuts established to service the haul-
boats that plied the river. "I come from Trecosann," he said. "I did not
know her." Not unnaturally: travel between settlements being limited
and the clan being one of the largest, or so Flint had been taught. He
had visited the southern river settlements only two or three times.

"I came from a village in Spinster's Spine," said Walkedfar. "I do
not recall its name. I left three years ago and travelled from settlement
to settlement, seeking faith, although I did not know it at the time."

Walkedfar could only be about fifteen years old now, so he must
have been young indeed when he set out.

"I met Sister Judgement in Beshusa and she showed me faith, and so I came to Restitution."

Rendel gave a shudder then, so intense that her back arched and she pushed herself up from the ground before subsiding. Immediately, Walkedfar reached for a leafsponge, dipped it in a pot of golden water, and pressed it to the fallen one's forehead.

"We pray that our fallen sister's change be painless, that there is still space in her heart for the Lord."

Flint stared at the sweat beading Rendel's pale face, forming narrow tracks down into her damp, sandy hair. Her eyes were closed, twisting and twitching beneath their lids as if she dreamed.

Rendel had been covered with a blanket, but it had worked loose at one side, twisted in her grip. Flint straightened it, and saw again that she had a fine bracelet on her wrist. He recalled noticing that it was the only thing she wore on her ill-fated attempt at faithwalking. The bracelet was made of rivershells, marbled blue and turquoise and threaded on cane fibres.

One of the shells was broken.

Amber!

Holding Rendel by the wrist, Flint said, "Where did you get this?"

Eyes still closed. No response.

"What is it?" asked Walkedfar. "What's the matter?"

Flint turned to him. "This bracelet," he said. "It belongs to my sister. She went missing from home . . . I'm trying to find her."

The tears. *I hate you! I hate you I hate you I* hate *you!* They had been play-fighting and the bracelet had broken and Amber had been distraught. It was only a bracelet, but he'd broken it and she had been as mad as any nine year-old could get. He'd repaired it, but imperfectly, a shell still broken, and after that she had worn the thing ever since.

"Had Rendel been here long before tonight?" Flint asked.

"A day or two," said Walkedfar. "She was the last to arrive. I don't think she was fully prepared."

If she had travelled straight from Tremellen she might have encountered Amber either there or en route. But why would Amber be in Tremellen?

He knew, of course. The only reason to be there was either to service the mutt trade or to be a part of it.

Just then Rendel's lips drew back from her teeth, an animal sneer, no sound escaping.

And her eyes opened, swivelled, resting on Walkedfar and then on Flint.

She didn't see him, he felt sure: she was looking into some other world entirely. He saw the pain and loss in her eyes. The horrible realisation of transfomation. The terror.

Her body bucked again, and Walkedfar leaned over her, held her shoulders to the ground. He peered up at Flint, and Flint felt exposed by the look in his eyes.

He turned away, heard the boy say, "We need to hold her. She's in pain."

Flint nodded. He put a hand on her hip, reached across to lean on her other hip too, trying to stop the convulsions that were contorting her body.

He felt bones shifting beneath his hands, and was struck by the intensity of the change, the speed.

She shuddered again, and Walkedfar called, "Lightfoot! Mercy! We need help."

Two other faithwalkers joined them as Rendel twisted and convulsed in a tangle of sleeping mat.

Flint pulled away, rocked back on his heels. He stared at the heaving figure, the three shadowy forms struggling to pin her in place.

She was groaning now, as if in labour. Giving birth to a new self.

Memories rushed him.

He stood, took a step back.

"Flintheart?"

Walkedfar was peering up at him as he wrestled with the fallen faithwalker. His face was a pale grey blob in the Communary's low light.

Flint stepped back again.

"Brother Flintheart?"

He turned, stumbled, rushed at the door, swung it wide, and staggered out into the cool night air. Stars pricked the sky overhead, crowding above him. A full moon hung low and swollen over the treetops. Moths whirred in light spilled from the Communary windows.

He ran, bare feet lacerating on the stony path, pain feeding his panic.

Brother Seesthroughlies found him in the square.

The small shelter they had constructed for him when he was a prisoner still stood, and somehow Flint had found it the previous night, curled up, and slept deeply.

Now, Flint peered up at the Riverwalker through eyes slitted against the glare of the morning sun. Seesthroughlies squatted, tiny bones jangling from his quickfibre headband. Some were tied into his beard, too, Flint saw.

"Rendel found her judgement before the Lord just before dawn," Seesthroughlies said softly.

Flint nodded, swallowed. He would never know, now, how she had come to be wearing Amber's bracelet.

He had abandoned Rendel when she needed his help. He felt that he had failed a test, although there was no judgement in the Riverwalker's eyes.

"I . . . I knew a man once," said Flint, compelled to explain himself. "I watched him change. It was his punishment. He had been found guilty of . . . attacking . . . my mother . . . me. . . ."

His tears stung his cheeks, salty moisture on dry, exposed skin.

He remembered. . . .

. . . The mutt stick, heavy in his hand. Too heavy, too big for a boy to handle comfortably. Thrusting and jabbing with the stick. Flint, Jescka, and Tarn at the front of an angry mob, all crowding in, baying for justice, for retribution.

The look in Cederotreco's eyes had haunted Flint ever since: resignation, perhaps even some traces of pity. A look held for a brief moment, engraved on his mind for life. The man who had been his teacher now pausing in his last moments of humanity.

The sharpened point of a mutt stick breaking the moment, forcing Cedero to step back. Onto the ramp that led down into the changing vat.

He remembered watching the actions of his parents, studying their anger and hatred, mimicking it and feeling it, savouring it, understanding the power of revenge, of justice. He remembered the intensity of the feelings that took a hold of him that night: the passion, the pride, the boyish triumph that he was at the centre of such an event.

And later, Cedero the teacher, lying alone in the straw of a holding pen, the fevers taking hold. Boyish triumphalism fading, passion detumescing.

Horror stealing in.

Flint was nine years old and had seen many changings, many mutts and beasts dipped in the vats to fortify the breeding lines.

But never before a man.

Flint had already endured, and subsequently blacked out, the attack, the beating, and now he was witnessing the true horror of the justice he had helped mete out.

Days later, Cedero was banished from Trecosann, sent out into the wilds to die. Moments before they took him away, Flint had looked into the man's eyes and there had been nothing there, a chilling blankness in one who had been so mentally engaging, who had been loved and hated by all around him for his intelligence and charm. Nothing.

Perhaps it was best for Rendel that the fevers had taken her from the world, that she had found her judgement so swiftly.

"We live in a time of trials," said Seesthroughlies softly. "It is a sad truth that most of our kind will fall before the Lord."

Time never passes at a constant rate, Flint realised. A mere day had passed, and yet the faithwalking ceremony, the passing of Rendel, and Flint's humiliation—all seemed so distant.

And most dramatically of all, the fallen had changed.

"Come," Tallofmind had told him, holding out a hand, beckoning for Flint to rise to his feet and follow the Riverwalker through the hard-mud streets of Restitution.

The Communary's dark stone walls stood before them, narrow windows revealing nothing. Inside: the three survivors of those who had fallen in the previous evening's ceremony, each being tended by one or two of the former novices.

Two—Patros and Mikkel—had taken traits common among the mutt population, a change Flint recalled from the dippings guided by Callum: a skeletal shifting, a broadening across the shoulder, a layering of new muscle across back, shoulders, neck, so much that the head appeared to sit lower. In their eyes, Flint saw nothing, a blankness he recalled again from the mutt dippings.

"Patros," said Tallofmind, putting a hand on the young man's head. Eyes turned. "Remember me, Patros?"

Patros nodded. "T . . . Tuh . . ."

Tallofmind shook his head, and turned back to Flint. He tapped the side of his head and said, "In here he is still Patrosbern Elpatros. No longer True, perhaps, no longer fit for the Lord's judgement, but all is not lost."

The third, Millice, was different. They came to stand before her.

She looked up at them and at first impression seemed barely changed
from the attractive young novice Flint had noted with interest the previous day.

But something had shifted, distorted. It was in her eyes, Flint
realised. Something disturbed him as her eyes found his face. He felt a
burst of relief when she turned to his guide.

"Tallofmind," she said to the short Riverwalker. "You bring
Brother Flintheart here to demonstrate to him the inevitability of
change. You wish him to see that change can be both tragic, as poor
Rendel found, and unsettling and hard to define, which is why you
bring him to me. Look." She said this directly to Flintheart, spreading
her arms, palms upwards. He could not help but study her, seeing
little sign of change, yet sensing that something was adrift. "You are
aroused by the sight of me, Brother Flintheart, and yet equally you are
repulsed because you know that I have changed and you do not know
in what way. You struggle with your deep-seated belief that all change
is harmful and corrupting, while the evidence before you indicates that
change is merely *change*. Brother Tallofmind wants you to see this; he
wants you to embrace his understanding that we live in the end days
for your kind. The last trump has wiped out most of True humankind,
and those who remain will face judgement—perhaps today, perhaps
tomorrow, perhaps in a hundred years. The True are kept artificially at
the top of the pyramid because all of nature has been engineered to
defer to your kind, and yet even that cannot preserve you as a species.
When you find your judgement, the world will be inherited by those
who have embraced change. We may be Lost, Brother Flintheart, but
only because you can no longer find us."

Tallofmind stood quietly to one side, waiting until Millice fell
silent. Sweat was running down her face now, effort swamping her as
she still fought to recover from her changing.

He led Flint away. "The interior change can be the most fundamental of all," he said. "Millice has become something of a savant."

"Why did you bring me here?" asked Flint.

"To show you the future," said Tallofmind.

They fed the body of Rendel to the natural changing lagoons where the faithwalking ceremony had taken place. Flint helped Walkedfar carry her all the way from the Communary.

The Riverwalkers chanted, but Flint did not know the words. Instead, he closed his eyes and thought of his sister. Was she alive still? Was she in some haul-boat with mutts and the Lost?

Afterwards, he showed Tallofmind the bracelet he had removed from Rendel's wrist. "This is my sister's," he said, "but Rendel was wearing it. Rendel came from a trading settlement on the main river route to Farsamy. I have to go to Farsamy."

Tallofmind nodded. "You won't get there on foot," he said. "Bide your time. We will see what can be done."

Flint stumbled, again, and all around children giggled.

He squatted on his haunches and grinned wryly.

"Stand," Sister Judgement said patiently. "Breathe and hold. Find the Joyous Breath, Brother Flintheart."

He stood, raised his hands above his head and pressed the palms together, savouring the way it forced his rib cage to expand.

"Rhythms and Clouds," Judgement said, and immediately the children started to slice air with flat hands, their mechanical motions keeping perfect time to Shuza's bone drum.

Judgement stood before Flint and looked up at him. Here, in a class of six- and seven-year-olds, he towered above his teacher, too.

"Patience," she said now, to Flint alone. "You must pass through the seven stages of clumsiness before your mind is free to roam through your body. Only then will you find that all parts of your body move as one, a single machine in tune with the Lord's will."

"But . . . you told me before that every part of the body must be allowed to move independently."

"As part of the Lord's pattern," corrected Judgement. "The two are not in conflict. Flow with softness and continuity, Brother Flintheart, and all will follow and you will be whole before the Lord."

Seesthroughlies had insisted that Flint learn the fighting meditation discipline they called Lordsway using the same phrase: "Learn to become whole before the Lord, Flintheart, and your mind and body will become a single machine."

Judgement placed the flat of her hand against Flint's naked belly, pressing the curled body hair flat. "Everything comes from here," she said. "Your true centre. Concentrate, Flint, and feel the stillness and balance coming from here."

Even after she withdrew her hand he felt the imprint of her fingers. And then he sensed something else, a feeling of calmness spreading.

"Rhythm and Clouds, Flint."

And he felt the drum's pulse instantly. He focused on the still centre Judgement had shown him, and started to slice the air with flat, stiffened hands—a man among children, although he felt more a dwarf among giants.

Tallofmind showed him the work they were carrying out on the podhuts just inside Restitution's stockade defences.

One of the first things he had seen upon entering the settlement had been the scaffolding encasing these podhuts, sculpted cane cages being used to guide the growth of new cells.

Now, the short Riverwalker scrambled up the scaffolding above Flint, beckoning for him to follow. "Most of these podhuts are grown from tubers supplied from the fields at Beshusa," said Tallofmind. "But here we are experimenting with growing our own. It is a skill that we do not traditionally have, but we Riverwalkers learn what we need. It is merely a matter of applying engineering principles."

"The Riverwalker way," said Flint, smiling to show that his comment was meant positively. He had come to understand that much of these people's beliefs could be summarised in the same way: applying engineering principles to the body, to the mind, to their surroundings. "We are all machines, no?"

Tallofmind grinned, and plucked at his dense beard.

They talked of themselves as machines, constructed by the Lord. They talked of the changed Oracle as a "lost wisdom machine"; of the changing vectors in the dipping vats as "tiny machines loaded with the power of the Lord."

"The Lord built us," said Tallofmind now. "And He built the mutts beneath us. He changed nature so that it deferred to True humankind and kept us at the top, through the destructive age of what some call Biogiddeon and others call Armageddon or the Fall and on into the end times in which we now live."

He waved a hand slowly, encompassing Restitution and beyond. "The whole world is the Lord's judgement machine," he said. "And it's thinning us out for eternal paradise or starting all over as new people, new beings. You stay saved, Flintheart, do you hear me?"

Seesthroughlies came to him at the Communary shortly after dawn the following day.

Flint sensed his arrival, somewhere in the periphery of his awareness, but he hung onto his centre, holding the Joyous Breath and the rapture of oneness of mind and body.

Seesthroughlies waited.

Flint released a breath that had been like sweet nectar in his lungs. Slowly, awareness grew of the morning dew on the moss beneath his calloused soles, of trumpeting dawn oaks celebrating the breeze, of an emerald-glinting millipede as thick as his thumb ascending the stone wall that surrounded the Communary's small shrine yard.

"Tallofmind tells me you want to go to Farsamy," said Seesthroughlies.

Flint nodded slowly, moving still with softness and continuity. Sister Judgement had taught him well and quickly.

He tightened the tie on his loincloth and took his cloak from the wall.

"We always send a delegation to Carnival," said Seesthroughlies. "Leave with us tomorrow."

CHAPTER 11

He had watched the Riverwalkers' boats from the stockade on many occasions, marvelling at the way they appeared to glide across the water, but this was the first time he had been in one.

Now, he sat at the prow of one of the long, narrow vessels, almost at the level of the water. The boat was constructed from a translucent quickfibre membrane stretched over a skeleton of ribcanes. When he placed a hand against the boat's skin it felt warm to the touch, and he could feel the river's currents surging beneath.

He sat with Tallofmind and Judgement and three others. Behind them, five rows of paired mutts worked the boat's treadles. Each mutt leaned slightly forward, holding onto a curved ribcane spar, raising one foot and then another and then pressing down on the angled, flat surface of a small bladder. Their actions pumped fluid around a living network of veins that lined the boat's walls, driving a series of paddles at the stern. And, when seen from a distance, the mutts appeared to be walking on the water.

Flint remembered the first time he had seen one of these boats. He had stared at it from the jungle in delirious wonder.

He turned to Judgement, now, and saw how the merciless sunlight picked out a tracery of lines on her brow, around her eyes and her mouth. "No goods?" he asked. Farsamy Carnival was the biggest market of the year, a time when clans from all around gathered to trade their specialist wares and produce.

Judgement smiled and placed a hand on the side of her head. "In here," she said simply.

Flint nodded. The Riverwalkers boasted the finest engineers of the

True, and they traded on their expertise. Many of the Riverwalkers on these four boats would not return to Restitution after Carnival, perhaps staying away for several years, joining other clans as bondsmen and spreading the Lord's word.

Already—it was still only midmorning—Flint heard the roar of the waters where the two great rivers joined, the smaller Transom feeding into the river Farsam.

He looked down and saw smudges of dark movement through the boat's thin skin. Snapping turtles, he recalled, and other tentacled monsters in the depths. Suddenly the boat felt far too flimsy for such a journey.

He gripped the side.

"This is where I nearly drowned," he said to Judgement.

There was an expression of sympathy on her face as she looked down into the waters, and then out across the river.

He could see the mouth of the Transom, now, and the clouds of silver gulls squabbling over scraps in the surf where the two rivers joined.

The boats passed below the chalky cliffs, and Flint saw that they were barely twice his height in places. They looked to be an easy climb, and yet the sheer sense of devastation he had felt upon reaching them before was still with him.

He breathed deep and held the air in his lungs, felt the panic-laden memories receding.

Up ahead, he saw a haul-boat heading south. He thought of Amber. Such thoughts were rarely far from his mind, but now they had a well-worn feel about them. They were an established part of his existence, something that gave his days shape.

He knew that his last realistic chance was rapidly approaching. If he did not find Amber in Farsamy, then he would have little chance of finding her at all.

"She is about so high"—a hand, held flat at the level of his breastbone —"with chestnut hair to her shoulders. The whites of her eyes are jaundiced from childhood illness. She is a True daughter of Clan Treco. She may be travelling independently, but I am fairly certain that she has been abducted and sold into servitude as a bondsman."

The same response: a regretful shake of the head, a shrug of shoulders, a mumbled apology, but no, they had not seen such a young woman.

Beshusa was a town made of flesh. Its streets were lined with podhuts, grown from tubers cultivated for many tens of generations by Clan Beshusami. The huts squeezed together, fleshy walls conjoined, held rigid by exoskeletal ribcanes and fibre-plates. The walls were transparent in places, networked with nerves and veins; in others they were the sheer black of night, or varied jungle colours; birds nested in nooks and crevices and in tangled tufts of body hair growing from the buildings. Vines and air plants grew from pockets in the walls, and hummingbirds and great, gaudy butterflies flitted and hovered before extravagant blossoms that may have been growing on the huts or may have been growing *from* the huts themselves.

Even the road surfaces were lined with networks of fibres, linking the buildings so that the city was, in truth, a single organism, a communal creature grown to house Clan Beshusami and its followers.

Half a day's travel downriver from the joining of the Transom and the Farsam, Beshusa was an ideal stopping place for the Carnival party from Restitution.

Flint moved on, away from the cluster of old men that had gathered by a bulbous drinking fountain on a street corner. The Riverwalkers were staying in a rooming house that overlooked the Farsam, but he had left them at the first opportunity. He would travel with them to Farsamy tomorrow, but now he had to take the chance to make enquiries, to see if, by any small chance, anyone knew of Amber.

He had been to Beshusa once before, travelling as a boy of eleven with a Trecosi group led by Callum and his wife of the time, Ann. There was a Treco clanhouse in Beshusa, and some clan business or other had demanded a visit from Trecosann. Flint had known little of the detail even then, and what he had known had been quickly forgotten—a wedding, or death, he supposed. But it had been an opportunity for young Flint to travel with his cousin and the others, and his abiding memory was the sense of freedom, a lifting of weight.

Now, he recalled that another cousin, Mallery, had been in the party, and the sisters Lessa and Nettie, and others whose names and features evaded the reach of his memory.

A handful of images lingered from that visit. He remembered the crowding, fleshy buildings, and their gaudy growths and efflorescences, but he did not recall the intensity of smell of the place: heady floral scents mingling with something sharp; an underpinning odour of decay, ever present; the meaty smell like split fleshfruit that could make you feel hungry or nauseous or sometimes both.

And he remembered the sense of being somewhere crowded, with people all about. Many were even strangers to each other, which was an unfamiliar phenomenon to someone not of the city—so many people passing in the street without even a nod of recognition.

It would be easy to lose oneself in such a place.

Night had fallen, cool and dark, the moon and stars lost behind clouds. The only light came from tubes of glow-water arranged in pictograms on the fronts of buildings, and spilling out from the podhuts' interiors.

There was someone in the clanhouse, or lights, at least.

He had found his way to another street-corner drinking fountain and splashed his face with cool water. Head clearer, he remembered his childhood visit here, staying in the Trecosi clanhouse. Stopping people in the street, he asked them the way to the clanhouse, asked them where a member of Clan Treco should go when new in Beshusa, and they had directed him here.

The clanhouse was a swollen two-storey podhut on an intersection between one of Beshusa's main thoroughfares and a side street lined with more brewhouses and brothels. Seminaked women—and mutts! —displayed themselves in windows and open doorways, chatting to each other, chewing gum, calling to passersby. He did not remember it like this from his childhood visit, but then he could easily have been ignorant of these buildings' functions at that innocent age.

He came to the clanhouse and saw movement behind translucent window panels, heard voices from the building's slitted vents. In the gutter, street rats pulled at emptied fruit skins discarded by passersby.

He paused, stood straight and inhaled, hanging onto the Joyous Breath as Sister Judgement had taught him.

There was a rattle by the door, which he spun; but no one responded, so he pressed at the door panel and passed through when it retracted from his touch.

He was in a small lobby, pausing in an arched entrance to the main hall. A bar counter had grown along the far wall, and the air was thick with the smoke of headsticks. Four men sat at a bench by the window panel, sucking on beer tubes and passing sticks around. A young couple sat in a corner, bodies pressed close, part-enfolded by their fleshy seat, giggling and murmuring. A woman stood behind the bar, stroking its smooth flank as if she enjoyed the feel of its leathery hide.

He approached her, aware of eyes following him.

"Good evening, Walker," said the woman.

A stranger here, they did not even recognise him as one of their own in his Riverwalker cloak and head chain, his new growth of beard.

He nodded in greeting. "Sweetwater," he said, and then he gestured at a dish of dried porkapple strips. "And some of these." He took a few shillings from the drawstring pocket in the cuff of his cloak, money that Judgement had given him shortly after they had arrived in Beshusa. He allowed the barwoman to take three of the ceramic coins from his hand, and sat at the bar with his drink.

After a time of silence, in which he ate and drank and gathered his thoughts, Flint said to the woman, "I came here once before, many years ago."

"That would be before my time here," she said amenably. Flint saw that her entire neck vibrated as she spoke, like that of a calling tree frog.

He nodded, looking back down at his drink, and then around the clan hall's colourless interior. "I am of the clan," he said. "I am Trecosi, from Trecosann."

"Looks to me like you turned your back on the clan," said one of the four men, coming over from his window table to stand at the bar. Upright, he was just tall enough to look down upon the seated Flint.

Flint glanced down at his cloak. "The Riverwalkers saved my life," he said, "and they took me in."

"You're returning to the clan, then," said the man aggressively.

Flint ignored the challenge. He did not have an answer, and even if he did, he felt no obligation to share it.

He remembered why he was here.

"I'm looking for my sister," he said. "Her name is Amberlinetreco Eltarn. She went missing from Trecosann"—how long ago? he had lost track—"some time ago . . . at the start of the dry season. I am spreading word through the clan, asking cousins to look out for her."

A glimmer of recognition flitted over the man's face. "The runaways," he said. "Tarn's kids."

Word had clearly spread already.

Flint stood. "Not runaway," he said. "I set out to find my sister after she disappeared. I believe she has been enslaved."

Now the man had been joined by one of the others, a taller man, Flint's equal in height and easily twice as bulky.

"Could be that you should go back to Trecosann," said the second, his voice slow, considering. "Not turning your back on the clan and parading around in the Walkers' clothes." He turned to his companion.

"What kind of Trecosi walks into a clanhouse looking like a mad preacherman from upriver?" he asked.

Flint made sure that his posture did nothing to betray his sudden fear. He remained seated, one hand on his sweetwater bladder, the other loose on the bar counter. He inhaled, clung onto the Joyous Breath, felt solidity deep in his belly, calm spreading outwards.

The two men were blocking his way to the exit. He noted that the barwoman had moved away along the counter, was looking studiously in the other direction. In the corner, the young couple were watching, silent.

He twisted at the waist, still seated but now facing the two men. "I am True Trecosi," he said softly. "And I am a Riverwalker, too. I am looking for my sister, and I hope she will find a true welcome if she finds herself in a clanhouse." *A truer welcome than this*, he refrained from adding.

Their movements were slow and clumsy, and he was surprised at how much time he had. He saw the look pass between the two men, and then the inexact lurch of the younger, taller man as he made to seize Flint's arms.

They were drunk, he knew, and also they did not have the control to move with smoothness and continuity as a Riverwalker did. Mind and body were disjointed for the two men, movements uncoordinated, independent of one another.

He swayed to one side, a slight, almost imperceptible movement, but enough to deflect the big man's lunge, leave him staggering forward across the bar.

He slid from the stool and stood in a comfortable pose, knees and arms bent slightly, ready for action.

Rhythm and Clouds, he thought, and he felt the steady pulse of the world around him, moved in tune with it.

The shorter man swung, hand open to slap or grab, and Flint swayed again, let the man stagger. Hands stiff, he jabbed, and took the big man in midstrike, fingers burying themselves deep in his assailant's solar plexus. The man's eyes bugged and he folded forward, gasping and coughing.

Flint stepped through the gap between the two men and turned, his back to the door now.

He stepped back, out into the darkness, and was immediately surrounded by the noise of the night, the flow of bodies. No one followed him from the clanhouse.

He followed the main thoroughfare and soon was able to let himself in to the rooming house where the Riverwalkers were staying.

Farsamy had grown out across the river from which it took its name.

Or, at least, that's how it appeared to Flintheart as the city came into view around a meander ahead of the Riverwalkers' boats.

Jetties and piers extended out from where the west bank must be, encalming wide areas of water to form harbours for the many craft toing and froing all the time. Spaces between jetties had filled in with floating podhuts, riding on great, air-filled bladders. Flint recognised Trecosi expertise at work there, remembering the 'huts that rode the floodwaters at Greenwater during the wet season. Judging by the scale of the docklands, great areas of the city must be permanently afloat.

Beyond, taller buildings rose above the podhuts. Some were clearly tuber-grown, but others must rely on the older technologies, built of stone, cane, and wood. North of the city, Gossamer Heights embraced Farsamy, a cupola of limestone hills bunched together at the southern end of Spinster's Spine. A similar distance to the west of the city and out of sight to Flint, the river Elver would be approaching its end, meeting the river Farsam just south of Farsamy.

The Riverwalkers waited on the oil-calm waters of a holding bay until a sullen-looking foreman gestured to them that a berthing space was clear. Instantly, the mutts started working their treadles and the boat glided up to butt softly against the pliant wall of the jetty.

Flint climbed out. He struggled for calm, tried to find his solid centre and let its influence spread, but it was futile.

In Farsamy, at last, he wondered what he would find.

"Is this Carnival?" asked Flint, uncertainly, some time later.

Away from the docks now, they passed along narrow streets, through jostling crowds, past stalls and basket-laden vendors, the air pierced by their insistent cries and calls. The press of people and activity here in Farsamy made Beshusa seem little more than an overgrown village in comparison.

Tallofmind shrugged, his head tipped to one side in a noncommittal gesture Flint had come to recognise in the old Walker. "It always feels like Carnival in Farsamy," he said. "It's the crowds, the scale of things—everything done bigger." Then he added, "But yes, Carnival is about to begin."

They continued on foot through the city. After some time of silence, Tallofmind glanced up at Flint and said, "The Riverwalkers take rooms in a hostel by the Sentinel. I hope you will join us, Brother Flintheart."

Flint met Tallofmind's look. He nodded. "Thank you," he said, grateful that his fellow traveller had voiced what had lain unspoken between them. Now that they were in Farsamy, their journey together was over. Flint might just as easily leave the Riverwalkers now, never to set eyes on them again, but he knew that would be unforgivable. "I am a Riverwalker," he added, which was what Tallofmind had really meant: no Riverwalker could be alone in the city. He was still among friends.

The hostel overlooked a narrow, cane-straight stream that cut through this part of the city, passing under streets and buildings only to reemerge a short time later. It carried refuse and effluent from the pod-huts, already part-digested, providing food for street rats and gulls and many smaller creatures. Across the stream there lay a small area of gardens, tended continually by a team of small mutts, and in the gardens' centre lay the sprawling mass of what the Farsamies called the Sentinel.

The Riverwalkers looked on the creature with caution and, Flint surmised, a distinct element of mistrust. It was what they called a wisdom machine, and what Flint would call an Oracle. He felt their attitude understandable: the only wisdom machine his companions knew, after all, was the Lost Oracle to the south of Restitution—a perverted and corrupted monstrosity, luring sentient beings from all around with its siren pherotropic lures.

But Flint had grown up at ease with Oracles, and now he felt drawn to the Sentinel's sanctity and insight into the ways of humankind.

He tried to ignore any intimations of wrongdoing as he left his companions practising Lordsway in the hostel yard, and headed across the narrow bridge to join the queues for the Sentinel.

If Amber had come to Farsamy, if by some chance she remained a free person, then Flint knew it likely that she would seek out an Oracle for guidance and comfort.

He stood behind a family group, come from a small settlement in Gossamer Heights. "Look," the old matriarch said, taking Flint's hand and pointing it towards the craggy horizon. "See where there is a nick in the skyline, just to the right of the highest point?" Gossamer Heights formed an irregular horizon above the city, lumps and crags making it hard to identify any one highest point. Flint nodded, and the woman continued, "That is where Farsamy Way passes through the hills and drops towards the city. And that is where we make our humble home."

"I came by river," said Flint.

"Walking!" cackled the old woman, pleased with her own wit.

Flint smiled. "My sister may have come by the Way, though," he went on. "She is so high, has chestnut hair to her shoulders, eyes yel-lowed by childhood illness. I don't suppose . . . ?"

The woman considered, then shook her head. "Many pass through at this time of year," she said. "The city is a big place."

That realisation was still only starting to settle around Flint: to find one person among so many!

He thought of the Riverwalkers, practising Lordsway. He sought the Joyous Breath and held onto it, calming himself.

Slowly, the queue shuffled forward.

Close to, he saw that the Sentinel had grown itself according to an entirely different scale compared to any Oracle Flint had previously encountered. Its great, swollen body bulged and pulsed, its bulk divided into many smaller compartments, much like the cells of a podhut.

It disturbed Flint, for some reason, to see similarities between Oracle and podhut, although each was part plant, part animal, part other, built by the Lord to serve the needs of humankind.

A sphincter opened, and the matriarch entered the Sentinel, having allowed the rest of her family to enter before her.

Flint waited, and a short time later the sphincter of another cell opened. He stepped forward, dipped his head, and climbed inside.

Sweet scents stole into his being. Trumpet flowers and sweetwater, honey and bracket ceps. Smothering him with calm.

"Tell me, Master." The voice was soft, reassuring. "Tell me of the world." This Oracle did not convey the usual sense of eagerness, and Flint knew that it must not hunger for input in the same way that Tre-cosann's Oracle did. But it wanted to know, still: it did not want to know of the world, but rather of *his* world. He sensed it as some kind of machine, fuelled by knowledge and understanding, using diverse inputs to compute its insights and wisdom.

A Riverwalker's understanding, he realised: he was seeing it as a wisdom machine and not the quasi-mystical all-knowing figure he had grown up with. Understanding pulling the clouds from before his eyes.

And then its pheromones did their work, teasing at his senses, tugging at his emotions.

He leaned back, felt steady pulsings against his spine, warmth.

"I am Flintheart," he said drowsily. "Flintheart of the Riverwalkers, Flintreco Eltarn of Trecosann. I come here looking for my sister, Amberlinetreco Eltarn." He thought of his sister, then, of her face, the chirpy facade she always put up to protect herself from the world. He thought of her as a child, curled up on the Leaving Hill, willing herself to be taken up to join the spirits of the Lost where she believed she belonged.

Instead, he saw Tarn, laughing and cursing amiably; he saw Callum and Petria; he saw Mesteb of Greenwater, and Janna and Hillery, too.

"They are here?" he asked. "They have been here?"

"Sentinel is one of several," said the dreamy voice inside his head. Flint had a sudden understanding of a network of Oracles through the city, smartfibre roots penetrating beneath the podhuts and streets to join them up. Not here, then, but other Oracles in Farsamy had held audience with members of the Trecosi delegation to Carnival.

He had known they would be in Farsamy, but it comforted him to know that they were not close, that they were staying elsewhere in the city.

He would see them, he knew. He had to. But he preferred it to be at a time and place of his own choosing.

He pictured Amber again. "My sister . . . ?"

Nothing.

"She travelled by river, down the Elver. I think she has been enslaved or bonded."

Still nothing.

Soothing scents, enfolding him. Telling him nothing he did not already know.

He left Sentinel some time later. He walked through the gardens, through neat rows of low hedges, beneath withy arches twined with vines and drape moss. He came to the cane-straight stream and looked down, watched rats tugging at what looked like the purple shell of a decayed fleshfruit.

Back at the hostel, he stood alone in the yard. In his head he found the beat, the pulse of Rhythm and Clouds, and his hands sliced the air as his mind found calm and clarity. Emptiness his only comfort.

CHAPTER 12

"**F**light of Eagles," said Judgement, and the Riverwalkers changed movements and rhythm smoothly, as one, to the beat of Judgement's bone drum.

Dawn's light spread silver across the city's rooftops. The River-walkers had been practising Lordsway since before the rising of the sun, and would continue for some time yet. Ritual discipline seemed to take on a new significance for them when they were away from their home.

Flint remembered this, now, from the old preacher Knowsbetter's visit to Trecosann many years before. He remembered the children crowding together, watching curiously as the old man, dressed only in a tangled loincloth, had practised these same movements, eyes seeing some distant place.

Flint wasn't concentrating.

He was not moving with smoothness and continuity—the independent movements of his limbs were not uniting in a single, flowing motion.

The rhythm evaded him.

He stopped, exhausted by his exertions. Usually, after practising Lordsway, he would feel exhilarated and energised.

The others continued, and Flint left the yard.

Pulling his cloak about him, tightening the cord at his waist, he headed out into the streets of Farsamy, felt their tight-packed cobbles beneath the soles of his feet. The streets were busy already, people heading purposefully in this direction and that, readying themselves and their city for Carnival.

Pausing by the front of the hostel, he heard the soft slap of bare feet on stone behind him and he turned.

Tallofmind stood before him.

"I'm sorry," said Flint. He felt as if he were deserting his friends, betraying their trust in him. "I'm not worthy of your faith." He slapped the side of his head with the heel of a hand. "I can't concentrate." The discipline Sister Judgement had taught him had deserted him this morning.

Tallofmind gave his tipped-head shrug and smiled. "Find your sister, Brother Flintheart," he said. "Carnival awaits."

The Riverwalkers' hostel was situated some distance from the city centre, but as soon as he set out Flint was aware of a sense of hyperactivity in the streets. He did not know what the city was normally like, of course, only that this tension and excitement could not be the normal state of things.

Soon, stalls lined every street, bedecked with canvas canopies in an array of colours and patterns. Entire buildings had been erected wherever space allowed, sometimes encroaching out into the street itself, an exotic assortment of speed-grown podhuts and lean-tos built from cane and canvas and smartfibre sheeting.

Traders sold rugs woven from tufted fibre that changed colour depending on the light; rings, necklaces, and brooches made from living fibres; jewellery that would grow with the owner, adapt itself to his or her moods. Body artists painted faces and hands. . . . Flint looked closer here, as he came to a stall where a beautiful young golden-skinned woman painted flowers on another woman's cheeks. Skin bubbled under the artist's brush, blistering into a staggering reliefwork of petals and buds.

Changing vectors!

The artist was painting with vectors, modifying the skin itself to give her artwork life.

The artist smiled at him. "I'll make you a crocodile," she said to him, voice low, seductive. "I'll give you scales, sir." She gestured to a man seated at the back of her stall—a Mollahdic preacher, Flint saw. "It's all certified safe," she continued. "Changes localised, decorative, fall away in days. You want me to make you someone new?"

Flint backed away through the growing press of the crowd. The artist was probably Trecosi, given her abilities with the changing arts, but her skill was not one practised in his part of the clan.

He sipped buttered tea from a stall somewhere near the city centre. He felt confused, his head crammed with images from the morning's exploration. Stalls selling fine leatherwear and bonework; performing dogs and goats tuned to the sound of their masters' drums and guitars; soothsayers, preachers, card-readers, and psychics, each selling promises of truth and insight. The latter had tempted him, even though he did not believe in their arcane arts.

Now he paused before a troupe of what he had at first taken to be some kind of performers: an old man in a lawman's painted and feathered finery, sitting before a man and a woman, the two arguing and pleading. It was a public arbitration, he realised, the couple laying their differences before the lawman and the audience, settling their marital differences as a form of public entertainment. Perhaps—it was not clear to Flint. So much that he had seen this morning seemed alien and bizarre to him.

A short time later, he came to a quieter place, some kind of roadside shrine, its air of peace and calm in stark contrast to its clearly rapid construction from ribcanes and banana leaves, lashed together to shield occupants from the day's sun.

A bald woman sat cross-legged within. It was hard to tell if she was young or old. Her skin was smooth as that of a fleshfruit, almost unnaturally so. He wondered how True she was, how crafted.

Flint entered, bowed his head, sat.

The shrine's peace was welcome after the hustle of the Carnival streets. He raised hands, palms together, above his head and took the Joyous Breath. Solidity, deep in his abdomen.

Opening his eyes some time later, he saw that the woman was studying him, patiently.

He lowered his hands and bowed his head towards her.

"It is not often that a Riverwalker takes the peace of the All," she said. Her accent was peculiar—southern, Flint guessed.

He looked around. He didn't recognise the figures represented by the statuettes, or the significance of the pictograms daubed on the back wall.

"I . . . I don't think I am a true Riverwalker," he said. "I'm not very good at it."

"Faith is not a skill," said the woman. "It is not a test, despite what your people say. Faith *is*."

"I'm looking for my sister," said Flint. "She went missing. She may have been abducted. I think she is in Farsamy, but I have no idea how to find her."

The woman touched the corner of one eye with a fingertip, then touched her lips. "Look and ask," she said. "And pray. How would one know your sister?"

"Average height," said Flint. "She has chestnut hair and her eyes are jaundiced from childhood illness. Her name is Amberlinetreco Eltarn."

The woman shook her head apologetically. "I have not seen her," she said. "There are many Trecosi at Carnival, though. Most have stalls in Willow Square." Then she went on, "And if your sister has had the misfortune to be taken against her will as you suggest, then you should go to Sun Street and the Pillories. Mutts and bondsmen are traded there, and freemen seek indenture."

Flint bowed his head. He rubbed his eyes with knuckled hands, then stood and backed out of the shrine, muttering thanks to the woman as she, in turn, called blessings upon him in a singsong chant.

Much of Farsamy followed a grid plan of streets and blocks, but Sun Street cut through the centre in a great diagonal slash. Many of the buildings here were constructed from stone, with podhut extensions grafted on and fibre reinforcements and modifications. The street's blackstone surface was wide and smoothed with age, packed so tight with stalls that even hand-drawn carts had trouble navigating a route.

Towards the northern end of Sun Street the stalls gave way to a series of low, fenced enclosures, some covered with canvas canopies, others exposed to the day's sun. The air here was heavy with animal smells, the press of bodies around the enclosures thick and eager.

Flint took a deep breath and tried to calm himself.

He heard a jabber of raised voices, a thick, southern accent letting loose a torrent of angry Mutter, a rapid clapping of hands to attract attention. A man in the nearby enclosure gesticulated at a group of mutts, cowering in the far corner. They were simian creatures: round, button eyes and compressed faces, thick black fur covering their bodies. The man spat something brown into the dirt and continued his tirade.

Flint turned away, pushed through the crowd.

At the next enclosure he saw more simians. These mutts were barely waist-high to him, their opposable toes giving them advantage in the fruit plantations.

He moved on.

In the next lot, the mutts were almost indistinguishable from True humans. Seven males and six females with pups stood silently, obediently, current bids chalked on the wall behind them.

"Walk!"

The command came from a man in the crowd, and instantly the mutts fell into step with each other, completing a tight circuit of their enclosure. They moved well, and would fetch a good price.

Some time, much later in the morning, Flint came to an area where men and women stood on small boxes, calling to the crowd, offering themselves into service. True humans with no clan affiliations or ties, Flint realised, seeking to become bondsmen. With chilling clarity, he realised that this might, ultimately, be his own fate.

He passed slowly through the crowds, studying everyone, asking questions of anyone who would listen: *. . . so high . . . eyes jaundiced by childhood illness . . . Amberlinetreco Eltarn, True daughter of Clan Treco.*

Willow Square was only two blocks from the main mutt-trading centre on Sun Street. It made sense for the traders from Trecosann to make their base here, as their expertise lay in the gennering arts and their main products were lines of change: not so much selling changed mutts and beasts as displaying the kinds of changes their skills could induce in the hope of striking agreements to govern longer-term trade.

Flint spotted his father—only two stalls distant! He felt no need to seek the calmness of the Lordsway, he realised. He was icily calm already.

He paused in the shelter of a sweetmeat stall.

Tarn lolled on a stool by an enclosure that contained three young mutts. Flint recognised them as among those that had been dipped on the day Amber had disappeared. One was barely more than a pup and completely hairless, sitting, rocking back and forth and singing softly—an oddity, a freak put here to attract attention. The other two were of a kind: probably no more than seven or eight years old, they were broad across the shoulder, heavily muscled. It was a type which had much potential for future use, Flint saw. It made him think of two of the fallen faithwalkers back at Restitution.

Someone came and spoke in Tarn's ear. Cousin Hillery: grinning, enjoying the freedom of Carnival, wearing a fold-around cloak that exposed a diagonal wedge of midriff and drew the eyes of Tarn and other passing men.

Flint approached.

Hillery stepped back from Tarn, giggling, and moved away.

Tarn did not recognise him at first: a bearded stranger in the Carnival crowd. When he did, he sat upright abruptly, eyes widening. "You . . ." he gasped.

Flint nodded. "I am still looking for Amber," he said. "Have you heard anything of her?"

Tarn rubbed at the black stubble on his chin. Finally, he shook his head, words clearly evading him.

A big, hirsute man in a golden cloak joined them. "Mesteb," said Flint, in greeting.

Again, there was a pause before his cousin from Greenwater recognised him. "Flint," he said, then. "I told your father you were coming to Farsamy. You . . ." He gestured at Flint, a wave of the hand indicating his clothing and the beads in his hair.

"I travel with the Riverwalkers," Flint said. "I left Greenwater with traders who turned on me. They were Lost. I thought you were more careful about who you did business with."

Mesteb shrugged. "Your Aunt Clarel arranged passage for you," he said. "I will warn her." After another pause, he added, "No sign of your sister, hmm?"

Flint removed Amber's bracelet from his wrist. "I have this," he said, holding it out towards Tarn. "Do you recognise it?" Blankness. "It's Amber's. I believe that she lost it in Tremellen." He did not need to expand on that: Tremellen could only imply the haul-boat trade.

"I think she's here in Farsamy."

Mesteb nodded. "I will look out for her," he said. Then he added, "Will you come back to your family after Carnival, Flint?"

"Family?" burst in Tarn. "Look at him, Mesteb! He has turned his back on the clan and gone with the evangelists." He leaned forward and spat at Flint's feet. "He is no more Clan Treco than his Lost sister."

Eyes peering up at Flint, watching for reaction, looking for another fight.

Flint held his breath, found solidity. He turned his gaze pointedly away from his father and addressed Mesteb. "I have clan news to pass on," he said. "Rendeltreco, a young woman from Tremellen, found judgement before the Lord at the Riverwalker town of Restitution recently." In response to a blank look, he clarified: "She died." He remembered the pale young woman, sweat darkening her sandy hair, eyes jammed shut, torso twitching. He remembered the wild bucking of her body, the sharpness of pain in her animal cries, the bones shifting beneath his hands as he tried to restrain her.

He remembered fleeing into the night, running from change.

"I would be grateful if you would pass on word to her family," he concluded, swallowing drily.

He turned and left, not even looking back when he heard the low rumble of the two men's voices, the word's "seed patch" amongst others with which his father taunted him.

If these men were representative of Clan Treco, then it was an affiliation Flintheart of the Riverwalkers no long wished to claim.

That night, when he had eventually tired of his search, he ate with the Riverwalkers in their hostel near to the Sentinel Gardens.

No one asked him about his day: if he needed to share his experiences he would tell them. That was the Riverwalker way.

They knew, anyway. They could easily tell from his withdrawn mood that he had found no success.

He drew solidity from their company, and then he went out into the gardens to find peace in solitude. Long queues waited by the Sentinel, but that did not interest Flint tonight. He sat beneath scented trees and tried not to think too hard about the future and the near certainty of the failure of his quest to find poor Amberline.

He slept on a thin sleep roll, in a room with twelve others. Or rather, he lay on his back, and then on his side, unable to settle, unable even to close his eyes. He stared at the dark shapes of the hostel cell's ceiling, the occasional pulsings of its walls, the slanted moonlight penetrating the building's open vents.

He recalled the words of the shrine-tender: *Look and ask and pray.* She might easily have added: And know when to give up, Brother Flintheart.

He walked with Judgement and Walkedfar, the morning sun searing, the air dry. Breaking with standard Riverwalker attire, Flint wore a wide-brimmed hat to shield himself from the sun.

Again, the streets were busy, crowded stalls forcing the people to pass through ever-narrower gaps. Flint found the press of bodies confusing, his senses muddled by the sensations of being in such a crowd.

They stopped for some time at a Beshusami stall, Walkedfar and Flint listening patiently as Judgement discussed podhut husbandry with two of the Clan Elders.

As the morning passed, Flint started to understand Judgement's techniques, to appreciate just how good a haggler she was: negotiating with clans before they realised negotiations were even taking place. Judgement manipulated what appeared to be casual conversation to gently probe, to plant ideas and possibilities: the Beshusami were second to none when it came to breeding and selecting podhut germ cells, channelling the processes of change to produce the finest seed material for new buildings and other structures. But the Riverwalkers' understanding of engineering meant that they could take what the Beshusami did a stage farther: using their skills to nurture and guide the further development of the podhuts as they grew.

When they left the Beshusami Elders, Flint knew that before Carnival was over the Riverwalkers would strike a renewed pact of cooperation with the clan, trading expertise for products, buying time with the Beshusami to spread the Lord's message.

They ate plantain stuffed with pecans and drank from a water fountain. Flint took the opportunity—as he had throughout the morning—to approach people, asking after Amber and always getting the same response.

Later, they stopped before a long stall in Peter's Square. The stall bore samples of smartfibre. Mostly it was unrefined fibre, bundles that had been skimmed and sorted for display; some had been woven, forming fine skins of translucent material, glimmering in the light, so thin as to appear flimsy and yet taut and rigid to the touch.

"Clan Ritt fibres," said a young man behind the stall. He was dark-skinned, well-fleshed although not grossly so, a ceramic chain around his neck and a slightly arrogant air betraying his high standing within his clan.

Flint looked at him closely, but the trader clearly didn't recognise him. This was Henritt Elkyme, son of the Ritt Elder who had recently visited Trecosann to find out about the Trecosi gennering skills.

Flint ran his hands through a tray of combed fibres, relishing the sensuous flowing sensation as they passed between his fingers.

"Perhaps the finest you will find in all of the eastern provinces," said Henritt.

"Most certainly the finest," an older man added, gently correcting his master, ignoring the dark look his interruption inspired.

"A fine selection of raw materials," Flint said carefully, addressing the younger man. "Tell me, what do you craft with these fine fibres?"

Henritt started to answer but was interrupted again. "We do not need to craft anything with our fibres for trade at Carnival," said the man. "Their quality speaks for itself."

He was covering for his clan's lack of engineering expertise, Flint saw. Clan Ritt were widely known for the high quality of the fibres they grew, but not for their skills in crafting finished products from the material. There was an opportunity there for the Riverwalkers, and

Flint happily stepped aside as Judgement moved in to pursue the conversation, the negotiations he had clumsily initiated.

He was becoming attuned to the Riverwalkers' ways.

"Alal?" he said, approaching a broad-bodied man who stood looking up at the men and women trying to sell themselves into service in the wide, tree-lined thoroughfare known as the Pillories.

The man turned, and Flint saw that it was, indeed, Alal. He was a labourer who had travelled with the group from Trecosann to Farsamy Way. Flint had shared a cell with him for one night on that journey. He remembered him as an insightful man who thought deeply and slowly. His fringe of blond hair hung over a dark face and—Flint saw now—troubled eyes.

"Alal, my friend. What troubles you?"

Alal's features cleared when he worked out who Flint was. He gestured, smiled, said, "You look a different man. You're still looking for your sister?"

Flint nodded.

Finally answering Flint's question, Alal said, "I came here looking for work." He waved a hand, taking in the ranks of men and women standing on boxes, telling onlookers of their strengths and skills, all seeking work as Alal sought work. "I am not alone in that."

Flint took the man's arm and led him through the crowd. He bought slices of fleshfruit from a stall and shared them with Alal, guessing that his friend had not eaten for some time.

"Are Jemmie and Lizabel in Farsamy?" Flint asked. "Are they well?"

"Probably," said Alal. "I left them in a small settlement in Gossamer Heights. They said they would follow me to Carnival, but we did not arrange to meet. They will be here somewhere." Brighter now, Alal asked, "Have you searched the auctions for your sister?"

Flint nodded. "I have been to every holding pen in Willow Way," he said. "And there is no sign of Amber. I tell myself that should be reassuring: it increases the likelihood that she is still a free person."

Silence, then Alal said, "There are many other holding pens in Farsamy. Willow Way is only the most well known."

Flint nodded. "I know," he said. "And I keep looking."

CHAPTER 13

Over the following days, Flint searched all of Farsamy—sometimes alone, often in the company of Alal or one of the Riverwalkers. It was a futile and disheartening search.

Sitting by the river one afternoon, staring out over turbulent waters where gulls and skimmers bucked and swooped, Flint and Alal shared a bladder of beer. It was a taste Flint had only recently acquired and one of which he had an uncomfortable feeling he might one day grow too fond. For now, though, he sipped and passed the bladder across to Alal.

"I've looked everywhere," he said. "Asked everyone. Half of them think I'm mad, or making up romantic adventure stories about myself."

"There are people who do that," said Alal. "People like a good storyteller."

Flint thought of the old Riverwalker, Knowsbetter, and his tall moral tales. He nodded. "I keep asking myself how long I can go on. How long I *should* go on."

Alal passed the beer back to Flint and after a long pause said, "Can you stop?"

He had cut through Flint's confused thinking. How could he give up? If there was the slightest chance that he might find Amber and save her from whatever mess she was in, then he could not possibly abandon his search.

"I have found somewhere to stay," said Alal.

"Good news," said Flint. For the last few nights Alal had been sleeping rough in the streets. "But how do you pay?"

"It's what the Farsamies call a trust lodge," said Alal. "It's owned by a group of traders. Young people looking for work can stay there,

174

making what contributions they are able to a fund that pays for maintenance. They ask us to make further donations when we find work and move on."

He hesitated, then continued, "It's pretty grim. Some of the residents don't respect the place. But it is better than the street. You shoud bear it in mind if you want to stay on after Carnival."

The auction pens were a depressing place to be. Flint had never found them so before, but now that his sister might be here he saw the place in a new light.

Mutts huddled together, trying to avoid the looks and demands of their prospective purchasers, trying to find shelter from the sun, and yet they were unable to refuse when told to walk, jump, run, show off their fitness. Love and fear filled their eyes whenever they looked at one of the True. Their existence was almost too awful to contemplate.

Flint felt as low as he had felt in all of the time he had been seeking Amber. He could not give up, and yet deep in his heart he knew that he already *had*, that as much as he persisted in his search he knew he would never find her.

". . . the whites of her eyes appear yellow, the result of childhood illness."

"Yes, I know the one."

Flint stared at the man, not believing his words, thinking it must be some cruel joke.

"A young one," the man went on. "Doesn't speak. Looked fit— Makki reckoned she'd fetch a good price."

"Are you sure?"

The man shrugged, suddenly defensive. "Yellow eyes, reddish-brown hair, about so high. Don't know if it's her, but the mutt Makki was selling fits your description."

"She's no mutt," said Flint. "She's my sister: a True daughter of Clan Treco."

The man shrugged again, raising his eyebrows as if to say, *Believe what you like, but she's up for auction with the rest of the mutts.*

"Where is she? Please?"

"Over in Minster Place," said the trader. "Ask for Makkibern Elthom. Has pens with forty-plus mutts in 'em."

Minster Place! All this time in Farsamy and she—if it really could be Amber—had been held in one of the small trading squares only a few blocks from Sentinel Gardens! Minster Place was a short walk from the hostel where Flint had been staying.

"Thank you," he gasped, turning away from the trader and pushing his way into the throng that filled Willow Way. He desperately hoped it was her, and yet equally he hoped it was not. . . . If it was her, then what hell had she been through? But at least he would find her. If it was *not* her, then he still hadn't found her, but at least it allowed him to hold onto the slim hope that she travelled freely and might still be safe.

Minster Place was a small square, dawn oaks in each corner, each tree's cluster of six smooth-barked trunks an exotic—*wild*—intrusion into the heart of the city. A shaven-headed, bearded Mollahdic preacher stood on a pedestal in the centre of the square accusing the mutt traders of all kinds of wickedness and deceit, the lightheartedness of the banter he exchanged with the traders somewhat belying his message.

The Place was divided into a grid of holding pens intersected by viewing paths. The structures had a permanency about them that was absent from much of Farsamy, and Flint guessed that this was a fixed market that continued even when Carnival was over. Farsamy was at the heart of the mutt trade, after all.

"I'm looking for Makkibern Elthom," he said, tugging at the sleeve of a squat man who leaned against a post, chewing spitbark and scratching at his crotch.

The man looked at him, carefully withdrawing his sleeve from Flint's grip. With a nod of his head he indicated that Makki's pens were deeper into the square.

Flint pushed through the crowd, oblivious to the cursing of those around him.

"Makkibern Elthom?"

Deeper.

"Makkibern Elthom?"

All the time, Flint eyed the traders, searching the pens frantically for a copper-haired mutt who was not a mutt at all but his kid sister.

"Walkers looking to buy, are they?" Makki was a short man, with a round belly barely contained by his filthy tunic. He had a bristly beard, growing unevenly across the lower half of his face, and his head was bound in a long strip of grey fabric—a form of headgear many of the traders here wore.

"I'm looking for my sister," said Flint, his look flitting between the man's face and the pens behind him. Then he called, "Amber? Are you here, Amber?"

Makki waved his hands in a silencing motion, and said, "Shush, shush, good sir. What's all the noise and commotion with, eh?"

All around, people were watching the two of them, curious on-lookers sensing that something out of the normal was happening.

Flint turned to Makki again. "My sister," he said. "I've been in-formed that you're trying to sell my sister, Amberlinetreco Eltarn, True daughter of Clan Treco."

The man looked confused, and he was doing his best to look con-cerned. "Only mutts," he said to Flint. "Take a look for yourself, good sir. Mutts out of the Beren transit camps. Take a look."

Flint was doing so. In the nearest pen there were some short mutts, mouths and nostrils mere slits in flattened, fur-covered faces. Beyond, others similar and diverse and not one that even vaguely resembled his sister.

"About so high"—hand held in front of his chest—"chestnut hair to her shoulders. Fifteen years old. Eyes yellowed by childhood illness."

The man's concern suddenly looked genuine. "I . . ."

"What? What is it? What have you done?"

"All my stock is genuine," said the man hurriedly. "All bought in good faith from the transit camps."

"And . . . ?"

"There was one," the man said, watching Flint nervously. "They called her Taneyes. She fit your description, but she was no True clan member, sir! She was one of the fallen. Couldn't even speak Mutter."

"'Was'?"

"I took her in good faith, sir, I tell you! And I sold her in good faith, too. Young master of high standing." He spread hands over his round belly and puffed his cheeks out for effect, then continued, "Lived the good life, I'd say. Eats well. Dark skin." He gestured to his neck. "Had a chain thing around his neck. Came and took her last night."

Flint's mind was working rapidly. He had spoken to a man like that earlier in Carnival . . . Henritt Elkyme! He had spoken to him at one of the Ritt stalls on Peter's Square.

They were still there, thank the Lord! The same selection of fibres was arranged over the stall—samples put there for display, rather than for sale. The real Carnival business for this group was to strike longer-term deals, much as the Riverwalkers had come to renew pacts of cooperation and exchange with the clans.

Henritt was clearly a senior representative of his clan, despite his age. Flint recalled him saying back in Trecosann that he was to lead his clan's delegation—a claim Flint had dismissed as mere boasting. Now,

Henritt sat back on a stool behind the stall, surveying his domain, and his dark, fleshy face bore the look of one well satisfied with his lot.

Flint stood before him, bowing his head deferentially. There was a look of fleeting recognition on the man's face as Flint said, "We spoke before."

He knew Sister Judgement had been back since then, negotiating indentures for two Riverwalkers to go to work in Rittasan in the fibre fields. "And?"

In Trecosann hierarchy was not so central to the clan's organisation, but Flint knew that the southern clans had a more rigid class structure. Henritt had an arrogance he recognised, the sweeping assumption of those with power that almost everyone they encounter will be a social inferior.

"I come from Minster Place," said Flint. "I have spoken to Makkibern Elthom about . . . about a mutt. Young, female, with chestnut hair and yellow eyes."

The Ritt master looked blank. "And?" he said again. "Why are you telling me this?"

Flint studied his face for signs of deceit but saw none. Only puzzlement, and irritation that his time was being wasted.

"She was bought by . . . someone who sounded like you."

The young Ritt master shrugged, any curiosity on his face disappearing as the reason for Flint's questions emerged. "Farsamy's a big place," he said. "There must be plenty of people who look like me." He smiled, now. "Anyway: plenty more mutts out there, aren't there?"

". . . young man . . . high standing in his clan . . . perhaps a little, er, *portly* . . . dark skin . . . wears a decorative chain around his neck . . ."

Most of the time he received the same responses he had when enquiring after Amber: sympathy, but no help.

"Could be Thombern Elpetre—has a stall over on Willow Way."

"Could be Jessritt Elfez. Last I saw he was working the pens on Square of Saints."

"Maybe Loutenka Ellou. Try the brewhouses on Gossamer Road."

But no, when Flint managed to track them down not one of these candidates admitted to having bought a young yellow-eyed mutt from Makkibern Elthom on Minster Place.

Exhausted, Flint sat with Alal, watching gulls skim the garbage floating in the waters of the river Farsam. "I felt so *close*," he said.

"Carnival is over," said Alal. "What now?"

"I know," said Flint. Today he had watched the stalls and lean-tos being dismantled as he hurried about the Elderman Quarter, still trying to track down another Ritt trader who, upon being confronted, had shown Flint the mutts he had bought. Not one came close to fitting Amber's description.

"I don't know what I will do now. I have until morning to decide. Then the Riverwalkers return to Restitution."

CHAPTER 14
HENRITT'S STORY

"Faster, faster!"

Henritt Elkyme leaned forward in his carriage's deep bucket seat. Banana-leaf screens shielded him on three sides, so that all he could see of Farsamy was the cobbled street, the jostling crowds, and the tight-packed buildings to either side. Henritt took a crop from its carved holder and flicked it at the sweat-streaked flank of the nearest mutt. "Faster," he said again.

This place had an air of transience, of lean-tos and podhuts thrown casually together—here today, but probably not the next—against a backdrop of trees, hills, the great river Farsam, luxuriating in their ancient permanence. It made him uncomfortable.

He flicked again at the nearest mutt, then, catching gentle old Pilofritt's look, eased himself back into the cushions. Pil had been with the clan for many years, a bondsman given in tribute to Henritt's father Kymeritt by the neighbouring Tenka clan, as part-settlement in some obscure dispute.

Henritt chewed on a jaggery stick, then tossed the sugary husk out into the street when he had finished. Pil would be right, of course: there was no hurry, no need to work the beasts too hard. It had been a long journey and everyone was tired. He closed his eyes, sick already of the sight of so much flesh, human and otherwise. Sick of the smells of shit and sweat and dirt, the babble of voices, the occasional raised beseechment to whatever gods these people worshipped. And yet . . . the clamour, the tension of mixing with the world beyond the clan— it was exciting, too. He, Henritt, purebred son of Kyme of the clan Ritt, had been to Farsamy many times before, but this was the first time he had led the delegation to Carnival. As Pil kept reminding him, he had much to learn. And also, so much to see and do!

He walked through the early-morning crowds, resenting all around him.

His head hurt; his stomach burned; his throat was dry and swollen, making it hard to talk or swallow. Not that he wanted to.

Pil had woken him too early—deliberately, he felt sure. Carnival was under way and he had stock to buy, a head to clear. Henritt recalled the night before, lying slumped at the roadside with the street rats sniffing at him, trying to work out if he was garbage to be consumed. He'd flapped at them, driven them from him. They should have been able to tell. He couldn't remember returning to the lodging house. No doubt Pil would fill him in on the details if he bothered to ask.

The delegation from Rittasan had established itself in one of the squares near to the centre of Farsamy. Here, Carnival filled every open space, with stalls and pens spilling over into streets and thoroughfares.

Dew lingering from the cool night gave the cobbles a surface slick with slurry and a smart algal scum that dissolved away any debris the rats had missed.

"Hey, Janos!" he croaked, waving at a young bonded behind the Ritt stall. Janosofritt looked moribund: hooded eyes sunk deep into his pallid face. Just as he should: for much of the night the two friends had matched each other drink for drink.

The boy smiled and waved. He was good company, even if his fawning did verge on the outrageous. He was a good worker, too.

Henritt stepped behind the stall, eyeing the arrangements critically, gesturing at Janos or one of the mutts to refine the display.

Under the canopy he was sheltered from the growing intensity of the morning's sun, but there was no respite from the heat and the pervasive smells of the stock. He sat on a cushioned stool, ready to do business, ready to take his first serious steps in multiplying the clan's wealth.

The delegation from Rittasan had brought samples of some of their best smartfibres to Carnival. Their livelihood was founded on the fibre beds, the techniques for farming and moulding the smartstuff jealously guarded, passed down through the generations. Clans would travel for days and weeks to buy in stocks of Ritt fibre and its products: the fibres had much in common with the coarse spider silk to be found in some parts of the wilds; refined over generations, when Ritt fibres were woven together they would bond and scab over, forming waterproof sheeting that could be used for clothing, bottling and other containers; depending on the aftertreatment, Ritt fibres could be used in the construction of buildings, boats, and carriages. The stock they would sell at Farsamy market would finance the trip and the purchases Henritt was to make; the longer-term deals and contracts initiated here were what really mattered.

Henritt had spent many such trips studying at the feet of his father, or Uncle Chardinritt. He was aware that he sometimes gave the impression of callowness, of disinterest even, but he was well taught and his brain was sharp. He would not let the clan down.

Give him a mutt, any day! Mutts were straightforward in their loyalty and devotion: a good mutt could be nothing but obedient, after all. They didn't have it in them to be condescending, to patronise their betters in the way that Pilofritt had perfected, to simultaneously obey their master's every word and yet undermine his standing in the company of equals.

And Janosofritt! The boy had loved it.

"Perhaps the finest you will find in all of the eastern provinces," Henritt told a wild-eyed Riverwalker, allowing him to run the loose fibres through his hands, feel their quality.

"Most certainly the finest," Pilofritt chipped in, simultaneously defending the clan's standing and undermining Henritt. He had been like that since the start of trading, and Janos had not even troubled to hide his delight each time the old bondsman corrected Henritt.

"A fine selection of raw materials," the Walker said. From the look in his eyes he was clearly impressed. "Tell me, what do you craft with these fine fibres?"

Henritt started to answer, but Pilofritt beat him to it again: "We do not need to craft anything with our fibres for trade at Carnival. Their quality speaks for itself."

Now, another Riverwalker moved over to join them. Older, with crow's-foot lines around her eyes and a steady, measured pronunciation, she said, "You are being disingenuous, no? Such riches! You must have many uses for these fibres. In Restitution we use smartfibres to enhance Beshusami podhut pods—I'm sure you do the same."

"Oh, we have many uses for our fibres," said Pilofritt. "But we always welcome exchanges of ideas and skills with our neighbours. . . ."

After several days of this, Henritt had had enough of Pilofritt taking over at every opportunity. "I am going to inspect stock," he said, addressing no one in particular one day.

"I will accompany you, sir," said Pil immediately.

"You do not trust me to choose wisely?" demanded Henritt.

"You are my master and superior, sir. I merely advise and help you to refine your judgement. It is my duty."

Henritt met the old man's gaze. Turning away, he plucked another jaggery stick from behind the stall and bit into it, enjoying the kick from the coarse palm-sugar snack. He knew Pil disapproved of such stimulants. He tossed the husk into the gutter for the street rats. Why should he care what the bondsman thought? Pil might be purebred, but he was no freeman.

He led the way towards the Pillories and Willow Way. Bodies pressed all around. The wealthier clansmen and freemen wore fabrics made from Ritt smartfibres, their poorer fellows and bonded in cottons and woollen cloaks.

Henritt knew that if he paused for Pil's advice he would be told to explore the engineering stalls in the Elderman Quarter. The Ritt clan might be blessed with the source for some of the finest raw materials in the region, but innovations in their uses came from elsewhere. There would be gadgetry and clever devices aplenty in the Elderman Quarter, but the real trade there was in talent and forging longer-term partnerships: talented engineers to be recruited to the clan; innovative clans with which to construct alliances.

But Henritt was young and, he would readily admit, easily bored. His older brother Willemritt was the one who had been groomed in the semimystical techniques of fibre production, and it was Willemritt who was obsessive about the clan's product. Henritt was smarter than that. He knew that the real power lay in marketing and politicking. Let Will bury his head in the fibre vats day and night! It was Henritt who came to town, Henritt who saw the sights and met the people from outside the clan's small world.

And he knew exactly what would please his father, Kymeritt, far more than any exotic gadgetry. "Okay, Pil," he said. "Let's go look at some livestock."

They were chained by the ankle to loops of smartfibre bonded to the cobbles. Thirty or forty, perhaps, in this one pen alone. The smell was almost overpowering: faeces and urine but, more than anything, a booming, musky body odour. It made Henritt wish it was still raining, something to wash some of the stench out of the air.

He stood before a group of five males. They varied in height from one that barely reached Henritt's chin to one that towered over the others, like a mighty tree amid saplings. Despite the variation in body size, they looked as if they were all from the same stock: flat faces with almost no nose at all, wide mouths that split open to reveal even teeth in an expression more nervous than threatening. Their fur was thick, matted, starting above the eyes and extending over the head and down across the upper part of the body where it became thick and tangled, like the pelt of a goat.

"Janos would like them, no?" said Henritt, half turning to address Pil. The bondsman chuckled, then looked pointedly downwards. Henritt reached over the stock fence with his crop and flicked at the loincloth of one of the mutts. "Ah," he said. "I see." They'd been gelded. "I'm sure he could find a use for one, even so."

The beasts had good broad backs and shoulders. They might be worth the reserve price.

Pil put a gentle hand on Henritt's arm and shook his head. "Good stock don't need gelding," he said. "They must have needed calming. Probably wild stock—didn't want 'em rutting."

Henritt nodded. It paid to be careful. Most of the mutts he had known were, by their nature, obedient and hardworking. But he knew that many were flawed in some way: sickly, untrustworthy, malignant. *Imbuto* was the term they used: superficially healthy, but harbouring corruption in the core. His father would not thank him for bringing imbuto stock into the clan.

A herd of hogs in a nearby stall attracted his attention, squealing and chattering excitedly. One had blood smeared across its face, its features a curious mixture of hog and other. A street rat was dangling, twisting and writhing, from a mouth disturbingly human in form.

The hog bit hard and the rat went limp. The beast tossed its head back and swallowed while all around the other hogs pushed and snapped and chattered in their singsong voices. As a child, Henritt had pretended to identify words in those voices, had imagined an entire language of hoggery. The beasts were vile things, but, bred true, they had a loyalty to humans ingrained in them as solid as that of any mutt.

Henritt took Pil's arm and they left the hog stall behind. "I want something special for Father," he said. A plaything, a toy that would ever remind him of his youngest son's devotion and fitness to take on the affairs of their branch of the clan. "A gift."

"The clan will be served well enough with the contracts we are negotiating today," said the bondsman. "Gestures merely impress. Good business sense repays the faith your father has invested in you."

"True," said Henritt. "But I want to impress him, too."

"You won't find better than this one in a year of Carnivals," said the trader, a squat man with a grubby headcloth and blackened teeth. "Bids have already passed double the reserve price."

Henritt smiled, nodding absently. This mutt was the best he had seen. A bitch, the top of her head barely reached his chin, but she was finely proportioned, the musculature solid around shoulder and thigh, but not too heavy. Her skin was a pale honey brown, furred with a light downy fluff that grew more thickly across chest and groin. She could almost have been human, but for the fur and the dark, dark eyes: black at the centre, fading to a glowing tan hue where the whites would normally have been. The hair on her head was dark with shades of chestnut and copper, cut short to emphasise the evenness of her features.

He stepped close, reached for her mouth, and pulled the lips apart to examine two even rows of teeth. Dugs firm, no sign of lumps or slackness. He turned her, checked for signs of rot or infestation; gestured with his crop for her to walk as far as her chains would allow. She moved well.

He glanced at Pilofritt. "The bidding will go too high," said the bondsman. "We have several of this type already. She wears chains—for what reason?"

"Ever the cautious one, eh, Pil?"

Before Pil could respond, Henritt went on: "Father would enjoy her, don't you think?"

The bondsman bowed his head. "He would be impressed," he conceded.

When Henritt returned just after the middle of the day, someone had upped the bid. He was glad to be alone now, with Pil remaining at the stall. "I'll match the price," he told the trader. "And up by a tenth."

Someone else was examining the bitch, pulling her about, pawing at her. The mutt stared resolutely at a point above the woman's head, waiting for her to finish.

There was something in this one's look, her stance, that marked her as different, Henritt thought. A defiance, perhaps. Not a good thing in a mutt, but in this instance it raised her above the rest.

He went to her, studied her again. "Are you a talker?" he asked. Many mutts were dumb, at best communicating only with grunts and some simple Mutter. Some could be quite fluent, though, he had heard.

She looked at him, opened her mouth enough to expose her neat, off-white teeth. No sound passed her lips, though. Her expression lacked anything human, and in that instant Henritt was struck by the animal nature of the thing he was buying for his father.

"Clan Coltar have confirmed orders through to Hawksrise," said Henritt over a stick of beer, celebrating another good day's trading. "Clans Treco and Willarmey, too."

"And did Pil tell you of the deal he is negotiating with the River-walkers?" asked Janosofritt.

Henritt put a hand on his friend's arm. "He tells me everything," he said. "I'm in charge, see? He has to tell me, doesn't he?" The Riverwalkers were from an engineering enclave upstream from Farsamy. When Pil completed the negotiations they would supply bonded engineers to Clan Ritt in exchange for mere promissory notes for supply of materials.

So much business! Henritt's first trip in charge had been a huge success.

And to complete his triumph, Henritt had managed to see off the rival bids and only a short time earlier he had taken the female mutt into the protection of his clan's trade delegation. Now she was in a wagon at their lodgings. It had been a good day.

Just then, a girl at the bar caught his eye. She was plain, but well proportioned. He leaned even closer to Janos, nodded towards the girl. "Whaddya think?"

"I suppose you don't have to look at the vat while you're stirring the fibres," said Janos.

Henritt clapped his friend on the back and stood, then went across to the bar. It looked to be a promising night.

Back at the lodgings. Head aswim with drink and narcotics, Henritt leaned on a door frame to steady himself.

He'd come back alone. Janos was still out there with some white-wood salesman he'd met earlier in the day. Wendoftenka, the girl at the bar, had been fun, had rutted like the world was about to end, but had had to get back to her lodgings before her clanfolk came looking for her.

So here he was, drugged and sexed out, end of a long day. . . . Why didn't he just go on up to that feathered mattress the clan was paying for?

Their wagons and carriages were out back. This was where their mutts slept, under the shelter of the clan's vehicles. The new one . . . she was still inside one of the wagons.

His eyes were already adjusted to the dark, but inside it was even gloomier.

He knew where she was from the sounds she made: feet on floor, breathing.

"It's okay," he said. "Just checking."

He could make out her shape now, backed into the farthest corner, hands held in front of her as if to protect herself. "No touch," she gasped.

"You speak?"

Her voice was quiet, the words strangely formed.

"Good girl work hard. No touch."

He couldn't place the accent. "Where are you from?" he asked. Then, "What town is it you been outta?" he added, trying to remember how to talk Mutter.

"No touch," she repeated. And, again, he was struck by the animal in the human, the human in the animal, of her nature.

He backed out, locked the door, pissed long and hard against the wheel of the wagon, then made his way inside the lodging house.

He dreamed of her, the bitch, although by morning all that lingered were a few fleeting fragments, startling in their mundanity. A half-formed image of her backed into a dark corner: *No touch*. Her easy, rolling gait as he had led her back to the lodging house after his successful purchase. Dark eyes: brown on golden tan, as if cast in resin.

He ate fleshfruit on the way to the market, drank copiously from the bladder Janos carried, trying to clear his head for the day's trading and negotiations. He thought, again, of Wendoftenka, heard her cries repeated in his head. He wondered if he would see her again later. He felt suddenly reinvigorated, ready for the day and night to come, for the triumphant return to Rittasan the day after.

Later, the wild-eyed Riverwalker returned to the stall, his manner agitated, as if he had been chewing jaggery all through the night.

The Walker just stood there, head lowered, staring at Henritt with upturned eyes.

"We spoke before," the Riverwalker finally said.

"And?" said Henritt. The trade deal with the Riverwalkers was in the bag, and he felt in no mood for confrontations he did not understand. He could afford to dismiss this fool, he calculated.

"I come from Minster Place," said the Walker. "I have spoken to Makkibern Elthom about . . . about a mutt. Young, female, with chestnut hair and yellow eyes."

"And?" Henritt repeated, wondering why a Riverwalker would be so taken with a particular mutt—even one so fit. "Why are you telling me this?"

"She was bought by . . . someone who sounded like you."

Henritt shrugged. "Farsamy's a big place," he said. "There must be plenty of people who look like me." He smiled, now. "Anyway: plenty more mutts out there, aren't there?"

He turned away, exchanged a few words with Janos, and when he looked back he saw the dejected back of the Riverwalker, heading off through the crowd.

Clans Coltar, Treco, Willarmey, Tenka, Beshusami . . . Henritt stood back and allowed Pilofritt to recount the long list of settlements they had made at Farsamy. He was tired from the journey home, and he took the opportunity to rest and to observe Kymeritt Elkardamy. His father was attentive, the clan head absorbing the success of the trade delegation with customary efficiency.

But he was drawn . . . like a child with a new toy, a new pet. He wanted to investigate the goods they had purchased, the bladderpumps grown by a new technique developed by Clan Treco, the quickfibres harvested from wild, imbuto-tainted beds in the far west—a new germ-line of much promise. He wanted to talk to the two Riverwalker engineers, now bonded to Clan Ritt. Their expertise and innovation would be a valuable addition to the clan's production base as surely as their preaching would prove an irritation.

And yet, as Henritt had known, he was drawn more than anything to the mutt called Taneyes. Now . . . now that Pilofritt had run out of momentum, Kymeritt circled her, checking her over for corruption, for signs of ill health.

"She is well muscled," said Henritt. Sometimes it paid to state the obvious. "The cleanest mutt in Farsamy. She is docile—no sign of any taint. Speaks a little Mutter. I think she will work well alongside Stutter and the others in the fibre pods."

"We don't really need any more in the pods, or elsewhere, for that matter," said Kymeritt. "But yes, she looks like good stock. Sedge can isolate her until we know she's clean; then you can supervise her training. Pilofritt tells me you paid far too much for her."

Henritt nodded. "Nearly twice the appropriate rate," he admitted. "Clan Beren saw me as a naive and foolish trader to pay so much over the odds. Their swagger made it far easier for me to negotiate such a good rate for the fibre contract we arranged with them the following day. And anyway, I thought you would like her."

Kymeritt barked a short laugh and put an arm around his son's shoulders. "You are a Ritt through and through, my boy," he said.

"She haunts me," he confessed. "In my dreams . . . my waking thoughts. People talk. I heard Janos this morning, gossiping with Sedge. He said I'm losing my grip, that my balls must be bigger than my brain."

He was half dreaming now, drifting in the lucid-trance induced by Oracle's all-enveloping pherotropic mist.

The Ritt Oracle was discreetly tucked away on an overgrown island halfway down the stepped terrace of their main paddyfield area. It was approached along a narrow, raised track, either side fringed by bamboo and tall rushes with rice lagoons beyond. Oracle itself was a fleshy dome, its skin pocked with throbbing veins and grossly bulging tumours, with tangles of vine and creeper heaped high across its arched roof. Some said Oracle had formed the island itself, as silt accreted around its deeply rooted neural network of smartfibres.

Now Henritt sat cross-legged in Oracle's inner cavity, the entrance-way sealed over, the only light glowing redly through Oracle's fleshy walls. The only sounds, apart from his own voice, were the liquid rush-ings in Oracle's vascular system, the steady, low boom of its hearts.

Oracle spoke, its melancholy tones so intimate it might be com-municating directly with Henritt's mind. "You are young and free. There is no shame in what you say."

"She's a mutt!"

A new scent, a musky, sweaty, after-sex thing, subduing him, pla-cating him. "Mutts are human too."

"But . . . tainted . . . corrupted."

He'd been supervising Taneyes' training, as his father had in-structed. Making sure Sedge didn't treat the newcomer too harshly—he knew how territorial the mutts could sometimes be.

Supervising too closely, Janos had said this morning. Too atten-tively.

"You could keep the mutt as a plaything."

But . . . he was fearful of what may follow. "I can't get her out of my head."

Another change in atmosphere, in intensity. "The mutt: she has been isolated?"

He nodded, shying away from the implication of Oracle's words.

"But you have been monitoring her progress closely?"

"She's clean! No sign of taint."

"Except in your thoughts, your dreams. Perhaps your affliction runs deeper than mere masculine urges."

Oracle was toying with him, he realised. Trying to frighten him, and succeeding. "No," he said decisively. "I am healthy. I am clean. The mutt has not tainted me!"

"And, like any young purebred man, your balls are sometimes bigger than your brain."

He was about to reply but stopped himself, recognising Oracle's wisdom, its manipulation of his reasoning so that he could see himself as he was: a randy young man, no more. He smiled, bowed his head, was thankful again for Oracle's presence among them.

He wanted to be alone with his thoughts, but instead he encountered Pilofritt and Janosofritt where the track from Oracle joined the main track from the paddies into Rittasan. He could tell immediately that they knew where he had been, and why he had needed to consult Oracle.

He met the two bondeds' looks steadily. Janosofritt's smirk was irritating enough, but Pilofritt's casual arrogance was infuriating. "Do you not think that you should show me some respect?" Henritt demanded.

Pil paused—through insolence, rather than hesitance—and in that time his eyes never left Henritt's. "I am a bondsman," he said finally. "Not a mutt. Unthinking subservience is ingrained in mutts, but not in me. You are my master and I am bonded to your clan, but my respect is something you must earn, just as your father has done."

In that instant, in Pil's defiance and Janos's amusement, Henritt saw himself as others did. Perhaps it was a clarity of vision retained from the pherotropic atmosphere of Oracle's interior, perhaps it was simply the attainment of a final level of insight. Now he finally understood that in others' eyes he was immature, a fool, a source of amusement and ridicule.

He pushed past the two bondsmen and stalked towards the settlement. He was angry without understanding where to direct his wrath, within or without; his head was hurting, a result of his temper and the aftereffects of Oracle's intimacy. And he was mightily embarrassed.

Back in Rittasan things were no better. He saw accusation, ridicule, in people's eyes. Where before he would have seen admiration and respect, now he saw that they humoured him, laughed at him, undermined him with their gossip and rumour.

He came to the low arched building where they dormed a lot of the clan's mutts.

With barely a thought, he pulled the door aside and passed within. He turned automatically to the left, eyes coming to rest on the enclosure at the far end where Taneyes and some of the other young females spent much of their time. The flap was open, but the figure within was not the mutt he had bought. He looked more closely and saw that it was Calig, a male mutt he and Willemritt had played with as children.

The mutt was sitting on the floor, rocking back and forth as if demented. When he looked up, Henritt saw immediately what must have happened. "What did you do?" he demanded of the creature.

There was pain and confusion in Calig's eyes. "Pretty one," he said, in his stumbling Mutter. "Pretty one done run out this place."

Again: "What did you do?"

Calig's hand reached down under his loincloth and tugged at his genitals. He smiled now. "Calig done want pretty one be make manthing happy." Then he stopped smiling, let his hand fall away. "Pretty one done hit Calig. Pretty one done run out this place."

"Which way?" Even to his own ears Henritt's voice sounded pitiful, the desperation painful to hear. "Which way pretty one done run?"

He had been on the road for some considerable time before realisation dawned on him. This was the first time he had ventured beyond Rittasan unaccompanied, a purebred human on his own in the wildlands between clan territories.

What was he doing? What was it that had stolen into his thoughts and drawn him into such a rash course of action?

He paused, looked all around. To one side of the track pink canes as thick as his thigh loomed high, forming a near-impenetrable barrier between Henritt and the jungle. They looked like bellycane, but he could not be sure. Here in the wildlands, so much that looked familiar was impure, corrupt.

To the other side of the track, ragged thornbushes and clumps of tall grass clustered tightly, as if stacked one on the other. What looked like thicket oaks towered over the bushes, multiple rubbery trunks bursting from the undergrowth in groups of six and twelve. Up in the canopy, bunches of meat fruit hung and, camouflaged against the leaves, a small party of tree martens grazed.

He had left without thought, without even pause to gather provisions. He was thirsty, but did not dare pluck any of the fleshfruit from nearby branches. He had simply rushed from Rittasan in the direction indicated by poor, distraught Calig. The mutt could not be blamed: it was in his nature to respond to Taneyes' powerful sexual signals, just as it was in his nature to be pathetically subservient to all purebred humans. He was only a mutt.

Henritt continued on his way. With dense jungle to either side, she must have stayed on the track. She could not be far ahead. They would both be back in Rittasan before nightfall.

But with the sun swollen and red above the hills, Henritt had still not found her. Already, he had crossed several junctions where he might easily have guessed wrong; the jungle all around was thinner, too—she might even have left the track altogether. If she was scared then that was even more likely.

She was lost, he realised. All he could hope was that she would eventually find her way back to Rittasan on her own.

Yet still, he was drawn onwards, unwilling or unable to abandon hope.

Ahead, he heard voices. He was sure they were voices and not mere animal babble. Perhaps these people would have seen Taneyes; perhaps she was even with them.

Pil and Janos might think of him as an object of ridicule, but he was no fool. He approached cautiously. These were the wildlands, after all.

There was a small group of travellers resting at another junction. Henritt recognised this place from his journeys to Farsamy: he had only ever taken the fork to the left before. The travellers were wearing poor clothing, coarse fabrics that may have been woven from the wool of the goats they had staked by the roadside. There were three men, five women, and seven children, from toddler to a rangy adolescent girl.

The men were bearded and all of them looked hardened to the world, but they looked to be purebred humans, although not from any clan he knew. Itinerant craftspeople, he guessed from the wagon stacked high with what looked like bales of fabric. Weavers travelling from market to market. There were many such bands in the region, he knew; they called regularly at Rittasan, knowing it to be a wealthy settlement. It was a peaceable, domestic scene before him.

He emerged from cover and approached the junction in the open, careful to hold his hands freely at his sides to show that he posed no threat. When he saw that they had seen him he raised a hand, palm held flat towards them, a universal gesture of amicable greeting.

As he came closer to them he saw that they looked puzzled by his appearance, more than anything. He was an unexpected sight, he supposed: a purebred human, travelling alone.

"Greetings," he said, lowering his hand. He did not know what language they would speak, but it would be an insult to address them in Mutter. "I wonder if you can help me?"

He saw that one of the women was not looking directly at him, but rather at a point just over his shoulder. He paused and half turned to glance behind him.

The girl—the tall, gangling, adolescent one—had doubled up on him, emerging from the bushes with a brutal-looking club raised above her head. She laughed when she knew he had seen her, then rushed at him and swung the club down towards his face.

He raised an inadequate arm to fend off the blow.

The girl was still laughing when he hit the ground, lay there unable to move, senses drifting, floating away like in a lucid-trance, blackness spreading, enveloping. . . .

Voices woke him. Not human. Not mutt. Voices punctuated by moist snuffling sounds.

He was cold, his body slick with moisture—blood or water, he was not sure. He tried to move and felt a sudden stabbing pain in his chest, his ribs.

He opened his eyes and saw that it was still light. Perhaps it was morning now and he had spent the night unconscious. He drifted.

The snuffling sound again. Then something cold, wet, sharp with bristles, pressing against his face. He opened his eyes and saw frighteningly human eyes staring back at him over a wide snout. There was fear: the beast squealed, spraying him with spittle, and backed away with a hammering of feet.

He remembered the hogs from Farsamy market, toying with a street rat they had caught. This beast . . . there was a lot of hog in it, but there were other traits too: the disturbing eyes, the long canine fangs protruding from its wide mouth, the sleek fur on its body, rising to a tufty crest along nape and upper back. A true beast of the wildlands, malignant and corrupt as anything he had ever seen.

The fear had been temporary, an artefact of surprise that was rapidly departing. The thing took a step towards him again.

He was naked, he realised. The travellers had beaten him and stripped him of all that he possessed and left him to the wilderness.

He made himself sit, and scrabbled about in the leaf mould for anything that might serve as a weapon.

He was in some kind of clearing in the jungle. The travellers must have dumped him somewhere away from the track.

His hands closed on a stick, but under the brittle bark it was soft to the core, rotten. He looked around for possible escape routes.

And that was when he saw that there was more than just one of these mutant boars. There was another adult nearby, standing crookedly to support its heavily goitred neck, and beyond it two smaller, possibly younger beasts.

He returned his attention to the nearest boar and, abruptly, a stick emerged from its left eye socket. No . . . not emerged: *planted itself* in the thing's eye. The shaft of an arrow!

The beast took an age to realise what had happened. It stood, rooted to the spot, tipped its head slightly, as if puzzled, then shook vigorously. It raised a front leg, pawed at the ground, tried to step forward, and staggered to its front knees. Then it groaned, a disturbing, near-human sound, and finally it sagged to the ground.

The other boars stared for a drawn-out moment, then—emitting brief, startled squeals—turned and stampeded out of the clearing.

Henritt slumped, releasing the breath he had been holding.

A man stepped out from the trees, tall and bald with bulging eyes.

He wore many layers of rough clothing, made from animal skins, coarse-woven fabric, and stripped, braided leaves. A bow was slung casually across his shoulder.

He stood over Henritt, studying his pathetic form.

"I expect you have a story to entertain me over some pork, eh?" He laughed, turned to the boar, and started to work his arrow free.

The man, who called himself Cedar without claiming any clan allegiance, was not alone. He introduced his companion as Herrel. She looked to Henritt to be a mutt, with densely matted hair across most of her visible features and a wide, animal mouth. She didn't speak—couldn't, according to Cedar. Illness had deprived her of the ability.

Henritt knew what kind of illness the man's words implied: the corrupting illness, creeping into its victim's core and twisting what it finds, transmuting, leaving human not-human and animal not-animal.

Now Herrel approached Henritt, and he was suddenly aware of his nakedness before these two strangers.

"Let her heal you," said Cedar. "The Lost have talents your kind ignore: the inner change is not always malignant."

She had a wad of chewed leaves in her hands, some kind of herbal poultice. She pushed them against Henritt's chest, where the skin was torn and puffy. Pain lanced through his rib cage and he fought to stop himself crying aloud. It subsided rapidly, and a numbness spread through his side.

"Thank you," he gasped.

And all the time, sounds of wet cutting punctuated Henritt's healing as Cedar worked at the dead boar, stripping back its hide and carving chunks of meat from its body. He had lit a fire, and already strips of pork were cooking, suspended in the flames from skewers stuck at angles in the ground.

The man studied him patiently. He had asked for Henritt's story, and so now, falteringly, Henritt started to talk, of Farsamy, of Taneyes, of Rittasan and his father. Soon his words flowed more freely. It was like confessing to Oracle again, seeking advice from the ancient one.

As he talked, Cedar rummaged in one of the packs he and Herrel carried, emerging with a coarse cape. He handed it to Henritt as his story was nearing its end.

"I . . . I have nothing with which to pay you," he said.

Cedar shrugged, dismissing the matter. "Your obsession with this mutt, this Taneyes," he said. "From what you say it does not sound like a natural thing, an infatuation. You had little chance of finding her out here, and yet you still tried: your senses must have been clouded, corrupted. It sounds to me as if you have had a lucky escape, in more ways than the obvious. You still intend to seek her out?"

He felt the desperation again, but it was less intense. He shook his head. "I don't think so. She has gone, and it is probably good that she has gone."

"She was not the normal true-breeding mutt, in any case."

Cedar's words had a certainty that surprised Henritt, and for a moment he wondered how this man could say such a thing.

"What do you mean?"

"It's inbred in a mutt that it should always be subservient to any purebred human: they can't help it. If your Taneyes was of true stock then she would not have been capable of running away from her master. The fact that she fled proves that she was not pure, that she was tainted."

There was a sudden bitterness in the man's words.

"You . . . ?"

Cedar nodded. "I have seen everything, experienced it all. I was once a purebred just like you, and then the changing fevers stole my humanity away, corrupted me, wiped what I was and left me as I am: tainted and impure. My clan drove me out because I had become one of the Lost. But is it really so bad?"

He took a skewer from the ground, held it out towards Henritt.

Henritt hesitated, then reached out and took the strip of pork from the skewer and stuffed it hungrily into his mouth.

Later, he said, "If Taneyes was dangerous, then surely Pilofritt would have known? My father, even. Why did they not do anything?"

"Maybe they don't like you," said Cedar. "Or maybe they were testing you to see how you would handle the situation."

He wondered what he would do when he returned, how he would handle this kind of knowledge.

"I will not forgive them," he said.

"Does it matter?" asked Cedar. "Your kind always regard yourself as the freest of the free, and yet you are bound by your self-imposed position. I remember exactly what it is like. Now, for the first time in your life, you are truly free. You don't have to return to Rittasan. You can do whatever you like."

That hadn't occurred to Henritt. He had just assumed that he must return.

He settled back, comfortable in the heat of the fire. He could decide later.

Henritt pulled the cape tightly around himself, keeping the sun's penetrating rays from his naked body. Cedar had shown him more kindness than he had ever known—and that from a man who had lost everything.

As he entered Rittasan, he was aware of the stares, the comments. He must look odd, frightening even, clad only in a rough-woven cape, his face so sore it must be heavily bruised despite Herrel's poultices.

He straightened his back and kept walking. Let them stare.

He could have done as Cedar had suggested: left all this behind him and looked for a fresh start. But he had resisted the temptation to run. This was his home and these were his people—good, bad, and everything in between. This was where he belonged.

He saw Pilofritt and nodded. The bondsman studied him with narrowed eyes. Finally, the old man dipped his head, looking away. Things would be different now.

Henritt smiled grimly. He was a changed person—stronger now. Not tainted in any way, just different.

In a world where traits migrated from species to species, carried by plague and fever, where people were judged on what could be divined of their breeding . . . in a world like this any transformation was a frightening thing. But also, he now understood, it was a natural progression.

He had become a different person, and he was learning to embrace the change.

CHAPTER 15

Flint stood on a floating bladderplant pontoon, rising and falling with the pull of the Farsam's current. Out over the water the early-morning light slanted silver, casting a million flickering gems on the water's surface. Gulls swooped and skimmed, beaks dipping in the water to drink and snatch morsels of food.

And a line of mutts strode in steady unison, at this distance looking as if they were walking on water.

The Riverwalkers were going home.

Flint watched until they had long since passed out of sight.

"Move with smoothness and continuity," Sister Judgement had told him, leaning close and kissing him on the cheek. Reminding him that he was a Riverwalker, even when he was alone.

Now, he took a deep breath and held it, searching for a deep internal solidity in the Riverwalker way.

Calmer, he turned away from the river and threaded his way through stacked bales and sacks, back to solid land.

"Floor sweeping's done by rota," said the wiry young Tenkan Alal had introduced as Nimmocoll Elphilamy.

Flint surveyed the interior of the rooming lodge. The lodge occupied the basement level of a city centre brewhouse, and the floor was packed mud with a thin scattering of rushes and unidentifiable debris. "Whose turn will it be this year?" he asked.

Nimmo laughed. "I like him, Alal. This one'll fit in like you says."

Nimmo was the lodge's overseer. Alal had explained that this meant he looked after the place for the owners, dealing with any trouble and making sure no one stepped too far out of line. Flint had sensed a hint of dark undercurrents here—that he was sinking lower into the underclass of Farsamy—but did not really understand. All he knew was that he had some quick learning to do if he was going to make his way in this foreign city once the money Judgement had left him had run out.

"What work do you do?" asked Nimmo.

"I . . ." Flint stopped. "In Trecosann I pretty much ran the family fleshfruit plantation. I helped change mutts and stock at festival times. I . . ." He did what was required to keep a drunken and violent father solvent. And since then . . . he had learnt to pray, he supposed.

"We'll go to the Pillories," said Alal. "We'll work something out."

It was still only midmorning, but it felt much later. The Riverwalkers had set out early, the upriver journey being a greater challenge for their crews of mutts.

"Farsamy is hungover," said Alal.

It was true. The place had an air of dejection today, in the aftermath of Carnival. An air of imminent violence, too. Flint's father, too, had always been at his most volatile when hungover—liable to lash out at the slightest provocation.

Flint hunched his shoulders and walked with Alal. He was wearing trousers and an oversized shirt, borrowed from fellow lodgers. He had even, reluctantly, removed the fibre strand of beads from his hair. No one would employ him if he was dressed as a Riverwalker.

He said nothing as they walked. Maybe it was just his mood, a sense of anticlimax after he had felt so close to finding Amber the previous day.

There was more activity in the Pillories than in other parts of the city. People still needed work, after all. The crowds were thinner than last time Flint had been here, leaving more space around the men and women who stood on boxes and low walls, silent or engaged in a reasoned monologue.

". . . if you should employ me, good sir, I can guarantee as how you wouldn't be disappointed. I'm fit and strong, and I'm a family man so I stick at a job to make sure I gets my money. My last . . ."

". . . been work hard. Me been carry letters of sat'sfaction from . . ."

". . . learnt to cook in the kitchens of a Beshusami brewhouse. I'm good and I'm clean and . . ."

Flint found it all terribly disheartening.

He watched as Alal found a space on a low platform. His friend was the silent type: he stood and people saw that he was healthy and strong. He had said earlier that he could never be one of the "Pillories braggers."

Alal beckoned to him, shuffling along to make room.

Flint looked around, then climbed up beside his friend. He felt exposed. He felt as if all eyes had suddenly turned on him. He thought about how he should stand, and that only made him even more conscious of his every move, and of his discomfited posture. He moistened his lips and tried to think of something he could do or say, but his mind was blank.

Some time later, a man stopped before them. He was a wealthy man, by the look of his clothing, or he was in the employ of a wealthy man, at least. He peered up at Flint from under the peak of a flat straw hat.

Flint nodded, making eye contact.

The man's gaze moved on. A short time later he gestured at the young woman who claimed to be a Beshusami-taught cook, and moved away as she followed behind him.

"I felt like a mutt," said Flint.

He and Alal sheltered from the midday heat beneath the spreading fronds of a tree-fern in a small square just off the Pillories.

"Like the auction pens at Carnival," he added.

Alal nodded. "Get used to it, Flint," he said, after a time. "You are a freeman now, not a clansman. The best you can hope is to get by as a freeman or to find a place in bondage to one of the clans. It's not always a bad way of life."

Alal led Flint down another side street and into a brewhouse. "Nimmo stands door here some nights," he said. "He recommends it."

"But how can we spend money in a place like this when we have no work?" asked Flint.

Alal shrugged. "Things come along," he said. "You can't suspend your life while you're waiting, though."

He ordered two beers and paid before Flint had managed to fumble for Sister Judgement's money in his cuff-purse. The ale tasted fine after the dusty heat of the Pillories.

Some time later, there was a disturbance among a group of young men and women at the bar. Alal smirked at Flint's worried expression. Leaning across the bench so that Flint could hear him above the raised voices, he said, "This is nothing, Flint. You should come here at night."

Two men pushed against each other, each with his arms raised to fend the other off.

"Let's go," said Alal, standing.

Flint followed him towards the exit, but as he did so a rotund man backed into him and turned, cursing.

Flint raised his hands. "I—"

The man's face was pink—from heat and excitement and drink, Flint supposed—and his eyes narrowed angrily. He stepped towards Flint and pushed him square in the chest.

Flint sprawled back across a low bench, knocking drinks across the floor.

He staggered to his feet and found that the fat man had followed him, fist drawn back to his shoulder like a snake coiled to strike.

Rhythm and clouds.

Sister Judgement's voice hung in his head, so intimately! He remembered standing surrounded by seven- and eight-year-olds, each kicking and chopping in a poetic, disunified synchronicity. Patterns in chaos. He remembered the feeling as he had learnt to find the rhythm, to move with softness and continuity, as Judgement had taught.

He stared at the man, saw sweat shining his stubbly features like snail trails.

He felt time coalescing around this moment as he found solidity deep within and his body settled into an easy, prepared stance.

The man's meaty fist stabbed at him, and Flint swayed to one side, felt the man's forearm glance off the side of his head.

Off balance, the man staggered forward, and Flint stiff-fingered him in the midriff and stepped out of his path.

Coughing, the man turned.

Flint seized him by his tunic and threw him across his out-stretched leg.

Now, his awareness spread, and he realised that at least two other fights were going on, as the original disturbance had been catalysed by his skirmish with the man now sprawled on the dirt floor.

He twisted as a hand settled on his back, then relaxed as he saw that it was Alal.

"Come on," said the labourer. "This isn't our fight."

They left the bar and returned to the Pillories to seek work.

All the time he stood on the low wall, Flint held onto that inner solidity, enduring the appraising looks of his prospective employers and, more often, those of onlookers and fellow paraders.

He wore a hood against the sun's glare, and from beneath its shade he surveyed the crowds, always looking for a flash of chestnut hair. He had little hope, though, convinced that it was, indeed, Amber who had been sold at auction during Carnival. She would be travelling now, with her new owners. Probably heading for one of the Tenkan gang-farms, though Flint could hope that—bought by a man of standing, as the trader had insisted—she would have as acceptable a life as possible for a True human being treated as a mutt.

Back at the rooming lodge, he drank rancid water from the fountain and then washed the day's dust from his face. Rubbing water into his hair and beard, he felt refreshed.

A man called Lorin was strumming at a banjar and singing a song that Flint half recognised. It was a song of new love, but its jolly words were undermined by the wistfulness in Lorin's soft, high voice.

Flint joined Alal and the others, gathered around Lorin. Someone struck up a headstick and passed it round. When it came to Flint's turn, he hesitated and then sucked deep.

Instantly, he felt a rush of heat pass across his face, as if he were suddenly leaning close to a fire. His nose and throat were burning, tingling; his chest felt as if it were about to burst.

Eyes bulging, streaming tears, he took the stick from his mouth and held it in front of him. A hand floated into view from the left and plucked the stick from his fingers.

He took a deep, burning breath and held it within, seeking calmness, inner stillness.

And still, Lorin sang.

Later. Cool evening air. A hollow feeling deep in his gut. Flint stood supporting a youngster whose name he did not know as the boy coughed up the contents of his stomach into a latrine pod.

The boy straightened and rubbed sheepishly at his mouth. "Thanks," he mumbled.

"Lorin's song," Flint said. "Why . . . ?"

"Lorin married a year ago," said the boy. "Back home in Tenecka. Two days later she was raped by Lost raiders. They gave her the changing fever, too. Poor sod."

Flint watched the boy's retreating back, then turned and relieved himself into the same latrine pod. Smells of vomit mixed with urine and the pod's digestive juices reached his nose, which seemed to be overly sensitive tonight.

"Flintheart."

He turned, nodded at Nimmo who now stood at the next stall absently pulling at his penis before sending an arc of glistening piss into the waiting mouth of the pod.

"I hear how you handled yourself today," said Nimmo. "Muddy says you sees off that fat bastard, Guligan."

Muddy was the barman who ran the brewhouse where Alal and Flint had gone earlier.

Flint arranged his clothes and shrugged. "He was drunk and I didn't want trouble."

"Sure," said Nimmo. "Listen: I may be able to find some work for you. Standing door, maybe going out on the Night Watch. What do you reckon?"

"Beats standing in the Pillories like some Beshusami whore," said Flint. "Do you think there's work for Alal, too?"

"Maybe. I'll ask."

Working the Watch suited Flint well, leaving much of the day free for him to explore Farsamy, continuing his search for Amber. And at night, he went with four or five others to patrol the Elderman Quarter of the city.

They were paid by a collective of brewkeepers, and much of their work consisted of hauling drunks out of the brewhouses. A dousing with water from a drinking fountain was usually enough to bring them to their senses, but sometimes they needed more forceful persuasion to go on their way. On rare occasions the Watch actually had to intervene in brawls, and it was then that Flint made grateful use of his brief training in the martial arts of the Lordsway.

Most of the time, though, they walked the streets from bar to bar, chatting idly with the whores and waiting for something to happen.

"Pastey tells me you're a Tenkan," Flint said to Lorin in the dark hours towards the end of one such night.

Lorin nodded. "I'm a freeman now," he said. "I had to leave the clan. I couldn't stay in Tenecka. I expect Pastey has told you all he thinks he knows."

Flint nodded. They rounded a corner, trailing a little behind Alal and Sweet. Street rats scampered in the shadows of the buildings, and somewhere a dog yapped.

"From what I hear Tenecka sounds a harsh place," Flint said. "Tell me: how do they treat the mutts on the gang-farms?"

"I've heard about your search for your sister," said Lorin. "So I know why you're concerned. You think she's working the fields?"

"If she's been dragged into the mutt trade then it's not unlikely, is it? Most end up there."

"She may be lucky," said Lorin, after a pause.

Which, of course, meant that she may be *un*lucky, too, Flint knew.

"I want to go there, I think. Look for her. You think I'll get by on my own out there?" It was an idea that had been slowly taking shape. His best remaining chance, he supposed.

It was a while before Lorin answered, and then it was indirect.

In silence, they stopped by the docks and shared bladders of the dark beer Muddy brewed in his basement. The sky had a yellow haze above the city, Flint saw, light pooling from Farsamy's streetlamps— suspended knots of smartfibre that gathered sunlight by day and leaked it out through the night. Out over the water, bats plunged after small fish, their irregular, loud splashes oddly unsettling to Flint.

Lorin turned to him now, and Flint saw that same dark wistfulness in his eyes. "I met some old friends at Carnival," he said. "Did a lot of catching up. They tell me there's going to be another purge before too long. It's been building up that way for a few years now: more and more Lost settling in the wilds around the settlements. Bringing the fevers with them . . ."

A purge. Back in Trecosann they had regular purges to drive any Lost out from the lands around the settlements, driving out the agents of change. But from what Flint had heard they were nothing compared to the purges held in southern lands, where the Lost were more entrenched and the scale of everything much greater.

"It should have been done long before now," said Lorin bitterly.

Flint nodded. He supposed that Tallofmind would disagree, arguing that it was impossible to hold back the final reckoning, but how could you take that line with one who had lost as much as Lorin?

"Why are you telling me this?" asked Flint.

"If there's a purge then they'll be recruiting," said Lorin. "I'm going back, Flint. If something is finally being done to drive out the Lost, then I'm going back to join the fight. And if you really want to look for your sister in the Tenkan plantations, you might want to come with me."

It was several days before the occasional gossip about an imminent purge turned into anything substantial. Flint became convinced that such talk was simply the kind of rumour that idle young men used to fill their days and make life potentially more interesting.

Then, one day, word came back from the Pillories that the Tenkans were there, rounding up volunteers to join the purge force.

"I'm going to the Pillories now," said Lorin, to those gathered in the gloom of their rooming lodge. "And you are all welcome to join me."

Flint followed him immediately, pausing only to clasp hands with Alal and wish his friend well. Young Sweet came, too, along with four others. Finally, Nimmo stepped forward to join them, looking suddenly pale and childlike. Licking his lips, he said, "Been here too long. Reckon it's time I travelled a bit, don't you reckon?"

Lorin stepped out into the street, and Flint and the others followed.

CHAPTER 16

There were four longboats in this convoy alone, each carrying upwards of sixty men. From what people were saying, several such convoys had already set out, and more would follow in the days to come.

This was no mere purge he was heading into. This was a war.

Leaning against one side of the boat, he was standing below the waterline, which was about level with his waist. A small gangway passed along either side of the boat, which was divided into four cargo bays like the one in which he stood. Above his head, fibresheet canopies kept the sun's harsh rays from burning them.

He turned to Nimmo. "You realise what this is, don't you?"

Nimmo looked at him, eyes big in his narrow, bony face.

"It's a haul-boat," said Flint. "It's the kind of boat Clan Beren use to transport mutts downriver in the trade." He remembered travelling on a similar boat from Greenwater—memories of a time that seemed so long ago.

"You ever killed someone?" asked Nimmo abruptly.

Flint thought immediately of the time as a boy, prodding at Cedero, forcing his former teacher into the changing vats. "No," he said quietly. "Not killed."

"You will soon," said Nimmo.

Flint stared at him, not sure whether Nimmo's agitated state was caused by fear or by some other sense of anticipation.

They landed in Tenka territory well into the afternoon. Lorin called this area the Ten; Flint was unsure if that was its full name or a local abbreviation.

The docking area consisted of a small cluster of podhuts and lean-tos surrounded by a high stockade. Beyond that was a wide area of razed ground, a buffer zone before the wilds took hold.

They trooped off the haul-boat. Flint felt tired, even though he had spent most of the day standing and sitting around.

They joined a crowd around the podhuts, the rest of the day's volunteers. A short time later, a grey-haired man with a thick moustache and a crossbow slung across his back climbed up onto a small platform and addressed them.

"Welcome," he said. "Welcome to the Ten, my friends. My name is Marshall Maltenka Elmarc, and I will be commanding this division of the purge force. We may come together as strangers today, but by the end of this all you will be closer than brothers. It is my task to organise you into a working division as soon as possible." He pointed towards the stockade, indicating the wilds beyond. "The Lost are out there, men. While we prepare ourselves they continue to spread. They continue to raid and steal. They continue to rape and kill. It is your job to stop them."

His fighting talk had a rousing effect on the volunteers, and the mood became markedly different: upbeat, boisterous, high spirits verging on rowdiness. Flint felt it himself, a righteousness swelling within.

Nimmo clapped him on the back. "Come on," he said. "Lacey says there's beersticks if we're quick."

"Sounds good," said Flint.

He looked, then, at Lorin. His friend was still staring out beyond the stockade and into the forest, where Marshall Elmarc had indicated the wilds. He was ready for the fight, Flint realised. Probably more ready than any of them.

They slept in the open, sheltered only by the stockade and the sleeping rolls they'd been issued. Flint lay for a long time staring up at the stars, listening to the night calls from the wilds.

They could have set out that afternoon, but Lorin had told him the

Marshall had decided that it was too dangerous, as they would be finishing their journey after sunset. Instead, they would wait until morning.

Dawn came with a lightening of the sky and the coarse calls of the
Marshall's officers, chosen from among the volunteers the previous
evening. Lorin was one of them, known to the Marshall as a returning
Tenkan. "Come on, men," Lorin said, standing over the sleeping forms
of his fellow volunteers. "New day. Time to organise. We'll be on the
move again soon."

Flint rubbed at his eyes, and joined the general chorus of grumbling
at the early start. He sat, and saw that already queues were forming.

"Kit or grub?" said Nimmo, squatting at his side.

Flint rolled his bedding and attached it to the loop at the back of
his belt. "Hnnh?"

"Kit, I says," Nimmo went on. "Food can wait, but kit's with us
for the duration. Come on." He rose and, with a backward glance at
Flint, hurried over to join one of the queues.

Flint joined him.

Slowly, they moved forward. "Bow or crossbow?" Nimmo asked,
more than once. "Crossbow, I reckon. The Tenkans make 'em well or
at least that's what Lorin says. How about you, Flint? What're you
after?"

Flint shrugged. The only weapon he had ever used was a mutt
whip, and then only in show.

Lorin already had one of the finely crafted Tenkan crossbows. He
had shown it to Flint and Nimmo the previous evening. It was the preferred Tenkan weapon, technology founded on a combination of their
own engineering skills and refined smartfibres supplied by the neighbouring Ritt clan. They were supposed to be more manoeuvrable and
accurate than the conventional long- and shortbows Flint had seen

some of the Tenkans carrying, but the time needed to crank up the tension between shots made them slower in action.

They came to the long bench, where three old Tenkans were dispensing equipment: clothing, weapons, drinking bladders. One of them thrust a pair of boots at Flint, strapped together with gum tape and good intention. "No," said Flint. "I'm okay as I am." He took an empty bladder, instead.

At his side, Nimmo was arguing with one of the men, trying to convince him that he should have one of the small number of crossbows. Flint looked at the longbow offered to him and again said no. Instead, he gestured at a fighting staff, sharpened at either end. He took it, felt its balance in his hands, and nodded. It felt like the staffs the Riverwalkers used in some variations of the Lordsway. "This is good," he said. The man behind the bench shrugged and turned to the next in line.

As they ate a breakfast of dried bread and cane cheese, Marshall Elmarc stood above them on the stockade. He assured them again that before long they would be a smoothly functioning fighting unit and not a disparate group of strangers. He told them that they were heading today to what he called a settlement camp on the Leander Plain, where they would be based for a few days while they awaited deployment into smaller purge squads. He reminded them that they would be travelling through the wilds, the home of great numbers of the Lost, only too willing to attack and rampage and destroy all that was True. "Be prepared," he concluded. "You march through enemy territory."

Soon, they were out there, forest closing in around the well-worn trade route they followed. Its surface was cracked and buckled blackstone, and it was as wide—wider, even—than Farsamy Way itself.

Silence had rapidly stolen over the purgist division when they set out, the boisterous mood of the previous night now departed. Occasional murmurs broke out over the sounds of the wilds and the padding of booted feet on the road's surface. Flint walked barefoot in the Riverwalker fashion, occasional sharp edges of the blackstone uncomfortable under his calloused soles. The boots he had been offered earlier may have helped, but he suspected not.

He kept looking around, searching the shadows for any signs of movement, of Lost. He felt scared, and he felt ashamed that his own fear overrode any concern he had for Amber and what she must have felt if she had travelled this road.

Judging by the anxious looks of the others, he was not alone in his sudden trepidation.

In the imposing screens of jungle to either side, Flint recognised stands of whitewood and a few dawn oaks and thicket oaks, but most of these southern trees were new to him. Thick drapes of moss and vine wove barriers between the branches and trunks of the trees, and gaudy fungal growths erupted in sudden splashes of orange, red, and sickly flesh brown. Occasional movements were birds—the darting jewels of hummingbirds and barkcreepers, the startling crashes of forest fowl and pigeons—or butterflies and bees.

Early on, a mist clung to the ground in places, but soon the sun burnt it off and they all had to remember to ration the contents of their drinking bladders against the day's heat.

At some point, Flint realised he had simply been marching—vigilant, but no longer expecting every mysterious shadow to hide an assailant, every movement to be the first sign of attack.

He thought again of Amber, wondering if she had come this way, part of a group of mutts being marched south to the gang-farms of the Ten. Joining up for the Purge seemed to make sense back in Farsamy, but now he wondered how he would ever find the opportunity to look for his sister.

They reached Camp Sixteen in the middle of the afternoon, having broken their march only twice to drink water and chew on dry breadcakes.

Sixteen was a stockaded settlement that had clearly expanded greatly in recent years. A central core of long-established podhuts and wooden cabins was now surrounded by ranks of dormitory huts, and two sides of the stockade had been dismantled and extended outwards to accommodate the growth.

"It's what we call a settlement camp," Lorin told Flint as the three climbed up onto the stockade later that afternoon.

Up here on the camp's defences, Flint could see that the jungle formed a cliff of greenery to the west. To the east, the land was open, divided up into a patchwork of fields and plantations where the Tenkans grew massive quantities of fibres, meat fruits and canes, boll-cotton, and other crops. A slender river, some tributary of the Farsam, snaked through the fields. Here and there, Flint saw small figures working at the plants and some even climbing high in the trees to work.

Mutts, working the plantations.

He thought of all he had heard of the brutal conditions endured by plantation mutts, and even by their owners, and now it did not ring true as he surveyed what appeared to be some kind of rural idyll. It all looked so peaceable at this distance.

"Why do you call it a 'settlement camp'?"

"It's on the edge of the settled territories," said Lorin. "Mutt teams stay here and clear the land, and then the camp becomes a proper named town."

"So we're bunking in a mutt camp?" said Nimmo.

Lorin nodded. "At least we're inside the stockade," he said. He indicated the ground immediately below the defensive wall.

Flint and Nimmo leaned over and saw a few lean-tos and fibresheet screens below. Around to the right there were more, and Flint guessed that the bulk of the encampment was out of sight from where they stood.

"The mutts sleep outside to make room for us," said Lorin.

Nimmo pinched his nose and straightened. "I wondered what the stink was."

They went back down to find some food.

Nimmo had been right about the smell: a rich melange of bodily odours, both human and animal in nature.

In all his travels, Flint had not been anywhere as alien as the mutt encampment felt to him now. After being allocated space in one of the dormitory huts, Flint had slipped away to shin down some climbing rungs he had spotted on the outside of the stockade.

All around, mutts sheltered from the late-afternoon heat under canopies suspended from stout canes. He had never seen so many mutts in one place, gathered in small groupings, queuing for food, dozing in the shade, singing Mutter songs that were the same as the songs they sang in Trecosann.

He walked through the encampment, studying the mutts, struck both by the great variety and by the constancy of type within that variety. He was familiar with many of the types: the short, muscular labourers; the tall, willowy race favoured by Clan Beren; the small simian tree climbers known as Mutties. The others he knew less well or not at all: the dense-furred aquatics with their breathing slits and webbed hands; a type that was almost entirely hairless, with slender heads and long fingers; groups of small, hyperactive creatures he first took to be children until he saw that they were in fact adults, chasing each other and chattering and squabbling over scraps of food.

At every opportunity, he stopped them and asked his well-worn questions. "Me master outta Trecosann," he said. "You speak? You been know me words? Me been look for mistress outta Trecosann. Her got red in hair, yellow in eye, her high like this." He held his hand level with his chest. "If an' you see her you treat her plenty good. You been know me words?"

He spotted a bondsman—an overseer—and spoke to him. "I think my sister has been taken in the mutt trade by mistake," he said. "Her most distinctive feature is the yellow in her eyes from a childhood illness. Have you heard of anyone like this?"

The bondsman shook his head. "Not here," he said.

It was the same response he always had.

He climbed back onto the stockade and down into Camp Sixteen. Outside the camp, the atmosphere had been one of domesticity; within, it was taut, close to boiling point. So many young men in close confines, waiting for action.

There was a brewhouse, packed so tightly that its customers had spilled out into the street. Flint went on past and eventually found a relatively secluded spot near the cookhouse.

He inhaled deeply and held his hands palms-together above his head, struggling to find and hold the Joyous Breath. For a long time it evaded him, his attention diverted by the comings and goings of the purgists around him.

Then he realised that darkness had fallen and some time must have passed. He felt solidity deep in his centre, and moved smoothly into the rhythmic chopping and kicking of Rhythm and Clouds. There was a whole repertoire of the Lordsway that he had never learnt, but the moves he knew he knew well.

Much later, he found his place in the dormitory hut and spread his sleeping roll in the narrow space on the floor between Nimmo and a snoring Beshusami.

It was four more days before they were finally despatched to the front line of the purge. They spent much of the time in what the Tenkans called training, but which was clearly an effort both to assess their fitness for action and to fill their time while decisions were taken and arrangements made.

They ran with water bladders slung across their shoulders. They fired bows and crossbows at still and moving targets—a set of concentric rings on a board, a barrel set rolling across the ground by some brave or foolhardy volunteer. They wrestled, barehand and with clubs and staves, despite the broken bones and bruisings that frequently ensued. Some— mainly returning Tenkans, including Lorin—retreated to the settlement camp's one brewhouse and debated tactics of assault and pursuit.

Flint did as he was asked and was neither among the strongest and fastest nor among those that struggled or suffered injury.

"You scare them," said Nimmo, at one point. "You stand out from them."

Flint bowed his head, holding his friend's look. "It's not a bad thing to be different," he said.

A short time before this exchange Flint had been involved in a wrestling bout with a pale-skinned labourer from one of the Willarmey settlements in the west. It had started out as just another exercise, with reputations and side-bets at stake. But then . . . Flint had met his opponent's look and known there was more, some undercurrent he had missed, something more than mere physical competition.

He dipped his head towards the man, the traditional sign that he was ready. His opponent spat in the dirt and took a few paces towards Flint. All around them, a crowd pressed, as close as they could without encroaching on the fight circle marked on the ground.

The man ducked down and swung. His fleshy fist missed Flint by a long way.

Closer, the man swung again and Flint swayed backwards, out of reach again.

Flint kept control of his breathing and clung onto that point of stillness deep within. He had the Lordsway on his side, while his opponent had only his clumsy strength and innate aggression.

"Come on, muttfucker! Fight like a man!"

The labourer lunged, trying to get a hold on Flint, but again, he was left clutching at air. Almost immediately, the man turned and swung and Flint sidestepped smartly. At each swing he leaned this way, that, ever a short distance out of reach.

There were complaints from the crowd, abuse and insults. They wanted a real fight, not one man outsmarting another.

Buoyed up by the support, the labourer charged again and this time Flint met his assault with a chop, and then a well-placed kick as the man sagged to the ground. He stepped back and stood quietly, looking at the Tenkan overseer who was supposed to be in charge of this bout. The man raised a hand, the signal that the bout had come to a close, shaking his head as he did so.

"I heard 'em," said Nimmo now. "Asking what kind of a way's that to fight a fight?"

"It wasn't a fight," said Flint. "It was a wrestling bout, a test. I did what was needed. It wasn't entertainment; it was training. Or at least, that's what they tell us."

"They're not used to religious men out here," said Nimmo. "They think you're setting yourself up as better or something."

"I'm not a preacher," said Flint. "I just learnt from them."

"They're calling you the muttfucker," said Nimmo. "All that time you spend with the mutts."

"I talk to them and ask them if they have seen my sister," said Flint. He was aware of the insults, but had not dwelled on them. The atmosphere here among the purgists was juvenile at times—playful and vicious, as childish gatherings can so easily be. Flint knew that he stood out as an easy target, simply because he acted differently. It did not seem a big issue.

But now Nimmo added, "You should be careful, you hear? The troubles they've been having in the Ten makes everything different for us. Don't want to be mixing it with the mutts at times like this. People . . . they're looking for differences, for ways to mark people out. You don't want to stand out too much, Flint."

Nimmo was right. The normal rules were different in this place, at this time. Flint nodded. "I'll be careful," he said.

Lorin came back from a discussion with Marshall Elmarc, and Flint knew that things were changing again.

"Flint, Nimmo," he said. "It starts."

Nimmo tipped his head up, eyebrows raised. "How's that then?" he asked. "What's happening?"

"We head north," said Lorin. "About a day and a half on foot, and then we head west into the forest for a short way until we find a small logging settlement by the river Leander. There's been trouble there— some kind of skirmish, a raid by the Lost."

They weren't the first to be sent north from this settlement camp, but still Flint felt surprised that their time had come. He realised that he had not really known what to expect of this purge. At first he had expected to be right in the thick of things from the moment they entered the Ten; later, their time in this settlement camp had seemed interminable, and the purge little more than a distant rumour.

"There will be five of us," said Lorin. "And some bondsmen and mutts. Are you ready?"

Flint nodded, uncertain.

Lorin led them into the jungle.

The squad consisted of Flint, Nimmo, and two barely adolescent Tenkans, Slater and Jona. Ahead of them the bonded mutthound handler, Martoftenka, chaperoned his team of four hounds with a ceaseless sequence of whistles and claps. Fanned out in the trees were thirty mutts, armed with canes, spears, and hardened-fibre swords.

Flint swallowed, trying to find calmness, trying to keep his head clear because at any moment his life might depend on his speed of reaction and thinking.

He held his staff, sharpened at both ends, tight across his chest and followed the narrow path through the trees.

A sudden crashing sound made Flint freeze in his tracks, and then he realised that it was just a bird, startled from its roost in the trees.

He glanced at Nimmo, who had a short bow raised, ready to fire. "Fuck," said Nimmo. "Just . . . *fuck*."

They carried on their way, catching up with Lorin and the young Tenkans, who had barely paused.

Some time later they came to the settlement. It would have been much quicker to follow the main riverside trail, but purge squads had been ambushed in that way too many times in the past.

They could see the podhuts of the settlement over the top of a low defensive stockade. It was a small place: maybe fifteen families had lived here.

Lorin gestured at Martoftenka and the bondsman whistled to his hounds, sending them off across the razed buffer zone. The four big dogs raced across the open ground and over the stockade in flowing movements.

The squad waited and listened for the baying calls that would come if the mutthounds found a fresh scent, but there was none.

A short time later, Lorin led them across the buffer zone, and, all around, his team of mutts emerged from the trees.

The settlement had been stripped bare. Some of the podhuts had been slashed—some time ago, judging by the dried wounds of the deflated buildings. Others had been left undamaged, but their contents looted.

"There was a raid here," said Lorin. "The Lost came in one night and ransacked three homes, killing their occupants, before they were driven away. The next day everyone left. Some of the settlers are hopelessly overoptimistic when they set up camps like this: you saw their pathetic attempt at defences. . . ."

He turned away from them. Flint saw that the Tenkan was crying.

They spent the night at the settlement, mutts and hounds deployed around the low stockade to warn of attack.

Flint drank soup from a wooden beaker with Nimmo and Lorin, the three of them seated on a log by the river Leander. The river, whilst a mere stream compared to the great rivers of the region, was still wide enough to provide the settlement with some degree of security. The fetid pools along its banks also gave home to legions of biting insects, and Flint was continually swatting at the things and scratching at the bites they inflicted on any exposed skin.

Lorin lit one of the candles he had brought from Camp Sixteen, and it helped keep the insects at bay.

"You lived in a settlement like this?" asked Flint. "Before you left the clan?"

Lorin nodded, his movements just about visible in the gloom, the whites of his eyes flicking nervously, awkwardly. "Other side of Tenecka," he said. "A place maybe twice the size of this. More established."

"Back in Farsamy, Pastey told me your home was raided."

"It was," said Lorin. "I kept warning them. They felt safe because we weren't out in the wilds like some of the other settlements. We had stockades, but they had never finished building them. I kept telling them, and then one night there was a raid. They killed my cousin Marc with a stick through his gut. Killed his wife, too, but more slowly. These attacks are mindless: they stole very little.

"I heard the disturbance, and then cousin Marice came raising the defences. We saw them off, killed two and hunted down six more over the next few days."

"Pastey—he says they got your wife, Lorin," said Nimmo, rocking back and forward on his seat.

Flint thought Lorin was not going to respond, and for a long time no words were spoken. Then Lorin said, "That's what I tell people."

Another long pause ensued, and Flint stared at Lorin, trying to make out his expression, trying to make out his mood.

"I was out with my neighbours for much of the night, chasing off the raiders and checking to see what harm had been done. When I returned home, the podhut was in silence and darkness. I was puzzled. I couldn't understand how Tora could have gone back to sleep on a night like that. I went up to our room and stroked a light patch. Our mattress was red with her blood, and she lay there staring up at me. Her face was relaxed. The muscles must have gone like that when she died."

"Had you missed some of the raiders?" asked Flint. "Were they hiding while you saw off the others?"

"That's what I thought," said Lorin. "And then I heard a sound. In the doorway . . . there was Redgrass, one of our mutts. He was covered in blood and he was naked and he had come back for another go at her. He didn't seem to understand that he had done anything wrong. He smiled at me—*smiled* at me—and pushed me out of the way.

"He was on her again by the time I managed to gather myself. I had my bow and a spear. The spear went through them both."

Nimmo was shaking his head. "No, Lorin. No," he said. "Mutts don't do that. Mutts *can't* do that. It's impossible."

"That's what Marshall Fostenka and the others said. Even when confronted with the evidence of the two bodies . . . They said I was confused in my grief. That I had come in and found them like that, a tableau of dead bodies left by the Lost raiders. It is not unknown for them to do such things."

"No one believed you?" asked Flint, unsure if *he* even believed him.

"No one. That's why I had to leave. No one would believe that a mutt could act like that, breaking one of the most fundamental elements of their nature: their bondage to True humankind. No one would contemplate the fact that one of our clan's greatest fears had come true: there are so many mutts in the Ten—how could we control them if some changing vector stole in and robbed them of their bondage to our kind?"

Later, much later, it was Nimmo's turn and, characteristically, he came
directly to the point.

"Me?" he said, still rocking back and forward on the bench, but
faster now, his movements more staccato.

"I came here to kill someone."

"Who?" asked Flint, aware that Nimmo was waiting to be
prompted and Lorin had retreated within himself for now and would
say nothing.

"Oh, no one in particular," said Nimmo. "Just someone. The Lost
are as good as any. I want to see what it's like to be the one who snuffs
out someone else's light, to be the last thing another person sees, their
last source of hope. I want to experience that moment when they're
about to take their last breath and then the moment immediately after
and I want to see if anything is different."

Suddenly, he stopped rocking, and his head swivelled, lizardlike, to
fix on Flint.

"Does that shock you?" he asked. "Does it disgust you?"

"I—"

"Good. It does me."

He started rocking again.

"Last year, right at the end of Carnival. I'm standing door at
Muddy's. Big fight starts up and there's only me and a couple of others
to try and sort it all out. Me, I picks out one of the big guys. Little fuck
like me takes out the big guy then everyone else is gonna think twice.
That's my thinking. So I take him with a chair leg and he goes down
like a bag of shit.

"We drag him out later and dump him in Mason's Way and I wait
behind, still surprised that I took out this big guy. So I kick him in the
guts. Feels odd . . . no resistance 'cause he's out cold. Makes me mad so
I kick him again, and in the head, too."

Nimmo swiped at his face with the back of a hand. "Fucking bugs," he said, even though the flies had dispersed now.

"I had to make myself stop," Nimmo went on. "But ever since I wonder what it would have been like if I'd carried on. It's been haunting me, scaring the shit out of me. I have to find out, Flint. You can see that, can't you? It's not that odd, is it?"

CHAPTER 17
FLINT'S STORY

Lorin had some sticks of beer. Rather than share them out, he cracked them open one at a time and the three passed each around until it was drained. "The Tenkan way," he had called it.

A half-moon hung over the trees, and Flint found that he was staring at it, keeping himself awake.

"So," said Lorin, eventually. "What's your secret, Flintheart of the Riverwalkers? What's the dark truth in your heart of stone?"

Flint swallowed, but said nothing.

"You know Lorin's," said Nimmo. "You know mine. So what is it, Flint?"

"I changed a man," said Flint. "Or at least, I helped. I was one of the ones who pushed him into the changing vat with a mutt stick."

"Why?"

"That was the judgement, the verdict of the Clan Elders. My teacher, Cedero, was to be changed and then banished."

"What did he do?"

Flint dipped his head. He had suppressed these memories ever since, or at least tried to.

"What did he do, Flint?"

"Nothing. Cedero did nothing."

Nine years old and festival time and Flintreco Eltarn was in his element. He had dumped little Amber on Aunt Clarel and he had done all his chores and now he was free for the rest of the evening.

He met up with cousins Mallery and Jenna at the foot of the great stone wall that enclosed part of the yard behind the Hall.

"Hey," he said, in greeting. Mal and Jen were two years older than Flint. They'd taken to holding hands when they thought no one was looking. But Jen liked having Flint around, or so she said.

"Hey, Flint," she said now, and Mal grunted a greeting of his own, his voice gravelly, breaking.

Within the enclosure, there were sounds of partying. "Stiffs," said Mal. That was what they called the grown-ups. In the Hall and its grounds there was a party for the stiffs. Clan members had descended on Trecosann from all around for this festival.

"So?" said Jen, pulling her hand out of Mal's and pouting.

"Come on," said Mal, heading past her.

Soon the stone wall ended and they passed into the area at the southern end of the enclosure. Here, there was a scattering of fibre cabins and some new-grown podhuts. Festival guests would stay in these buildings, and there were noises and light within some of them even now. Grown-up things, Flint knew: festival parties usually moved indoors at some stage, for drinks and smokes and sex and whatever else they did.

Fires burnt high, over in one of the cleared areas, and people moved about and danced to the music of the drum and banjar players.

Mal walked confidently in the open, and Jen and Flint followed. No one bothered about them. They had been told this wasn't a party for children, but no one seemed to care now that they were here.

Mal took a beer stick, bit its top off, and tipped it into his mouth. He passed it to Jen and she drank. Flint coughed and spluttered at the smoky taste of the brew, not at all what he had expected.

Jen taught him to dance later that evening, forcing Mal to watch and be patient. Flint thought the beer probably helped him with this, but he couldn't be sure. The rhythms seemed to keep changing just as his body found time, his limbs uncoordinated. Not like Jen, who had a natural knack—he now saw—for moving with smoothness and continuity.

Exhausted, he wanted to rest afterwards, but Jen was excited, teasing Mal about the way his voice jumped from low to high, demanding that the two boys chase her through the seed-patch thickets. "First to the river," she cried behind her. Flint never did know what she had been promising, although many years later he had, indeed, gone with Jenna to the river and had held her and kissed her and had been stunned at the intensity of feelings it inspired: the passion and awe and the dark fear that had made him turn and run—from Jenna, from this *thing* that made people feel so intensely that they became different people altogether.

On this festival night, though, alone and nine years old, he had wandered. Had he abandoned Jen and Mal, or they him? He did not really know.

The sounds of the party seemed terribly distant, and he feared for a moment that he had gone too far, stumbling beyond the safe confines of Trecosann and into the wilds.

But no: fibrecane grew in a boggy bed to his right, a twin row of dwarved fleshfruit trees to his left. He was still in the seed patches, where the mutts were encouraged to grow supplies to supplement their keep.

Voices.

A woman: laughing, drunken, teasing. *First to the river*—those were not her words, but her tone.

And a man: his voice softer, less excitable. "Old times' sake, eh?" he said, and laughed.

Oddly, it was the man's voice Flint recognised. It was Cederotreco Elphil. Cedero was a wanderer, a man who was both popular and unpopular. He had argued with Clan Elders many years before and left to live in Farsamy. When, eventually, he returned, many Trecosi thought he had been allowed back into the clan too readily, while others envied and admired the life he had led.

Cedero had become a teacher, living on the charity of the Elders in return for teaching the clan's young about the dangers of the wilds and the big city, and the importance of following the established ways. He had managed to do so with double meaning at every opportunity: the city is dangerous, the city is fun; the wilds will kill the uninformed, so be informed; your elders are wise, but they have not seen the world as I have!

The ladies liked Cedero, too. The teacher is a dangerous man but, oh, how safe your husband is! That was what Mallery, Jenna, Shemesh, and the others said of him, anyway, and Flint always nodded, as if he understood, just as he laughed when they laughed and swore when they swore.

The path twisted away from the river here. Flint came to a wall of bellycane and peered through the slotted screen it formed.

There was a clearing, and there was a man, naked, standing with his back to Flint. Dark hair grew over his body, and for a moment, Flint thought it might be a mutt.

But no, the man reached up and scratched at his head. He half turned as he did this, and Flint saw that it was indeed Cedero, standing naked in the clearing, his penis standing out a long way from his body in startling fashion.

And the woman—how could he have failed to recognise her voice . . . ?

Eyes drawn to her by sudden movement as she discarded an undershirt on the ground, Flint saw his mother, Jescka. Her dark skin caught the light of a candle one of them had lit, and that of the moon, too.

Shorter than Cedero, she was broader at the hips, and whilst not greatly overweight, her flesh settled in gentle swellings around her belly and butt. Her breasts hung flat, her nipples dark pools like the wedge of black at her groin.

She moved towards Cedero, and Flint felt himself drawn towards them, driven to flee, the forces balancing out and so rooting him to the spot.

She kneeled before Cedero, her hands on his hips, and took him deep in her mouth.

Flint saw a sudden twitch in his teacher's buttocks as she drew him in, and he felt excited, sickened, amazed.

Cedero's hands worked the hair on the back of Jescka's head, kneading, caressing. He shifted, moved a foot between Jescka's thighs, and she drew her head back, gasping, before dipping forward again, running her hands over his legs, and then between them, one hand passing up, finger sliding along the dark crease between his buttocks, parting, prying.

"Wha—?"

A dark figure staggered into the clearing, started to speak, stopped.

More words were exchanged, slurred and excited. Flint could not make them out.

Cedero pulled away from Jescka, trying to cover himself with his hands.

Jescka stood, partly shielding Cedero from the intruder.

Tarn! It was Flint's father. . . .

"Tarn," Jescka said, then more words that Flint could not distinguish.

She stepped aside and then reached for Cedero, took him in her hand and started to rub him, still talking, still teasing. *First to the river*—that tone again.

Cedero said something, raised his hands defensively as he flinched back from her touch. Jescka laughed—at him, at Tarn, Flint could not be sure which.

Tarn lunged, arms flailing, and Cedero tried to step back, but somehow Jescka still had a hold on him and he cried out. Tarn swung at him and still Jescka laughed, rubbed, doing her utmost to taunt and humiliate both men.

Cedero swung his fist, striking Jescka across the side of the head. She fell away, finally releasing him, and he ducked to gather his clothes, then ran from the clearing.

It was over! Flint felt a breath releasing, realised that his trousers were wet, his face soaked with tears.

Tarn made as if to follow, but stopped. He was drunk. He would not catch Cedero tonight.

He turned to Jescka instead. She was still standing, despite reeling under Cedero's wild blow.

Tarn thumped her and she fell.

He kicked her, and when she tried to crawl away he kicked her again, knocking her over onto her side, the blow almost enough to lift her from the ground.

"No!"

Flint did not know that he had called out aloud, but moments later Tarn's hands were on him, hauling him into the clearing.

And then the beating began.

Later, he lay, unable to move, and the only sounds he heard were his mother's whimpering, his father's rhythmic grunts and cursing, and the distant sound of courting dawn oaks, their flowers calling to birds and bats, offering up their dark nectar.

"You changed a man—it was Cedero, wasn't it?" Lorin's voice was subdued, gentle.

Flint nodded. The dawn oaks were calling, even now.

"There was a hearing," he said. "Jescka was hurt so badly . . . and so was I. They had to act. Tarn said Cedero had attacked Jescka and then attacked me. Jescka told them Cedero was responsible—those were her words: *Yes, Cederotreco Elphil is responsible for this!* The Elders asked me. 'Yes,' I told them. 'I was there. I saw it. I saw . . . Cedero . . .

hit her. . . .' I could hardly speak; I could hardly think. I agreed with my parents before the Elders."

"Would they have believed you if you had claimed any different?" asked Nimmo.

Flint shook his head.

"Then it's not your fault, is it?"

"People don't believe what they don't want to hear," said Lorin now, reminding them of his own story.

"I held the mutt stick," said Flint. "That night, at festival. I helped prod and poke him into the changing vats. I saw the moment his life stopped and he became something else.

"That night, I slipped back into the stock pens and saw Granny Han tending him as his bones shifted and the changes stole over him and he became something different." He smacked the side of his head. "I'm there now: I can see him; I can hear his cries of pain and fear."

"You're in the wilds of the Ten," said Nimmo. "And you're talking shit."

Lorin cracked another beer stick and passed it around. It tasted smoky and acrid and it was like the first beer Flint had ever drunk. But it was cool and it was wet and it was the only beer they had. They drank, and talked shit late into the night.

CHAPTER 18

CEDAR'S STORY

Such a pretty young thing.

Strong and clean-looking. Soft, golden down covered her exposed skin. Her night-black eyes were stained honey-gold around the edges. Distinctive.

She could almost have been human.

So why had he hit her again? He'd spoilt her pretty face.

First time . . . well, the first time he *had* to. Quickest way to stop her. But this time . . . this time he had enjoyed it.

It made him wonder just what he had become.

He'd found her the day before. He didn't have a name for her then: didn't know that she was called Taneyes.

They'd been travelling north when he found her. Through the wildwoods, skirting around the settlements and roads of the truebreds, wary in this time of unrest.

Too much violence in the south. Too many panicking truebreds clubbing together to slaughter anyone who was different.

Purge was too clean a name for mass murder. That's what Cedar thought.

But he knew not to argue. Arguing against crossbows and spears—

with people who sneak up on you at night and burn you out—was not a good idea. He'd had too many near misses recently, enough to tell him to move on.

Herrel had accepted his decision to head north without question. She would not speak aloud, of course—in all their years together Cedar had never known her to speak and still he did not know if she had a physical impediment to speech or a mental one. She had other ways of communicating, though: gesture and sign were the obvious ones, but she also had more subtle senses heightened in the way some Lost do. Sometimes he thought she read his mind, but he didn't really believe it. She spoke to him through body language, and she understood his own language of the body intimately and often responded to this even before he had voiced his intentions. She sensed the moods of the body and its traumas and ailments, too. He had owed his life to her healing hands on more than one occasion.

And so they had travelled, walking side by side, burdened by towering backpacks that carried all their possessions and supplies.

The day before this day they had come across signs of settlement: plantations and paddies and tended roadways.

"We're in Ritt territory now," Cedar said, although he suspected Herrel already knew. "No longer in the Ten. Best we stay clear of them, though. Panic may have spread."

Finding a trail through the jungle, they had bypassed the settlement, their journey longer but safer, too.

All the time, Herrel walked at his side.

She was a short woman, with a broad body that was higher on one side than the other. Her deformed shoulders may have been a fault of birth or a result of later change; Cedar had never discovered which. She wore a coarse woven skirt and a knitted sable leaf vest, but left the rest of her thickly furred body exposed. Her face was flat, as if someone were constantly pressing it backwards, and her mouth—that silent mouth!—was wide, lipless, like the mouth of a river turtle.

She was the most beautiful human being Cedar had ever known, one whose company he never felt worthy to share.

Towards the end of the afternoon they came to an old woodman's hut, from the days when truebreds still dared live and work in the jungle. Long abandoned, it was covered in thornbush and tangleweed but, within, it was clear of growth and clean.

He deposited his pack, but kept the long bow slung across his shoulder. He kissed Herrel on the brow and she turned away, already intent on gathering herbs and fruit from the forest, reliant on her sense of what was good and what corrupt.

He explored the vicinity of the hut. There was no sign that this part of the jungle had been visited recently by truebreds or others: no trails or traps, no signs of encampment or harvest.

That was good.

Truebred or Lost: Cedar knew that you could never trust anyone in the wilds.

But . . . such a pretty young thing!

There she was: wandering, staring around herself like a pup who'd never been out. He could see wonder in her eyes. Pausing to cup a trumpet flower in one hand and sniff its pungent scent. Staring up at the trees towering over her, slivers of blue showing through the canopy mosaic.

And pausing every so often, looking about, a nervous animal wary of predators.

She wore the rough tunic and leggings of the enslaved, but he saw immediately that she was no mutt: she was Lost, blessed by change.

He stood motionless. Watching.

She came close before finally she spotted him and stopped, eyes wide. Her mouth had opened abruptly and stayed open, but no sound emerged.

He smiled.

There was something about her that disturbed him. Something frightening. Some stirring of long-lost memories.

Maybe that was why he would hit her the first time.

"Don't run," he said, his voice sounding hesitant and weak.

But he knew she was going to flee. Years with Herrel had attuned him to the language of the body, too.

He stepped towards her and punched her.

That was all it took. A single, well-aimed blow.

The feeling of his fist as it struck her: soft flesh, bone beneath. That nearly made him turn and run away. More fear, more memories that wouldn't find their shape in his head.

He squatted over her, stroking her short chestnut hair away from her face. "Never trust anyone out here," he told her unresponsive form. "Didn't they ever tell you that?"

Herrel had the appropriate herbs all ready by the time he dragged the girl back to their camp, the first time he had hit her.

Not just for the girl, but for Cedar too. She knew he was hurting.

"You are the most beautiful human being," he told her, for the twentieth or thirtieth time that day. He waved towards the slumped body of the girl. "And this one is the prettiest," he said. "So why am I so greatly disturbed?"

He decided not to tie her up. Maybe she would learn to trust him, even though he had hit her and dragged her through the jungle, and even though later he knew he would picture her in his head as he made love to Herrel.

He sensed her movements when she roused, late in the night.

He sat in the doorway of the woodman's hut, buried deep in layers of clothing. He liked the sounds of the jungle at night. It was something he had grown accustomed to, for he rarely slept for long. Years ago, he had gathered from Herrel that he should accept it as part of his condition, just as he should accept his oversensitivity to cold and the fact that not a single hair grew on his body.

When she moved, he turned his head, aware that although he could not see her, she would see him in the doorway, lit from without. "Sleep," he said. "You are safe, my love."

There was a sudden eruption of squeals and grunts from the jungle. They were distant, but near enough for Cedar to be wary: there were few large animals in the wilds, but the various forms of feral hogs were among the largest and, often, most dangerous.

Both Herrel and the girl were awake in the hut—probably woken by the sounds. "Wait here," Cedar said, standing in the doorway and unslinging his bow.

He went out into the dawn light, senses alive to the dew-fresh scents, the calls of tree crickets, frogs, and songbirds, the touch of leaf mould on bare feet.

So sharp the swings from low to high! He did not understand the shifts in his mood over the last day and night, but now he knew the exultation of a new day, of a man at one with his environment.

He pulled his marten-skin coat tight around him. The morning air was cold as ever to Cedar.

He headed towards the sound of the hogs and soon saw signs that people had passed this way in the night or maybe the previous evening.

There!

A herd of six or seven of the beasts in a clearing formed where a great jelo tree had fallen. Some of the tree's roots had remained in the ground, and now, horizontal, the tree had thrown up a row of new limbs from its fallen trunk.

The offshoot saplings screened Cedar's approach.

There was a young man in the clearing, stark naked and fumbling pathetically in the leaf litter. He was looking for some means of defence, Cedar deduced.

A big boar was closing on the man. Stiff bristles stood up in an uneven crest along its spine, and its fangs were already stained red—perhaps from this man or perhaps from earlier fighting or prey. The naked man was injured, Cedar saw, but there was no obvious sign that he had been gored by a hog.

Cedar took an arrow from his quiver and drew his bow. He made a clicking sound in the back of his throat, and the beast turned its head towards the sound.

Instantly, the arrow buried itself in the boar's eye.

The beast stood, tipped its head to one side, started to shake from side to side as it tried to free the arrow. Pawing at the ground, it went down on its knees and then collapsed.

Already, Cedar was up and over the fallen jelo tree, clapping his hands and shooing the other hogs away. They stared at him and then, as one, turned and stampeded off through the trees.

The young man sat back in the dirt, trembling.

"I expect you have a story to entertain me over some pork, eh?" Cedar said, chuckling at the look of horror on the man's face as he wrenched the arrow from the hog's eye.

Not long afterwards, Herrel joined them, carrying their backpacks slung over each shoulder. With a brief hand sign she reassured him that she had bound the girl and left her behind.

Cedar saw the young man watching their exchanged signals curiously. "This is my partner, Herrel," he told him. "She does not speak. The fevers stole her tongue."

Again: the horror on the youngster's face—this time at mention of fevers, implications of change.

He would enjoy taunting this one.

Cedar gave him food and listened to him and offered him gentle guidance.

And young Henritt Elkyme gave him a name for the runaway with the honey eyes and the naivety of a child. He called her Taneyes.

It was an exchange loaded in Henritt's favour, and soon Cedar was bored with him, the spoilt child of a village Elder, blind to the limits of his own shuttered, unchanged existence. "Your kind," Cedar told him, "always regard yourself as the freest of the free, and yet you are bound by your self-imposed position."

There was a flicker of understanding in the boy's eyes, the briefest moment of insight, perhaps.

Cedar regretted lighting such a good fire to cook the pork. Now, the boy was too comfortable before it, entranced by the flames.

But the cold! Even now, as the day's sun grew stronger, Cedar felt chilled through, cold inside.

Finally, he held a hand aloft in farewell.

He took the two backpacks and indicated to Herrel that she should stalk the young truebred to make sure he was on the right road back to his home, and also to make sure he planned no trickery. You should never trust anyone out here.

Taneyes was there in the woodhut, staring at him from deep in those dark eyes. Herrel had gagged her and bound her with shrinking vine around her wrists, knees, and ankles. She had hauled boughs of thornbush across the doorway, too, hiding their captive from view and preventing her from shimmying out like an eel if she should be so inclined.

Cedar slid an arm beneath Taneyes' back, another behind her knees, and lifted her, disturbed more deeply than he thought possible by the feel of her, the smell.

He put her down in the sunlight

Herrel had painted a poultice on Taneyes' cheek, where he had hit her. He wondered why he had struck her so readily. He was not a violent man. Not that he could remember, at least.

"It's okay, my love," he told her.

And then he paused to wonder why he called her that.

His life had really started when Herrel found him, however many years ago that was.

Before . . .

Fragments. A few images of places and people, the knowledge that he had been a truebred man as good and as blind as any other before the change had found him and he had been banished from his clan.

Memories were like nervous butterflies: approach them direct and they always evaded him. Approach them at a tangent and just occasionally they would offer him more; sometimes, too, they would explode in a dazzle of colour and movement at unexpected moments, triggered by scent or sound, or by some abstruse association.

And now . . . he sensed them flitting about, just beyond his reach.

So banishment, yes: driven out from his home because of the change that had ripped through his body and his head. (And was there something more?) He remembered the confusion, the aimless wandering through the jungle he had always been taught to fear.

The driving hunger and thirst vying with the ingrained terror of what he might eat, what he might drink.

Fevers taking him in their grip, cold sweats drenching his body as he desperately clawed at the few possessions he carried to wrap himself in his blanket and even, eventually, to rip open his backpack with brute force so that he could wrap himself in its fabric. Fighting the cold. The bone-deep cold of the changing fevers.

He remembered that first bite of a jungle fleshfruit, the bloodlike juices running down his chin. He had seen tree martens grazing these fruit, so he hoped that indicated that they were untainted.

More fevers: the fruit or simply a continuation of his change? He never knew. Never knew anything but the frightening deepness of the chill.

And warmth!

Heat, sinking into his body. Moist compacts of chewed leaves, pressed against his head, smeared over his scalp, which was now bald, unprotected—he had shed his hair as he had shed his humanity. The poultices bound him in their warmth, drawing the chill from deep within.

A face, a woman, her features wild and distorted. Scaring him, as he had not yet learned to abandon his fear of the Lost and changed.

Later, wanting to talk, and unable to utter a sound. Wanting her to talk to him, and not understanding her silence.

He did not know how long that time had lasted. Or the time afterwards, when Herrel—as he had decided to call her, a name derived from some fleeting memory of a woman in a city—when she had led him by the hand, feeding him from the wilds and teaching him, patiently and tenderly, how to survive.

Yes, his life had started when Herrel had found him and when she had started to teach him to be whole.

He realised he was shivering, hugging his legs tightly to his chest. There was moisture on his face, and he flashed back to the fevers.

No, not fever sweat: tears.

The girl, Taneyes, was staring at him.

She looked scared, and suddenly he felt angry that she should be there, that she should be staring up at him with fear and anger in her eyes.

Herrel came back and signalled that all was okay. Henritt Elkyme would be back in his home now, trying to explain why he should appear from the wilds wearing only a badly patched sun cape. The thought gave Cedar some bitter amusement.

"You have a name?" he asked Taneyes when, later, they sat with stripped pork and tiffany nuts spread out on a flat palm leaf before them. "You want to eat?"

He took a strip of meat and bit off a piece.

Even though her mouth was now unbound, Taneyes said nothing. As well as removing the bonds from her mouth and hands, Herrel had removed the poultice from the side of her face. There was no sign of bruising where Cedar had struck her.

"My name is Cedar, and my friend is Herrel. We are Lost, and you, in case you do not realise, are Lost, too." He chuckled. "The days of humankind are nearly over," he said. "We, who have been blessed by change, are the natural successors. You should be proud."

He saw accusation in her dark eyes. She thought him a madman.

"We must decide what to do with you," he went on. "We should move on, and we do not want any trouble. Do we take you with us? Do we turn you loose and hope you will not draw trouble in our wake?"

But Herrel wanted to stay a little longer. He knew she had found good supplies of the herbs she used in her healing, and he supposed that must be the reason. He shrugged, sensing her unhappiness that he wanted to move on. "Another day, perhaps," he said, and he saw her relax. He could never deny Herrel what she wanted.

And sometimes their wants were mutual.

He took her piggy-style outside under the stars, away from the pretty young runaway.

Herrel, her great rear thrust up towards him, trembling buttocks nut brown in the moonlight; Cedar, parting his layers of clothing only as much as was necessary, still fighting off the cold.

She grunted softly and rhythmically, the closest she ever came to speech, and he loved her more than ever. And, despite the intensity of his love, when he closed his eyes he saw the runaway, was staring into

her wide, dark eyes, felt her hands around him, running over his buttocks, stroking and separating with her tiny fingers.

He rolled clear of Herrel and lay staring up at the patterns the stars
made in the sky.

She arranged her clothing and moved away.

He could sense from her movements that she knew he was disqui-
eted, that she probably knew he had been betraying her in his head.

He sensed again when Taneyes roused, late in the night.

He sat in the doorway, as before, listening to the sounds of the
jungle. Sleep had evaded him again.

When she moved, he turned his head, aware that she could see him
in the doorway.

And she spoke, for the first time.

"Please," she said. "I need . . . I need to go outside."

The voice! Soft, smooth . . . to be hearing that voice again!

"Of course," he mumbled. He went into the hut, avoiding Herrel's
sleeping form. He leaned over, found the line of the girl's arm, ran his
hand down until he found her hip, her leg. He left the bindings around
her knees, releasing those at her ankles. Thus hobbled, she shuffled
towards the door, and outside.

"My hands."

He untied her wrists, and watched as she pulled at her clothing,
squatted and pissed on the forest floor.

Silence. A straightening of clothes.

"Please," she said now. "Let me go. I . . . I heard the two of you earlier. I can do that . . . Untie me. I'll do whatever you want if you'll
untie me and let me go."

He went to her, put a hand to her cheek and caressed with the
broad pad of his thumb.

"Jescka," he said. And then again: "Jescka." His other hand reached behind her, pulled her towards him. "Oh, Jescka. You know I can't deny you, my love."

Memories, startled into dazzling life, like a butterfly in a bolt of woodland sunlight: Jescka, his darling, murmuring to him with that voice! Down in the seed patches where she told him—gleefully: she so loved to shock!—she always took her lovers. Out at night, under the stars. Just the sound of her voice: he never could deny Jescka.

He dropped to his knees, found the knot behind her legs. He pressed his cheek against her belly, basking in her warmth, and untied her.

He should have anticipated her next move, the sudden upthrust of her knee into his face.

More butterflies: violence was never far from darling Jescka. It followed her like a faithful mutt. That was why they had changed him, why they had punished and banished him. The violence. He remembered hitting her, hurting her.

She seemed surprised that her blow did not fell him. Staggering back onto his heels, he shook his head and laughed.

When she turned to run all he had to do was slap at her trailing foot and she went facedown in the dirt.

By the time he reached her she was scrambling to her feet once again. "You came back to me, darling Jescka."

She had come back for him to carry on where they had stopped before. And that was when he hit her the second time.

Morning came, but its sounds and scents did not awaken wonder in him as they so often did.

It was time to move on, and so he gathered his pack and he pulled his marten-skin coat around him, tightening its sable leaf belt. He pulled his sun cap down over his face.

When he looked back, he thought he saw sadness in Herrel's expression, but now he knew that he could not be sure. He realised that he had never really known much of the inner life of Herrel: had only interpreted from her signs and her expressions.

He could not bear to go near the prostrate body of the runaway called Taneyes. She was unconscious, and he knew bones had broken when he hit her in the night. He did not think she would live, even in the care of Herrel.

Such a pretty young thing.

He'd spoilt her pretty face. Spoilt her pretty young life.

And lost his love, again.

CHAPTER 19

The mutthounds found a scent early the next morning.

Someone had visited during the night, climbing the stockades to look within. Someone who was not a True human, leaving a trail of scent distinct enough to excite the hounds.

Flint pulled his reinforced fibre vest over his head and felt it tighten to his form. The garment was hot and uncomfortable, but it afforded him some protection from attack, at least.

He exchanged looks with Lorin and Nimmo. They nodded. The two younger Tenkans, Slater and Jona, hung back as the five stood in the settlement's small square. It was as if they sensed that something had changed, something that now bound Lorin, Nimmo, and Flint together.

One of their mutts swung the settlement's low gates open, and then the bondsman, Martoftenka, unleashed his hounds. Waist-high blocks of muscle, the dogs charged out, baying at the sky, their tails whipping ferociously. They raced along the foot of the stockade and then off into the wilds, finding a slight parting of the green curtain.

Martoftenka set off in pursuit, and Lorin ordered the mutts to fan out in the trees and follow the sound of the dogs. And then the five True members of the purge squad set off after the bondsman and his hounds.

"It's when they fall silent that you need to be ready."

Flint remembered Martoftenka's hurried briefing before they had set out from Camp Sixteen on this mission. The hounds knew to go quiet when they came near to their quarry.

Now, the dogs were quiet.

Flint rubbed at the sweat on his face, wishing he had taken the time to tie his hair back before setting out. They had been in pursuit for some time now, and the sun was much higher in the sky, from what Flint could see through the thick canopy.

Lorin was a short distance ahead, the young Tenkans to either side, Nimmo with an oversized crossbow just off to the right.

The only sounds were his breathing, the chitter of insects and birds, the soft crunch of footfalls on dry leaves.

And then: a soft whistle from ahead.

Lorin was signalling. Something was happening.

Flint passed through a trail of lianas, holding them aside with his staff, letting them fall behind him. Lorin was on the ground ahead, down on one knee. The bulky shape he had found was a mutthound. A nervous tic still quivered in its hindquarters, but the animal was dead. The stubby shaft of a crossbow bolt protruded from the side of the hound's head.

Lorin glanced back, nodded, rose to a crouch and continued.

They found Martoftenka a short time later, another crossbow bolt sticking out of the bloody mess of his face.

"This is crazy," hissed Nimmo as they paused by the houndmaster's body. "We don't know what we're up against. Could be fucking millions of them!"

"We're up against the Lost," said Lorin. "That's why we're here."

Light broke through the canopy up ahead where a stream cut a winding path through the jungle. On the far bank there were signs of encampment: flattened patches of woodrush where someone had made their bed, moss scuffed off waterside rocks where someone had moved without care.

"Not many of them, then," said Lorin.

"Unless they made more than one camp," answered Nimmo.

He was interrupted by a soft whisper of air and then a thud. Flint looked up and saw a crossbow bolt embedded in the soft trunk of a tree fern, not far above Nimmo's head.

They dropped to the ground and scrambled on hands and knees for cover.

Upstream, one of the squad's mutts emerged cautiously from the undergrowth, oblivious to what had just passed. He fell almost immediately, but Flint had seen movement as their assailant changed position to fire. He tapped Lorin on the shoulder, pointed.

Lorin tensioned his bow, aimed, fired. There was a cry and a man fell, wounded, from his perch in the trunks of a thicket oak.

They waited, but there was no more sign of movement.

They worked their way up the stream towards the bodies of the mutt and the Lost.

The man hung from the oak, his hips wedged low down between two of the tree's sextet of slender trunks. Nimmo stooped and seized his hair, pulled his head up.

The man's thickly bearded face was smeared with blood, and a fist-sized growth emerged from one side of his head where his ear should be. The tumour looked like some gruesome parasite, a bulbous leech sucking out the man's life.

But he was still alive.

His eyes flicked open; he grunted.

Lorin's bolt protruded from where his neck joined his left shoulder —a wound that would normally be instantly fatal.

"Where are the rest?" asked Lorin.

"Fuck . . . you."

At a glance from Lorin, Nimmo raised the man's head farther and then smashed it down against the hard ground.

Flint gasped and turned away.

"So?" said Lorin to Nimmo. "How did it feel?"

"Shit," laughed Nimmo. "I forgot. Reckon I need to find me another one."

They found more in a clearing some distance farther into the woods, drawn by the hollering of battling mutts.

It was another encampment, and this time there were several family groups of the Lost there. By the time Flint and the others arrived, the Lost were cowering behind a defensive screen of logs, greatly outnumbered by the surrounding mutts.

When Flint reached the camp, Slater and Jona had already felled several of the Lost with crossbow shots, but it had rapidly become a standoff, as the cowering Lost were armed with crossbows, too.

"Flint, Nimmo, Jona: go round behind them to cut off any escape."

They made a wide loop through the jungle, always fearful of ambush, but none came.

They arrived behind the log pile just as the Lost seemed to decide that they should make a break for cover. Two fired crossbows at the distant mutts while the others started to run across open ground directly towards Flint and his two comrades.

Nimmo raised his crossbow and fired. The weapon kicked against his shoulder and he cursed. Its shot lamed one of the fleeing Lost, but the others continued to run towards them.

Flint stepped into the open and held his staff before him.

The first of the Lost came close and stopped, eyeing Flint, fear and confusion in the man's eyes. He looked perfectly normal, and it seemed incongruous to be facing him like this.

And then he took a knife from his belt and threw himself towards Flint.

Flint waited, timing his move carefully, and then swung his staff with rigid arms.

He struck the man in the midriff, and turned instantly, drawing his staff back before the man could seize it. Stepping closer, Flint swung the staff down across the man's neck, then raised it and thrust down with one of its sharpened ends, driving it into the fallen man's chest.

Instantly, he pulled it clear, sidestepping as a Lost woman swung at him with a hardened fibre sword. He caught her with the point of the staff, slicing her neck.

Another man charged, and Jona fended him off with a sword until Nimmo managed a second, more accurate shot and the man fell, clutching at the bolt in his chest.

Those in the log pile had turned now, and were firing crossbows at them.

Flint, Nimmo, and Jona retreated into the trees.

It would be a matter of time now. A standoff until the Lost ran out of ammunition or patience. The outcome was never in question.

Another time . . .

As part of a general sweep of the wildlands between camps Twenty-three and Thirty-five, they found an encampment where the Lost were clearly well established.

The fighting lasted for two days, a time Flint spent in the jungle, with only flatcakes to eat and sweetwater from bladder flowers to drink. He was in the second line, watching for anyone who escaped. There was no one, and he felt a curious disaffection: a disjointed sense of tedium that seemed out of place when the sounds of fighting came regularly from such a short distance away. He found it hard to concentrate, even though he knew how dangerous it might be to lapse.

After the two days, he followed Lorin and Nimmo into the Lost settlement. Most of the cabins had been gutted and burnt out.

Two remained, and that was where the screaming came from.

Flint joined a crowd of purgists at the doorway to one of the cabins. Inside, a naked man was being beaten with a cane that had been pulped for half of its length to produce a flail of abrasive fibres. The man had the distorted body-frame of one who had undergone severe change at some time in his life. It was impossible to make out what his normal skin colour would have been.

There was a woman, too, and that was why the purgists were pressing to enter the cabin. Not to join in—fear of contamination still gripped these men firmly—but to watch her with Overseer Coletenka's mutthounds.

Flint left, feeling excited, sickened, disbelieving. The sickness won, even after all that he had already witnessed in this campaign, and he emptied his stomach into the ashes of a cabin.

He recalled Marshall Maltenka's oft-repeated call to arms: *We are fighting the forces of change. We are fighting for the very life of True humankind. You should feel proud to be joined in such a noble campaign.*

Another time . . .

Lorin, Flint, and Nimmo, leading a squad of twenty mutts, found a group of travellers, six children of varying ages, a man and woman of middling years hauling a hand wagon piled high with fibre-weaving, an old man leaning heavily on a twisted stick, struggling to keep up.

All looked terrified. All looked pretty much human.

"Oh, what a relief to see you!" gabbled the woman, hands clutched protectively around the head of a pup held in a sling across her chest. "Good men of the purge. What a relief for us pure True traders to know that we go protected on our way!"

They were clearly terrified, and from the many indications—the father's distorted skull, the old man's catlike eyes that he had the sense to keep turned away, the abundance of body fur on two of the children—they were clearly also Lost.

"You travel far?" asked Lorin. He knew, Flint saw.

The woman nodded eagerly. "Oh yes, good sir. We're heading straight out of the Ten just as fast as my old father can walk."

Lorin stepped back and, after a moment's hesitation, Nimmo did too, leaving room for the group to pass along the trail.

Flint watched them go. He doubted very much that they would get far.

And another time . . .

The small town of Minster had its own Oracle, but it was much in demand and the queues of weary purgists stretched halfway around the town centre.

Instead, Flint went to a quiet place by a pool formed from a trapped loop of the river Leander. He stripped to his loincloth and felt the small hairs on his body standing up in the chill evening air.

He breathed deep and stood with his feet a short distance apart. He raised his hands above his head and pressed the palms together, enjoying the sensation of his ribs being stretched up and apart, drawing the cool air deep inside.

He tried to find the Joyous Breath, the deep solidity within.

He tried for much of the evening, but he never found it.

He tried to find the memory of Sister Judgement's words, the calming tones of her voice, but they escaped him.

He was, he realised, a Riverwalker no more.

"Tenecka," said Lorin grimly, as he brought more bladders of ale to Flint and Nimmo.

The three sat in a canopy's shade outside the brewhouse in Camp Twenty-six, their seventh posting in the short time they had been a part of the Tenkan purge.

"Tenecka itself?" asked Flint. "What's happening there?"

"It's the mutts," said Lorin. "No one will admit it, but I heard it from Marshall Maltenka Elmarc himself: some of the mutts are in open rebellion. The Tenkans' worst fears: mutts who have lost their ingrained devotion to their masters."

He drank deeply. "It was inevitable," he added grimly. "We go there in the morning. The purge is turning inwards."

CHAPTER 20

After the great cities of Beshusa and Farsamy, Tenecka was a disappointment. Like many long-established settlements, the Tenkans' capital had grown up around the ruins of some ancient place. Some of its stone buildings must date back long before the Fall.

But even those ancient constructions struck Flint as squalid and poorly formed: square buildings of an ugly grey stone; blackstone roadways, buckled and cracked yet still conforming to a grid plan. Most of the buildings were made from whitewood and oak, the timbers split and regrown together with admirable craft, but little flair. Accustomed to the flowing bulbosities of podhut architecture, Flint found the straight lines and angles of Tenecka oppressive.

Everywhere, a layer of dirt coated all surfaces. Flint even felt that he could taste the grime on the air he breathed. Lorin had told Flint about the great dust storms they sometimes had towards the end of the dry season, powerful gusts taking up the soil from the drained rice and bellycane paddies and driving everyone indoors to shelter.

There were crank-handled sirens mounted high on some of the boxy buildings. To warn of storms, Lorin had said. Yet now, everyone knew, if the sirens sounded it would be for a different reason. Now, if they sounded, it would be a signal that what they were calling Shade's Rebellion had spread to the city.

Flint marched three abreast with Lorin and Nimmo, part of a long line of purgists that had arrived at Tenecka late on this afternoon.

People lined the streets, and every so often cheers and whistles broke out to welcome the purgists.

"They all look so poor," said Flint. Their clothes were grey and brown, made from natural fabrics and—at this distance—simply looked dirty and ragged. Their faces were gaunt, eyes bulging, shadows beneath; some children ran naked in the street, despite the sun and the cysts on their backs.

Lorin looked around, as if noticing for the first time. "It is the Teneckan style," he said. "We are not as outrageously decadent as those in the western cities, that is all."

Flint looked around again, and it was then that he realised how few mutts there were in this place, a city at the heart of the plantation lands where it was said that mutts outnumbered humans several times over. They must keep them more in the rural areas, he thought. No need for them here in Tenecka itself.

So long ago, it seemed, he had come here hoping to continue his search for Amber. The reality had proved very different to his intentions, though. Now it was just a matter of enduring, surviving.

The purgists camped in makeshift tents in a field on the northern outskirts of the city, and that was where Flint started to get some idea of what had been happening.

They sat outside in the darkness, drinking tubes of the local jaggery spirit they called *burn* and sniffing coarse headsticks. The mass of canvas and fibre shelters was like some kind of transit camp, bringing to Flint's mind stories of mutt camps used by the haul-boats along the rivers Elver and Farsam. There had been crops growing in this field until recently—hacked off at the base, their flattened stumps still in the ground. Some kind of fibre-cane, he thought.

"Hey! Is that you, Sweet?" Flint called, louder than he had intended.

It was. Sweet turned and waved, and pushed his way through the crowd to find a space on the end of the bench. A few years older than Flint, he was of small build—a similar stature to Nimmo, and back in Farsamy some had joked that they were brothers, parted at birth.

"Flintheart, Lorin . . . hey, Nimmo!" he said, laughing. "Night Watch reunion, isn't it? Been here long?"

"We just arrived," said Nimmo. "How about you, Sweet?"

"Yesterday. Been up to Henika's today. Just back."

Henika's was where all the trouble was, or so people were saying.

"People say the mutts have found a way of changing themselves," said Nimmo. "A vector that knocks out their devotion to humankind. Is that right?"

Flint hadn't heard that version. He'd heard that the mutts had learnt how to hypnotise themselves to overcome their deep-bred sub-servience. He'd also heard that they weren't mutts at all: that they were Lost, or even True humans, passing themselves as mutts in order to trigger some kind of regional war. And that they had been possessed by the spirits of the dead. And that they were carriers of some virulent new changing fever. And any number of less likely scenarios.

"Dunno about that," said Sweet. "Marshall Albatenka says there's really only a small number of them that are behind it all, and that the rest are just there because they're stupid mutts who don't know any better. Henika's is a pissy little farmstead up the Leander. We got it surrounded. This whole thing won't last much longer."

"Why so many of us here, then?" asked Flint, head reeling under the onslaught of the burn and the sticks.

"The people of the Ten are scared," said Lorin. "They don't know how rife this new change will prove to be."

"And there's one other thing," said Nimmo. "Think about it: mutts have changed—God knows how, but they've changed. And we're right in the middle of the biggest fucking purge in living memory! Who's doing the purging? Sure, there are people like us, but has there ever been a time when there have been so many armed and trained mutts around?"

They drank and they sniffed and they swapped stories of their campaigns.

Later, one of the brewmaids came by, collecting empty bladders and discarded sticks. She had a tray suspended from a loop around her neck, and it was stacked high with more drinks and sticks.

"Hey," said Nimmo softly, "got anything for us?"

The girl was tall and slim, and she wore a tunic that emphasised her cleavage. She smiled, and said, "Burn, headsticks, ale as weak as piss is all I'm offering."

Lorin thrust some coins at her and said, "Burn, and three more sticks."

"Got anything more?" asked Nimmo, showing her a handful of coins. He had a hand on her hip, thumb working a tight circle.

Flint was aware of the looks of those around, sensed tension suddenly ready to erupt. "Leave her," he said quietly, leaning towards Nimmo. "Not the place."

For a moment, it seemed that Nimmo would object; then he subsided, letting his hand fall away, closing his fist over his money. "Anyway," he said, as the brewmaid moved across to another bench, "buy me three mutts with that."

Flint took a tube of burn and cracked its top with his teeth. He enjoyed the trail it left down his throat, tingling and raw.

"Sweet," he said later, when the night sky had fully darkened and they had filled their bellies with all the drink they could afford.

"Hnnh?"

"Why's it they call it 'Shade's Rebellion,' then?"

"Their leader. A white-skinned mutt called Shade. Henika bought him not so long ago. The Tenkans say Henika was always known as a vicious bastard. Seems he found a mutt who learnt to stand up to him. The mutt thinks he's been sent by God to sort out humankind for good. First people knew of it was when Henika's body came floating down the river. Took 'em a while to work out who it was."

"I saw a mutt like that for sale from one of the traders who passed through Trecosann," said Flint, clutching at vague memories. He laughed. "I had a good look at it. It had scars on its back. The ones with scars are always trouble."

Nimmo laughed. "Looks like old Henika wasn't as good a judge of a mutt as you, Flint. Could have saved himself a lot of trouble."

Darkness by the river. The sound of water helped: soothing, washing away the tensions and the fears. And the memories.

Flint sat cross-legged on the dry mud.

He had been unable to settle. Perhaps it was the mixture of burn spirit and headsticks—even now his head was a-jitter—or perhaps it was something else.

Where would he go from here? What was to become of his life? He had closed so many doors by choosing to travel, clutching at the vague hope that he might find Amber and they would then work out what to do.

He had been drunk, he realised, and maudlin; but he had come to this place and sat, and now the river calmed him.

He did not even try to find the Lordsway. He knew it would be futile. Calmness was as much as he could hope for.

Some time later, he heard the sound of feet. He looked around and saw the form of a woman, heading along the riverside path. It was the brewmaid from the camp, he realised. She ducked her head, aware of his presence and pretending that she did not know he was there, no doubt hoping that he would leave her alone.

And then she looked up, and he saw her attitude change.

She came over. "It's you, isn't it?" she said.

He did not know what the appropriate answer was.

"Thank you," she said. "For stopping the other one," she added, explaining.

"Oh . . . Nimmo," said Flint. "Don't worry about him." A platitude: Nimmo was most certainly a person to worry about.

"I'll go."

"No, it's okay," he said. "I was just . . . getting away."

She sat by him, legs crossed, arms resting on her knees.

"My name is Flint."

"I'm Wend."

After a while, she said, "Most men . . ." She hesitated, then started again. "You're not a Tenkan, are you?"

"Trecosi," said Flint. "And I am a Riverwalker, too—they call me Flintheart."

"Flintheart. I like that. Riverwalkers—they do that meditation thing, don't they? Is that what you were doing here when I came along and disturbed you? What's a holy man doing in the middle of all this?"

Flint smiled. He realised then how strange the expression felt, how unfamiliar. "The Lordsway has deserted me," he said. "And I don't think anyone would rightly call me a holy man."

She turned to him, skin pale in the moonlight, the whites of her eyes almost luminous, it seemed. She took his hand and eased it through the gap at the front of her cloak. He felt soft flesh, fabric stretched tight, hardness pressing into his palm.

"Times like this," she said. "You need someone, don't you think?"

He shifted position slightly, awed by the rising and falling of her chest beneath his hand.

"Most men . . ."

Memories held him back. Memories both recent and long ago. Stopping him.

This thing . . . these feelings. They *changed* people.

He was scared.

She seemed to sense his reaction.

She took his hand, pulled it back out from the opening in her cloak, and he thought it was over, that he had failed her, messing everything up in his confusion and guilt.

She moved his hand lower, to where she had pulled her cloak aside, to the parting of her robe.

He found thick hair, heat. Softly folding flesh. Wetness.

She leaned back, still cross-legged, and he saw her face tipped up to the stars, long hair trailing in a curtain of shadow behind her.

He found hardness again, pressed it, ran his fingers around it, fascinated by the way she responded.

Finally, shuddering, she turned to him, found his mouth with hers, working to find a way through his clothing until her hand found the cord of his trousers, eased it loose, moved down.

Her leg slid up over his hip, and she moved up against him, positioned him, gently guiding him, teaching him.

Afterwards he cried, and she held him, stroking his hair and pressing his face against her chest.

Later she led him by the hand, through passageways and side streets to the building where she shared a room with her sister.

Within, in the darkness, they shared Wend's small sleep mat, trying to remain silent so that they did not disturb her sleeping sibling.

Waking up had never been like this before.

Light angling into the small room through opened shutters, a stranger moving about, apparently unconcerned that he was here with her sister, Wend.

"I . . . I'd better get back," he said when he had dressed.

Wend kissed him on the cheek as he paused by the door, and Flint mumbled, "Thanks," before he realised that that was probably the wrong thing to say.

Descending the shared stairway, he heard the sisters' voices, the two relaxing into conversation now that he had left.

He walked back through the outskirts of Tenecka, wondering if he would find his way and realising that, for today, at least, he really didn't care.

"Off doing your funny standing all night, were you?" asked Nimmo when Flint reached their shelter. That was what they had taken to calling the Lordsway, whenever they caught Flint going through the meditative movements of the Riverwalkers' art.

"Something like that," he said.

"You haven't heard, then?"

He looked at Nimmo, eyebrows raised.

"We're going up to Henika's," said Nimmo. "Going to take out the mad white mutt."

The track led them through a wide floodplain, divided by low mud ridges into square paddies where bellycane and rice matured under the dry-season sun. White herons danced in the muddy pools, disturbing fish with their spidery yellow feet. And mutts worked, already harvesting the slimmer canes to take an early crop and leave room for the rest to fatten out.

Men and women armed with crossbows, bows, and canes watched over the mutts.

Nodding a greeting at one of these overseers, Lorin said to Flint, "A year ago the mutts would have been left to work unsupervised. But not now. These days we watch them. We watch their every move."

They marched in a column of around thirty purgists, silent other than the pounding of feet on the baked hard track.

Eventually, the ground rose ahead of them, a whitewood plantation forming a neat screen of pale trunks. Guards were posted where the road entered the plantation.

Soon they came to a cleared area where Marshall Albatenka was already giving instructions to another squad of purgists. "Ah," he said, looking up. "The last arrivals."

He gestured at a board where someone had marked a plan of the Henika farmstead. "We have squads in place all around the farm," he said. He indicated the lower half of the map with his hand. "You will reinforce those on the southern side of the clearance. When we are in place, the farm will be razed to the ground. No one is to escape. Our information is that we are dealing with one aberrant individual who has undue influence over the other mutts, but I am sure you have all heard the speculation. If these mutts are changed in some way that removes their devotion to humankind, then they must be purged."

Flint stared at him and felt completely empty. What if Amber had been bought by Henika? What if she was in there now?

The Marshall turned and spoke to one of his assistants and then walked away. Instantly, overseers for each of the two squads started to snap instructions at their men.

There was still some distance to go through the whitewood trees, and they moved as silently as a body of sixty men could move.

Eventually, Flint detected a thinning of the trees ahead, and a short time later he stood looking out over an area that had been cleared.

In the middle of the open area, two barns and a timber farmhouse sat, each squat and square in the Tenkan style. And from within, there came the sound of singing.

Nimmo nudged Flint and pointed towards the door of one of the barns. Inside, there appeared to be logged timber piled high, but suspended from the frame of its wide doorway a body sagged. It was hard to be sure at this distance, but the thing was naked and appeared to be covered with dark hair. A mutt, then. Had the rebels turned on their own, or was this a grisly memento of the way Henika had treated them, perhaps the catalyst for Shade's Rebellion?

Flint wanted to walk away from this, right now, but he knew that was not possible.

Nimmo said something about stringing them all up, but Flint had turned away from him and did not hear his words clearly.

"Okay, boys."

That was their overseer, Tontenka.

Flint looked at the farm again, just in time to see two arrows plunge their flaming heads into the building's bleached shingles. He swallowed. He had seen this before: arrows twisted around with belly-pulp and dipped in stick-spirit so that they would burn.

Flames skipped up the sloping roof. White flames at first, from the spirit, and then yellows and reds as the wooden tiles ignited.

More arrows, lodging in the farm's walls, and in the barns.

The singing in the farm had stopped now. They knew their end was near.

Purgists closed around the buildings, crossing the open area between trees and farm.

Flint was in the second rank.

So close! He thought they would have to go into the buildings after the rebel mutts. Indeed, if it had not been for their earlier singing he would have thought the place deserted.

And then, finally, doors opened and mutts spilled out into the yard, coughing and screaming, some of them fighting each other.

Purgists aimed with crossbows and fired.

Flint looked on, sick, studying each mutt that fell, each mutt that tried to flee or tried to go back into the burning building.

Smoke spread across the clearing, and someone ordered the purgists to slow their advance, not to leave any gaps.

Ahead, some of the men were in the farmyard already, some fighting at close quarters with the frenzied mutts. Flint had never thought he would see anything like this.

Shade stepped out of the farmhouse.

Through drifting smoke, Flint recognised him immediately as the mutt he had seen at market in Trecosann: short and ghostly pale, with teeth too big for his mouth and an unchallengeable expression that was out of place on a mutt's face.

The smoke appeared to part around him, and Flint sensed a sudden lull in the battle. The mutt had such presence about him it was little wonder that he scared the Tenkans so much.

He raised a hand, and Flint sensed that he had been biding his time. Then, when his hand fell, Flint heard a groaning, a shifting of large weight . . . like the felling of a giant tree.

He looked at the nearest barn, where neatly trimmed logs were stacked high to the eaves and the mutt's body still hung.

The logs were moving.

One at the top fell, careening down the sloped face of the woodpile, and then others shifted, started to tumble forwards.

Flint looked down to see what lay in the wood's path, and he saw perhaps a dozen purgists and only three or four mutts. It was as if the moment were suspended in time, and Flint was powerless to do anything.

The log pile collapsed, submerging those in its way.

And in its wake, the dangling body of the mutt now swung from side to side, having been struck by the racing logs.

The farm was burning well now, its structure collapsing, the heat intense as Flint moved closer.

He found the body of a female mutt, turned her over to see her face, moved on.

The fighting still went on around him, although more sporadically now. The logs had been Shade's gesture—he had known he had no chance against the Tenkan purge.

Flint had not seen Shade fall, but he had found his body, his head clubbed so that it resembled a mangled fleshfruit, but his pale skin and scarred back unmistakable.

Now, he found another fallen mutt, a male. He moved on.

Nimmo lay, curled up like a pup on Leaving Hill, what looked like a slender cane sticking out of his side.

Bizarrely, he smiled up at Flint's crouching figure. "I found it," he gasped. "That moment. Nearly there. Taking the last breath and then . . . what's after? Nearly . . ."

He stopped talking and tried to moisten his lips, but his tongue was clearly dry.

The smoke hung heavy around them, and so Flint was startled when a figure suddenly emerged. A woman, or a girl. Scared. She paused, then backed away and was lost. She would not get far.

When Flint looked back at Nimmo he was dead.

They were welcomed on the streets of Tenecka as returning heroes. Word must have passed ahead of them that Shade's Rebellion had been put down, and now crowds lined the main thoroughfare as the purgists trekked dismally back into town.

"They think we have won," said Lorin, marching at Flint's side. "They do not understand that this will happen again and again if True humans are to defend their position."

Many of the purgists believed that they had won, too, and soon the city was overtaken by a spirit of celebration.

Flint went to their camp on the outskirts and joined some of the others in a communal bath to soak the smut and blood from their bodies.

Later, he looked for Wend but could not find her in the room she shared with her sister, or back in the temporary brewhouse at the camp where she worked.

He found Lorin instead, and they drank burn spirit and beer, chasing one drink with the other like true comrades at arms.

"What next, Lorin?"

"Dunno. The purge isn't done yet, is it?"

"Never be done. Like holding back water with a stick."

They drank more at the camp—for Nimmo, and for all they had been through—and then wandered along the river path into the heart of Tenecka.

"What next, Flin'?"

"Dunno. My sister. Keep looking."

"You mean you really had a sister? Thought you were telling stories. A noble mystery to hide behind. Is what I thought . . ."

Flint thought. "I really had a sister," he said finally.

Later, somewhere in town where trees grew by the road and people were cooking meat over open fires, Flint joined a double line of people dancing in and out of the tree trunks to the sound of a drum band.

Head pounding, burning like he had a fever, throat raw, he leaned against a wall and coughed until he thought his insides were coming out.

Straightening, he saw Wend, out in the middle of the street, her fingers interlocked behind the neck of a man who was either a purgist or trying to look like one. They were dancing, pressed together, her head tucked into the gap between jaw and shoulder. She would feel his stubble against her temple, would smell the smells of fighting, the sweat and dirt and smoke—his clothes were filthy; he clearly had not bathed since returning from action. Another to share the small sleep mat in the room she occupied with her sister.

Flint staggered across the road, barging past dancing couples and racing children. His head was pounding again, his skin hot.

"Hey," he said, and they paused, looking at him.

"Leave it, Flint," said Lorin, from somewhere behind him.

He ignored the advice and slapped out at the man's arm.

He woke in the dormitory cabin, his head sore, throat dry and rough. He crawled out into daylight, to where a bladderpump spilled water into the dirt. He doused his head, drank greedily, turned to find Lorin laughing at him.

"He *hit* me! The bastard hit me. . . ."

Lorin shook his head. "No he didn't," he said. "He didn't have to. You fell over flat on your face when you went after him."

Later, he sat cross-legged by the river, trying to find inner solidity. She came to him, eventually. Somehow he had known she would.

Sitting by his side, a short distance between his left knee and her right, she said, "It was nice, Flint, but that's all. Do you understand?"

He shook his head. "Not really," he told her.

"I like you," she said. "We had a good time."

He could have used the same words and yet meant something else entirely.

"I'm leaving," he said. "I've seen enough of the Ten."

"What will you do?"

"I'll carry on looking for my sister. You see, she went missing from Trecosann—that's why I left home: to try to find her." He told her about his search for Amber, about how he had gone to Greenwater, and then decided to go to Carnival in Farsamy but was diverted along the way. "I came so close! One of the traders told me he'd sold a girl who fitted her description—sold her as a mutt. I spent a mad day trying to track down the man who had bought her, but didn't find him. I'm sure it was her: the description was so close, and she's so distinctive."

"How do you mean?"

"She has one feature that marks her out from most: when she was a small girl she had an illness that left her with jaundice for most of a year, and stained the whites of her eyes permanently yellow. . . ."

He let his words trail off, seeing a sudden change in Wend's expression.

"I . . . Oh my . . ."

"What?"

"I went to Carnival this year. I travelled with the brewkeeper Esher and his family. I met someone. Henritt Elkyme. He was fun, and he was so arrogant! I spent one evening with him, but then he lost interest. I thought he was probably keener on the young bondsman he went around with, until I found out that it was a mutt he liked better, the creep.

"He bought her, Flint. Henritt Elkyme bought your sister."

CHAPTER 21

He was deserting the purge, he supposed. He did not know if that was regarded as some kind of offence by the Tenkans, and he only cared as far as it might hinder him on his way.

Travelling alone along a route that connected Tenecka with the main Ritt settlement of Ritteny, he passed many groups of travellers, mostly heading north out of the Ten.

Some were Lost, he knew, although they did their best to hide any obvious signs.

They seemed harmless enough, though. For the first time he had a sense of two communities living in interlocking territories, as tree martens occupy the upper reaches of the canopy and yet give way to nub mice and cane kits lower down.

The wilds belonged to the Lost, and he had to pass through these lands to get to Amber.

He camped out under the trees on the seven nights of his journey. He listened to the sounds of tree crickets and frogs, the high chitterings of hunting bats and the soft cooing of oak flowers in the breeze.

As he walked, he wondered if he could really be nearing the end of his journey. What if he came to Rittasan and found that they refused to release Amber? He would deal with that if he had to. He could, at least, do his best to ensure that she was treated well.

He remembered Henritt Elkyme, all right. He had visited Trecosann, and he was the one at the stall who had negotiated with Sister Judgement about fibre trade and indentures for two young Riverwalkers. Arrogant, yes. Wend's description was fair.

Also, Flint had confronted him when he found that a mutt fitting Amber's description had been bought by someone sounding very like

Henritt. He had denied it, sending Flint off on his mad search for someone else who might be the one who had bought her. "Plenty more mutts out there," he had told Flint.

He had expected Rittasan to be far grander than this, given Henritt Elkyme's manner. The imperious representative of Clan Ritt at Carnival had, in reality, only been the representative of a backwater.

The buildings were an assortment of seed-grown podhuts and tent-like cabins made from stretched sheets of smartfibre, giving the place an air of transition. In some ways it was like returning to Trecosann. Rather than enfold itself with high defensive stockades, the town was surrounded by managed fields and paddies, acting as a buffer between settlement and wilds; only the inner cluster of buildings was enclosed by defensive earth banks, and that would be little help if subjected to the kinds of pressures Flint had seen in the gang-farms of the Ten.

He wondered how long this sense of security would last, given the upheavals only a few days' journey to the south.

He was stopped at one of the main entranceways to the settlement, where a semicircular fibre arch looped over a road that was raised on a ridge between rice paddies.

A man with a long whipping cane stood before him, two mutts armed with hardened fibre shortswords to his rear. The man was a head shorter than Flint, and several years older. He looked bored.

"I am a Riverwalker," said Flint simply. He knew there were Riverwalkers here, and it was known that their kind often travelled alone from community to community. It was only natural for him to call here.

The man nodded. "Certainly look like one," he said. "But you'll forgive me for doubting you. All sorts have been passing through recently—driven out of the Ten, so I've been told."

Flint nodded. "You have two of my fellow Riverwalkers here," he said. "Brother Watchful and Sister Oftheclouds. They will vouch for me."

Henritt Elkyme was not as Flint remembered him. He seemed older, and when Flint looked into his eyes the depths were greater than before.

A brief shake of the head was all the response Flint needed to confirm that Amber was no longer here, that his journey was not over yet.

Henritt took him by the arm and led him back to a lemon grove behind one of the larger podhuts. They sat, and drank from a jug one of the mutts brought out.

"I'm sorry," said Henritt.

Flint had expected this to be more difficult, a battle of wills, a struggle to extract the truth from someone who had already proved himself to be an adept liar. But he believed this young man when he said that he was sorry.

"You did not explain yourself clearly in Farsamy—you did not tell me that it was your sister you sought. And . . . I would probably still have lied to you. She was beautiful. She had me possessed."

"'Was'?"

"Sorry: *is*. She's out there somewhere." He waved a hand. The wilds. "She did not stay here long. She ran away. I can show you the direction she took and I can wish you well and offer you supplies, but I'm afraid I can't do more than that. I don't know where your sister is."

"Can you tell me . . . how she is?"

Henritt met his look. "She is Lost," he said. "But you knew that, I'm sure. There is great diversity in the Lost, and your sister passes easily as a mutt—too easily."

"I've heard stories that some of the traders can craft people like that. They use changing vectors that guide the transformations into types familiar to us." He smiled grimly. "It is a technology my own clan has refined." He thought of Callum and his changing vats, of how his cousin and Father Grey would try to guide the changes once the fevers had taken hold.

Henritt nodded. "I suspected that, when Cedar explained to me that she must be one of the Lost."

"Cedar?"

Cedar—*Cedero?*

"I went after her when she ran away," explained Henritt. "I was attacked by a group of travellers and later rescued by one of the Lost. He called himself Cedar. A tall man, completely hairless, clothed in animal skins."

When Cedero had emerged from the changing brew . . . when Flint had stolen down to the holding pens that night and seen him in the grip of the changing fevers . . . his former teacher's hair had been falling out in great clumps.

Had the past finally come back to haunt him?

"Had he seen her?" asked Flint.

He let loose the breath he had been holding when Henritt shook his head.

What would Cedero do if he found Amber? Probably, he would not even know her: so much time had passed, and Amber had only been a small girl when Cedero had been banished.

"Where was this Cedar?" asked Flint. There was still half a day's light to use.

Henritt stood immediately, sensing Flint's urgency. "Calig!" he called, and a big mutt came running. "Get Stutter to pack some food and water for Walker Flintheart. And get Fleet and Merit: we're escorting Flint up the Ritteny Way."

The track was a thin trail, worn through wood grass, but Henritt assured Flint that it was the main trail from Rittasan to the west. They passed a junction, and Henritt gestured the other way along the larger trail they had joined. "That way is Farsamy," he said.

"And the other?"

"More Ritt settlements. And wilds—what we call the Badlands."

It all looked reasonably familiar to Flint, the vegetation similar to that he knew from around Trecosann. Thicket oaks and bellycane, various tree ferns with dangling fronds of moss. Here in the wilds, of course, they could all be subtly different, subtly changed.

Eventually they paused.

To one side of the trail, a dense stand of conifers crowded towards the light, their trunks tall and naked, like the tines of an upturned brush. The canopy shaded out any undergrowth here, and Flint saw that it would be easy to leave the trail and pass through the stand.

"I came back through the finger pines here," said Henritt. "I remember wandering in them, thinking I was lost and that Cedar had tricked me when he gave me directions. And then: the relief of stumbling onto this track and feeling the sunlight on my skin.

"It was something like thirty days ago," he told Flint again. "They won't be there now."

"But they were," said Flint. "And if they have left behind any signs then I will find them and follow them."

Alone, he found the fallen tree, new trunks thrust upwards from its fallen length. New life amid death.

This fitted Henritt's description of the place where Cedar had killed the boar.

There had been a fire here, some time ago. Presumably it was where Cedar had cooked the hog's meat.

Beyond the tree, he found a shallow gulley, and that was where he found the grave. It had been disturbed by animals: branches pulled aside from where they had covered the body, bones protruding.

The skull was that of some kind of animal, and from the extended canine fangs, Flint decided that this must be where Cedar had buried the unused remains of the beast he had slaughtered.

Thirty days was a long time. Other than the fire and the stripped, half-buried carcase, he found little evidence that anyone had been here.

Then, later, as the sky burnt a fierce red, he found an ancient hut. It was almost completely submerged by growths of thornbush and scrub, but someone had been here and cleared the way through to the entrance.

Within, there was no more sign of occupation.

He chose to spend the night here, and look more closely the next day.

Nothing.

The sun was high above and the heat intense, despite the dappled shade of the forest canopy. Flint emptied the contents of one of his sweetwater bladders into his parched mouth.

Where might Amber have gone? He felt so *close*.

There were various indistinct trails through the jungle here. Animal spoor indicated that many were created by the regular passage of hogs—animals he had heard snuffling about outside the wood hut the previous night. Others perhaps indicated alternative thoroughfares used by the Lost in preference to the well-worn routes between the settlements of the True. If so, that made any hope of tracing Amber more remote—so many more, likely hidden, routes to find!

But then, the fact that Cedar had directed Henritt back to the trail suggested that he might regard the more established human pathways as the obvious routes to take. And if Amber travelled alone, and she was still able to think clearly, then he felt sure she would have stuck to the trail, heading away from Ritt settlements. She probably wouldn't know she was heading towards the region Henritt had called the Badlands. . . .

In any case, he had to choose one direction to pursue *somehow*, and heading away from Rittasan seemed the best bet.

He headed back through the cooler shade of the finger pines. When he found the trail again he headed east.

Ahead, where the track wound up a scarp face, he saw that he was catching a small party of travellers: six adults and several children and dogs running around them.

He remembered Henritt's story of being attacked. The group he had encountered were different in number, but the lesson held good.

He trailed them for some distance, straining to see if any of the tiny figures fitted the description of Cedar, or Amber.

It was impossible to see.

They might be legitimate travellers, freemen plying trades from settlement to settlement, or even genuine clanspeople on some business or other.

Equally, they could be Lost.

He did not know how to juggle the risks: if they proved to be violent, he was outnumbered and almost certainly outarmed, as he carried only his combat staff and a knife. But probably his only hope of progress was to ask people he met for information about other travellers.

Finally, the decision was taken from him, as one of the dogs caught wind of him and set up a mad barking. One of the adults raised a hand towards the dog and it cowered and stopped barking. The group paused, looking back down the trail towards Flint, and then they resumed their journey.

That was a good sign, he felt.

He watched to see if any of them slipped away from the path, again recalling Henritt's story of how one of his assailants had sneaked up behind him.

Trees obscured his view and he felt vulnerable, imagining them stealing back through the forest to ambush him. But each time the group became visible, above and ahead of him, their number was unchanged.

He allowed his pace to increase, the gap to narrow.

They looked a peaceable party, glancing back occasionally to scrutinise him.

He took comfort in the knowledge that people seemed to identify him easily as a Riverwalker: the occasional itinerant preacher between settlements a familiar and harmless figure.

They waited, when he came close. Watchful as the lone traveller approached.

Two of the children had the stocky physique of mutts. One of the men had only one arm, although it was unclear whether it was a defect of birth or the result of a later injury.

Flint bowed his head to them. "Greetings," he said. "May you travel in the Lord's peace." He felt slightly guilty playing up to his preacher's image.

"Greetings, master," said a man who appeared to be either their leader or spokesman. "Make you travel in peace. Be travel with fellows?"

The man's Mutter was indistinct, his accent strange. Flint was unsure whether he was asking him if he was, indeed, alone or if he wanted to travel with this group.

"I travel alone," said Flint, choosing words that answered both questions. "I am looking for someone. Two people. One is a man, tall and bald and dressed in animal skins. The other is my sister. She has chestnut hair, yellow in her eyes. Both are Lost."

Just as this group were Lost. Or Lost with two young orphaned or rescued mutts, Flint guessed.

"Done see plenty Lost," said the man. "None how you done say, master."

Flint nodded. He waved along the trail ahead of them. The ground here started to level out, the trees thinning on the exposed and rocky crest of the hill. "Where are you heading?"

"Been lookin' for Harmony, master. Some say it out here. Been lookin' long time."

Flint nodded to the man, and then to the rest of the group. "Travel in peace," he told them.

He left them mumbling farewells to him, and strode on ahead.

Soon the trees were around him, thicker again, and the group of travellers was lost to view.

He slept sitting upright with his back against a lime trunk. Lorin had taught him this technique when they had been forced to sleep out during the purge. It meant that you were never fully asleep, always ready to respond to strange sounds in the night. And it made the warm cavities of nostril and ear less accessible to wandering insects and bugs.

So it was that he heard the children singing early the next morning, dawn still bleeding the eastern horizon.

He had settled a short distance from the trail, and now he worked his way through the trees cautiously.

Another family group approached, heading west into the heart of Ritt territory. They were mutts, or Lost, their near-naked bodies thick with swirling fur.

He emerged and they saw him immediately, the children halting their song and two of the four adults reaching for bows slung across their shoulders.

Flint held his hands up in peace, and waited.

"Greetings. May you travel in the Lord's peace."

They nodded, but did not speak. Flint wondered if they had understood his words. "I am looking for two people," he went on, regardless. "One is a man, tall and bald and dressed in animal skins. The other is my sister. She has chestnut hair, yellow in her eyes. Both are Lost."

The adults conferred, and then a woman said, "Man been call Cedar?"

Flint nodded eagerly.

She pointed along the trail to the east. "Be find Cedar where the fruit trees grow."

CHAPTER 22

It was a grove of fleshfruit, the swollen cobs hanging in heavy clusters, their rich purple flesh cracked open and bleeding red juices.

There had been a settlement here once, but the plantations had long been left to run wild.

Cedar sat by the trail, sucking the flesh of a fruit.

He looked up as Flint approached. He looked confused, and protective, as if he thought Flint would steal his fruit when all around they hung heavy from the trees.

He didn't appear to know Flint, although Flint knew him. He looked little different from the day he had been banished, a gaunt, bald man with bugging eyes and a lost expression, walking in a daze down the trail that led to a life in the wilds.

"Cedar," said Flint, opting for the version of his name he used now. "I hoped I would find you."

"The fruit," said Cedar, holding up the pulped husk of fleshfruit he had been eating. "You have to know which ones to pick. Most of them are corrupt. Imbuto."

Flint stared at him. The man's body was rigid, trembling, his eyes possessed of some strangeness Flint could not identify. Was this truly the person his teacher had become, or was it the temporary result of what he was eating? Perhaps he had not chosen his fruit as wisely as he thought.

Flint eased the fruit from the man's hand and offered him one of the bladders of sweetwater he had refilled from a trumpet flower the previous evening.

Guiltily, he wondered if he could get through this encounter without revealing the history they shared, without exposing his own guilt.

"I spoke to Henritt," Flint said. "You helped him in the forest after he had been attacked. Like Henritt I am looking for the Lost girl they call Taneyes. Can you help me? Do you know where she might be?"

Cedar's eyes flitted from Flint's face to the trail, the trees, the sky. "Don't know any Lost girls," he said. "I'm on my own. Anyway: out here you don't talk about mutts and Lost. We're all people, blessed by the change or not."

"My sister," Flint said. "She is my sister. She has chestnut in her hair, yellow in her eyes."

"Pretty thing," said Cedar suddenly, his expression changing, softening.

Flint sucked in a sharp breath. He waited while Cedar drained the drinking bladder. "Pretty thing?" he asked quietly. "You saw her? You know where she is?"

"She came back to me," said Cedar. "Darling Jescka came back to me after all this time. I didn't believe it was her until I heard her voice."

Why did he call her that?

"Where is she?"

"I don't know," said Cedar. "Gone off. Haven't seen her again. Just haunted me the once, darling Jescka."

"It wasn't Jescka," said Flint. "Or a ghost of Jescka. It was her daughter, Amberline. And I am Jescka's son, Flintreco Eltarn."

Eyes wide, the man stared at him. "You got no right!" he moaned. "No right to come for me after so long. Her and then you. Isn't once enough? Didn't I pay enough for you?"

"You paid too much. I am sorry."

"What are you saying? What do you mean?"

Stumbling over his words, Flint told him about that night in the seed patch, about what he had witnessed. "It wasn't you. My father . . . after you had gone. He raped Jescka and beat her. I think he would have killed her if I had not revealed myself and so given him someone else to beat."

Cedar was rubbing the knuckles of a clenched fist. "I hit her," he said. "It's not like me to hit someone. I don't know why I did it, but I hit her."

"My father hit her worse. You were wrongly punished. They asked me at the hearing, and Jescka had already blamed you for the attack. They asked if I had seen it, and I said I had. They asked if I had seen you, and I said I had. I did not lie, but I did not tell them the full truth of what had happened. I did not contradict my mother and my father. I did not dare."

"You were a child," said Cedar.

Flint had not expected understanding.

"I don't remember much," Cedar went on. "Sometimes in dreams. I remember hitting her, and I remember the fevers. You say I was a teacher: was I good?"

"You were popular and so we listened and so, yes, you must have been good."

"I would have been good," said Cedar. Then he repeated: "You were a child. You wouldn't understand. You wouldn't know that change can be a blessing—that's what I say to people: we're not Lost, we're blessed with change. We are the beginning of what humankind will become."

Cedar was becoming animated, now, becoming more the Cedero Flint remembered.

"You've travelled, haven't you, Flintreco? You must have, to be here on the edge of the Badlands. So what did you see? You saw all your so-called True humans cowering in their self-imposed pens, like mutts up for auction. All of them, hiding in pockets of managed sterility, in the middle of all this richness and diversity! And living out here in the wilds, adapted to the wonders of our world: the Lost, the changed. Your kind think we are damaged, but we are not: it is the True who are stunted in their understanding of what it is to be human."

Cedar scrambled on the ground for the split fleshfruit Flint had taken from him earlier. Finding it, he pressed it against his mouth and sucked at its sweet insides.

"What is it to be human?"

"To be human is to be fluid, unfixed. Open to change. Humanity is uncertain. Humanity today is not what it was yesterday, and it is only the start of what it will be tomorrow. All the time, your kind cling on in desperation: biological artefacts fighting the stream of time. Out here we are truly *post*human.

"To be changed is to be blessed. It is to welcome the future with open arms. You should try it, Flintreco. You should move forwards. I will show you how, if you wish. . . ."

Flint stared at him, his mind racing to comprehend his arguments. The purgists of the Ten saw change as a force to fight, a fate to resist. The Riverwalkers saw it as inevitable, a force to be accepted, if not actively embraced.

And now Cedar wanted him to welcome change on a personal level, to step with him into the future of humankind.

"So tell me," he said, some considerable time later. "What do I do, Cedar? What is the secret?"

A fruit. A simple fruit.

Here, in the heart of the corrupted plantation, the fleshfruits hung thick and shiny.

"People used to live here," said Cedar. "Your kind. They couldn't keep the wilds at bay, though. They fled. Eat their fruit, Flintreco Eltarn. The fruit from their wild garden. They are packed full of changing vectors. I had a friend who knew this place. I think she grew up here. She knows each of the trees here, like a relative. I've been waiting for her, but she hasn't come yet.

"The vectors won't do you any harm, Flintreco. They were made that way: catalysts of change, communicants of traits that modify and enhance. They will rewrite you from within. They serve us: tiny mutts, if you like. Let them in, Flintreco, and see what you become."

Flint took one of the fruit and split it in two with his knife. It looked and smelled normal. He lifted a chunk on his knife and studied it: no different to fruit he had eaten a thousand times.

He looked up to see Cedar watching him intently. Was he fooling him? He always had had a way with words. Was this some kind of revenge, at last?

"It's your choice," said Cedar. "Are you ready for the future yet?"

The fleshfruit tasted just the same as they normally tasted.

Nighttime. They sat at a fire and swapped food: dried pork strips and berries for flatcake and rice biscuit.

"Is this it?"

"Give it time."

"But it's had plenty of time already."

"Give it time."

"You were making it up, weren't you? Seeing how much I would believe . . ."

"Give it time."

"You deserve revenge."

Silence.

"What is east along the trail from here?"

"A few settlements. Ritt clan. And then the Badlands."

"You have been there? What are they like?"

"The Lost live there. I haven't been."

"You are still clinging on, aren't you? Even after all this time you can't let go. Living on the fringes of the True. Hanging on."

"Many Lost live here, in the interstices between truebred settlements. The land is rich. And yes, some of us have not yet fully embraced the future. One day. I'll head out there one day. When I'm ready."

"When will it happen?"

"Give it time."

He hurt, deep within.

An ache, an internal shifting. Maybe he was just imagining it, picturing the changing vectors at work. *Tiny mutts*, Cedar had called them. *Little machines*, the Riverwalkers called them. Inside him. Making him something other than human.

When would it start?

Cedar sat a short distance away in the dark. Not sleeping, although the night was old. Wrapped in his furs, he looked like some grossly changed beast of the jungle.

This was the end, Flint realised. This was the end of his quest. He had travelled so far—from Trecosann and his family, from the foolish young man he had been. And now he was travelling farther, heading away from the True.

Blessed by change, if it would ever start.

Humanity is uncertain. Cedar's words from earlier. Cedar, still the teacher. *Humanity today is not what it was yesterday, and it is only the start of what it will be tomorrow.*

The journey Flint had started, the great distances he had travelled: his journey was the journey being taken by all humankind.

He lay, wrapped tight in his blanket and longcoat, and his body was wracked with trembling and sudden, spastic convulsions.

He cried out, and mumbled, and sometimes he laughed.

He tossed from side to side, and his arms lashed out, striking tree trunks and ground, becoming rapidly bloody as blow after blow met hard resistance.

He lay rigid, sometimes. Not even a breath entering or escaping his lungs.

He was alone.

Daylight hurt his eyes, and he whimpered and tried to bury his face in the dead leaves.

Pools of sunlight broke through the canopy of the abandoned flesh-fruit plantation, and he squirmed into them, wriggling within the wrapping of his blanket and coat like a dying caterpillar.

Sunlight moved across the ground, and he followed it during the course of the day, still shivering, still sobbing in inner pain.

Darkness.

He slept, still shivering.

CHAPTER 23

He walked through the jungle.

CHAPTER 24

The gentle sound of water formed an aural backdrop to the *kerchee* of a red-faced monkey, the nasal chuttering of a warbler, the pips of tree frogs and fleshpeckers. Misty droplets hung in the air, beading his skin, chilling him.

He walked.

Tall, his beard tangled, his hair ragged and long and littered with debris from where he had slept on the forest floor, he looked like a True human, and walked like a True human.

He did not speak. He had no one to speak to.

He walked through the jungle, following the singsong summons of the water.

The water was cold, running shallow over a bed of pebbles and small boulders in a gentle loop around a clump of silver-barked gum trees.

On the inner curve of the meander a bank of rocks had built up. Flint squatted here, bony knees protruding from the folds of his cloak.

Some of the stones were rounded, their creamy surface pitted with tiny holes as if pocked by disease. Some of these had split open to reveal the dark, shiny mysteries of their interior: glassy, polished, magical. It was as if they were two different stones, or a stone caught in the process of change. Inner and outer.

He took a nodule and struck it on a large rock.

He dropped it, gasping, clutching at his hand.

He tried again.

Third time, the stone split into two pieces and a shower of smaller fragments.

He placed the two halves carefully on top of a flat boulder, shiny side up.

He looked around and gathered up some more of the stones and put them into his otherwise empty backpack.

He walked through the jungle, sticking to patches of sunlight wherever possible.

He listened to the birds and the insects, to the calling of the trees and the tune of the earth.

They took him in and fed him. The Lost have a knack for finding their own.

"Be call me Treacle," said a young woman with a coating of fur on every exposed surface and a reptilian beak instead of a mouth. "What name they be call you?"

He gestured at the pack on his lap. "Flint," he said, his first word since he had changed.

He slept in a communal lodge, body heat and odours thick in the air.

In the morning, Treacle and an older woman washed him in a tub of cold water. He protested at the chill, but they soothed him with hands on his chest and back and words of kindness.

He subsided.

It was as if they still talked to him, but not with words. A music in his head.

He heard a forest wren trilling, felt hands and scrubbing stones on his shivering body. He clung to the music.

Dressed again, his clothes clean as if new, he clutched his pack to his chest. "I must move on," he told them. "I must keep going."

He thanked them and walked into the jungle.

The storyteller became known widely in the wildlands between clan settlements—known to True and Lost alike.

They said he was a Riverwalker. Such was apparent from the clothes that he wore and from the way he kept his hair and beard long and tied in bunches. It was apparent, too, from his fondness for telling stories that made moral points about the wickedness in the human heart and the time when trials would be over and Judgement would arrive, the time when humankind would find its destiny.

They knew he was a spiritual man because he spent long parts of every day in meditation, hands pressed together above his head, motionless and not breathing for longer than any normal person could manage. It was clear that he saw the world more deeply than they did, and that sometimes he saw into their hearts.

They said he was a madman. That was apparent to anyone who met him, but his madness was of a gentle sort—a look in the eye, an eagerness in the manner, a tendency to repeat himself and to forget whom he was talking to.

No one objected to a greeting from the storyteller as they passed along the thoroughfares between settlements. Indeed, some even went out of their way to encounter him and offer him gifts in exchange for his time and words.

He was a man who carried riverstones and left them, split in two, by the side of the road and at junctions. They were his message to the world, his signature: Flint has been here, and left a part of himself.

He was one of the Lost, of course.

Most knew. He was too different ever to conceal his nature—different inside—even if he had wished to keep it hidden.

Most of the passing travellers of True breeding chose to ignore this. Some of the more enlightened even invited him into their settlements to teach and entertain their children.

He learnt to spot those for whom his embracing of change was a problem, and those were the ones he avoided.

He was a wild-looking man, covered in sun blisters in the dry season for he refused to stay in the shade, preferring to bask in the sun's rays.

He learnt to heal himself, and then also to heal others.

In the wet season, he wrapped himself in many, many layers, and still he shook from the cold, warming himself by telling stories of the dry season. He did this even when he was alone.

People liked the storyteller, but they never knew precisely where they would find him, where he would turn up at any particular time. He travelled continually, through the wilds and the territory they called the Badlands, which were not bad at all, but merely less populated with the True.

Always seeking, although he knew not what he sought.

CHAPTER 25
AMBER'S STORY

lint! Flint!"

The woman who was now called Taneyes but once had been Amberlinetreco Eltarn hurried along the overgrown track. The roar of the rapids nearby reminded her always of the risks, although her son frequently wandered and had never yet come to any serious harm.

She paused, and looked for movement. Butterflies and the scarlet glint of a tree frog were all that caught her eye.

"Flint?"

She saw him scampering away, head of thick chestnut hair bobbing above a screen of woodrush.

She knew a shortcut, and so she sidestepped into the trees, finding a straight line to the path's kinks and curves.

She waited behind a tree, and when she saw him approaching she leapt out from her hiding place making animal roars. Flint was too young to be frightened by her antics, and he collapsed on his tiny rump, laughing at her and pointing.

"Flint, darling, you shouldn't run off like that," she chastised him now, stroking his thick hair.

His expression suddenly changed to one of childish anguish. "But Nana Herrel said—"

"Nana Herrel said nothing, and you know it." But she knew what he meant. Herrel could be stern with the pups at times, and equally Flint could be oversensitive.

"Is it true?" asked Flint now, shifting subject with ease.

"Is what true?"

"Denny and Mereck says the Tallyman gets you if Nana Herrel don't be liking you. They says the Tallyman shouts so loud . . . says he eats children."

She took him in her arms and hugged him tight. "Denny and Mereck like frightening little boys," she said. "They should know better. Anyway, Nana Herrel loves you, darling Flint. And there *are* no Tallymen here: we're safe here."

It's not the Tallyman you should fear, in any case.

She woke in the night, in the cabin she had grown with Herrel while baby Flint had taken root in her belly.

They lived in a small community on the slopes of a great mountain, where the forest gave them a living of abundance. It was a peaceful place, the happiest she had ever known. A good place to raise her son.

So why, now, did she dream of the past?

Flint's words, she supposed: fears of the Tallyman.

> *The Tallyman comes*
> *in the dead of the night.*
> *When the Tallyman comes*
> *you'd better take fright!*

Back in the land of the True, her son would not have survived to his Naming Day: he had the high, domed skull of one changed before birth—changed deep inside. He was a sensitive child now, one gifted with insight and smartness way beyond his years. He was like a little Oracle, she often thought.

Perhaps he had sensed something, now, found some kind of understanding, knew of change to come.

She turned and tried to find sleep again, never at peace with her
thoughts in the darkness. She had known too much darkness in her life.

She thought, then, of Leaving Hill. All the bones glinting white
like chalk in the sun. She used to wish she had been left there as a pup.
It would have spared her much.

But those times were long gone now.

She found little Flint on the main trail that ran across the flank of the
hill and down to the river.

"You mustn't keep running off like this," she chastised him.

But he just looked up at her, smiling in his impudent way. "You
always find me, Mama!"

She sat down with him and took his hands. "I used to run away,"
she said. "When I was a girl. I had a lot to hide from. My mother and
father did not love me as I love you, Flint. Do you understand?"

Solemn, Flint nodded. "I'm not really running away," he told her.
"I'm playing. That's what children do."

Maturity and impish cheek. He could be so exasperating sometimes. . . .

Suddenly serious, Taneyes went on: "One time I really ran away. Or
at least I tried. I was very unhappy, with parents who mistreated me
and a brother who found me a burden. I went to Oracle. Do you know
what an Oracle is?"

"A smart pod grown to understand," said the boy. "Melody says the
True use them because they don't have minds of their own."

"I had decided to run away, and I went to Oracle and that was
where I decided I would go to Greenwater to visit my Aunt Clarel. She
hated my father—her brother. She knew what he was like."

"What did you do?"

"I went back to my room to get some of my things. And my father, Tarn, was there. I told him I was going. He said that just proved that I was not True—that no True daughter of the clan would do such a thing and that I was no daughter of his. He said that if I was going then he might as well sell me like the mutt that I was."

"He did that?"

She nodded.

"He was a bad man. He spent most of his time being angry with the people in his life, the women in particular. It is not uncommon for the True to banish clan members who turn out to be changed. They leave the pups out to die, and they trade the older ones into slavery. Tarn arranged with his cousin Mesteb to sell me to traders. I expect they drank the profit between them."

"Are they far away?" asked Flint now. He looked scared, and she remembered that, despite his air of oracular wisdom and under-standing, he was still only an infant—one who could be frightened by stories of the Tallyman.

"They are very far away," said Taneyes. "All of them."

Flint ran ahead of her, on the trail down towards the river. He liked the white water, where the river tumbled over big, rounded boulders, kicking up spray and foam and making an almighty roar. He liked the shapes and the sounds, he often told her: never the same, always changing. He could stay by the river forever, if she would let him.

She kept a watchful eye on him as he ran and skipped ahead of her.

By the river, their trail joined a larger track, and she saw two small groups of travellers passing on their way. She hurried to catch up with Flint.

He was squatting, holding two stones in his hand.

When she joined him, he looked up at her, childish wonder in his dark eyes. "Look, Mama," he said, holding the stones up to her.

She saw that they were two pieces of a single stone, cleaved in two. Rough on the outside, polished on the inner, the two halves fit together almost perfectly.

Flints.

This stone did not occur here naturally. Someone must have brought it with them. . . .

She looked around, saw an old woman approaching.

"Luah," she said to the woman, holding one of the stones up towards her. "Did you see who . . . ?"

Luah pointed along the trail, and Taneyes turned to follow her gesture.

A man walked away from them. A slim figure, dark hair in bunches down his back, a bag slung across his shoulder.

She thanked Luah, took her son's hand, and hurried along the river trail after the man.

CHAPTER 26

He had seen much, the man they called the storyteller. He had travelled great distances, but whatever it was that he sought seemed to be beyond his grasp.

He had found people who spoke only in song: tunes that he sometimes appeared to recognise and could hum, but the words of which he did not understand.

He had slept in the trees with mutties, had allowed them to groom his hair and beard, had eaten blood grapes with them and shared in their dreams and visions.

He had visited communities of the Ritt and the Ten. At some of the former he had been welcomed as a wiseman, a traveller and healer, and he had told stories to their children and remembered an old River-walker who had done likewise, many years before. At the latter he had been threatened and stoned, and had on several occasions been lucky to escape. There was fighting in the Ten, he knew: humankind versus destiny. There could only be one outcome in such a conflict, but they did not like to be told.

Out here, though. . . . Out here there was peace. The many kinds of human welcomed him, and so he travelled farther, deeper into the lands he had once believed to be bad.

Seeking. Always seeking.

He sat on the bank and watched the movement of the water, the endless variation of contortions and folds in its surface. He could sit like this forever, it seemed.

A woman came to him, holding the hand of a child who was clearly her son. The two had the same chestnut in their hair, the same yellow in their dark eyes.

He nodded in greeting and then returned to his contemplation of the water. There was a solidity deep in his belly as he saw that the water moved with smoothness and continuity, a reflection in nature of the Lordsway.

"Flint?"

He looked at her again, and saw that the boy was looking at her curiously, too.

"It is you, isn't it, Flint?"

And then, finally: "Amber?"

He sat in the sun, in the open area to the rear of the podhut Taneyes and Herrel had grown. He laughed at something the boy said to him, and then turned as his sister came out with food.

She stopped, just a little awkward still, fingering the rivershell bracelet on her wrist.

"I found you," he said to her, now. He indicated the building, the boy, the village beyond. "I seem to have found much more, too."

She moved to him and kissed him on the brow. "You always find me, darling brother."

"Where . . . ?" he said. "Where is this place?"

She smiled. "This is Harmony," she told him.

They ate and drank, and said little.

"What will you do now, Flint?" Taneyes asked after a time.

"I could go back," he said. "Now that I know you are safe. I can pass as True, you know. They just think I am mad. I could go back and help spread the change. All those so-called truebred humans living in terror of the future . . ."

"They would destroy you."

"I would destroy them," he said. "Or, at least: I would *change* them."

Then: "I came to take you home," said Flint eventually. "That was always my intention."

"This *is* home, Flint."

She was right: this Harmony was where the True humans lived now. And home was spreading all the time.

ABOUT THE AUTHOR

KEITH BROOKE spent a long time as a promising young SF writer, with three novels published in the United Kingdom in the early nineties (*Keepers of the Peace, Expatria,* and *Expatria Incorporated*) and over sixty short stories published around the world since 1989. Now he's a promising mature writer and online publisher, launching the Web-based SF, fantasy, and horror showcase infinity plus in 1997 (www.infinityplus.co.uk), featuring the work of around one hundred top genre authors, including Michael Moorcock, Stephen Baxter, Connie Willis, Gene Wolfe, Vonda McIntyre, and Jack Vance. He is coeditor with Nick Gevers of *infinity plus one* and *infinity plus two*, anthologies based on the Web site. His latest books are the novel *Lord of Stone* (1997; revised edition 2001); a collection of short stories, *Head Shots* (2001); and *Parallax View* (2000), a collection of stories written with Eric Brown. Hiding his identity behind the pen name Nick Gifford, he likes to scare children, with several novels published by Puffin, the first of which has been optioned for the movies. Keith lives with his young family in the English seaside town of Brightlingsea. You can find out more about Keith and his work at www.keithbrooke.co.uk.